When God Ain't Lookin'

A Novel by

George Delmarmo

CCB Publishing
British Columbia, Canada

When God Ain't Lookin'

ISBN-13 978-1-77143-164-4
Fourth Edition

Library and Archives Canada Cataloguing in Publication
Delmarmo, George, 1936-, author
When God ain't lookin' / written by George Delmarmo. -- Fourth edition.
Issued in print and electronic formats.
ISBN 978-1-77143-164-4 (pbk.).--ISBN 978-1-77143-165-1 (pdf)
Additional cataloguing data available from Library and Archives Canada

Contact the author George Delmarmo at: Hogfarmer@aol.com

Disclaimer: This book is a work of fiction. Any names, places, events, characters or incidents portrayed in this book are through the author's imagination and have been used fictitiously. Any resemblance or similarity to actual events, locales or real persons, living or dead, is coincidental and not intended by the author.

Extreme care has been taken by the author to ensure that all information presented in this book is accurate and up to date at the time of publishing. Neither the author nor the publisher can be held responsible for any errors or omissions. Additionally, neither is any liability assumed for damages resulting from the use of the information contained herein.

Publisher: CCB Publishing
British Columbia, Canada
www.ccbpublishing.com

Contents

Characters

Ann/Carol
Elsie
Bob
Father O'Neil
Sister Edith
Detective Josephine
Doc John
Detective Larry
Mother Superior
George
Andy
Mary Lou
Janet
Jules
Norma
Sal
Monique
Curly
Jean
Adele
Maude
Jose
Maria
Mongombo
Joel
Richard
Barbara
Russ
John
Mario
Evelyn
Stacy

Preface

The story is about the relationship of a young man, George and an older woman, Ann. George did not know of their difference in age nor the fact that Ann was studying to become a nun. The story spans both of their lives as they meet and part periodically throughout their lives. George is never quite able to forget about Ann. The story is further complicated by the fact that Ann has stolen money from the church. She was giving it to George. The setting for the story moves around the United States and Mexico before ending in Canada.

Chapter One

The beginning of any story is supposed to start at the beginning, but in some stories, it is hard to tell where the beginning is. If two people meet, did the story about the two of them start at their first meeting, or did it start when they left their homes, looking for an adventure? Or did it start years earlier, when their lives started to take shape. No one is raised in a vacuum, so as outside pressures start to shape a person's life, is that the beginning? Is it when a person starts to form an impression of the type of person he wants to be or what type of person he wants to meet?

Ann—or Annie to those who were too lazy to call her Ann—came from a little town in Ohio called George's Run on the border of Ohio and West Virginia. The town was located on the Ohio River, just south of Steubenville, and north of Wheeling, West Virginia. The local residents referred to Steubenville as being nowhere. George's Run was just south of nowhere on the mighty Ohio River. In the old days, rafters would bring their goods to New Orleans on the Ohio River. Steubenville was one of the stops after leaving Pittsburgh. Nothing stopped in George's Run unless it was broken. As a child, Ann would run along the banks of the river with the rest of the kids from the town. From the path, they were all engaged in the major activity of the town—watching a raft or boat go by. The passing of one of these vessels was the highlight of the day. The tugboat operators would toot their horns, as the children would wave. The crewmembers would join in; for a few minutes life in town was exciting. After the tug with the barge was out of sight, the town went back to existing until the next distraction came. On each passing vessel were the dreams and the wishes of the town's people who saw it go. They envisioned that they too were going down to St. Louis or even all the way down to New Orleans. In New Orleans, they could get a ship that would take them anywhere in the world. Now that was a dream worth having at any age!

The river itself was so intertwined in the lives of the people that they would describe everything in terms of the river. Phrases such as "mad as the river," "calm as the river," or "fast as the river" were heard every day. A little park ran along the side of the river. Everyone went there at some point during the day. The pathway that was right next to the river was the most-used path in town. Interspersed along the path were plaques with the name of the person, business, or organization that was responsible for cleaning and maintaining that area. At night it was the favorite place to meet, walk, or just talk. It was the place where dreams came true or where dreams were shattered. The local jokesters would always say that the path was the place in town where the most accidents happened that resulted in children. During the late 40s and 50s, all of those things that shook the rest of the world touched the town but had little effect on it. If, while sitting in the barbershop, someone picked up a magazine, he didn't even bother to look at the date since yesterday was today, today was tomorrow, tomorrow would be just like today, which would quickly become yesterday.

Most of the people worked somewhere else; they just came to the town to sleep. The teachers from the local schools were the only ones it seemed that lived, worked, and died in the little town. Those residents who had jobs on the tugboats got to go more places. They never got off the boat so their world was always the same. The only difference was that from the boat they could see the world changing, even though they weren't a part of it. Those who worked in Steubenville or even Pittsburgh left their "big city ways" outside of town. The only intruders in town were the radio and television. They had little effect, for most people didn't believe what they heard or saw on them.

The schools used the same books that had been in the school forever. The school district was so poor that it would have to wait for another school system to want to change its books so that the other system's old books would become the town's new books. The high school sports program was the same as the other schools, except that no good athletes ever went to school there. The high school basketball team was invited to play in a tournament once. They lost by sixty-two points. The team never accepted an invitation to enter another tournament again.

The children only spoke of either getting out of the town or dying in it. Everyone wanted to go somewhere else as soon as he/she grew up—anywhere but here. Ann was no different.

Ann's parents were poorer than most. They had two boys a year apart. Ten years later, they had Ann. When Ann was eight, her brothers got a job on one of the barges. She never saw them again. Her eighth birthday was the last time the family was together. Her mother was like all the other parents; she wanted her three children to have the best, to do better, and to be able to get out of this horrible town that sometimes drained her of the very will to live. Ann's father could care less about what happened. On Ann's eighth birthday he got drunk, which was usual, but today it was to celebrate her birthday. In addition, his two sons were getting jobs. Her father staggered up and took a deep breath before saying in a shaky, slurred voice, "Today my daughter is eight; it will only be a few more years until she gets pregnant. After that, someone else has to support her. Now, my two boys got jobs; I don't have to carry them anymore. Soon I'll be free."

After his speech, to everyone's delight, he passed out. He had to be helped to the couch. His snoring was the background music as the two boys left their mother and baby sister. The two boys walked out of the house and never looked back. They went down the street and the older one said, "We're free now. Let's stay this way for a long time." One of Ann's earliest memories was standing next to her crying mother as they watched her brothers go down the street.

The next few years all seemed to melt into one long day. School was the major activity in Ann's life. She went from her home to the school. When school was out, she went right back home again. She didn't have any toys like the other kids, so she would stand off to the side on those days when she came outside. Some of the kids would make fun of her, while others invited her to play with them. Ann felt inferior to the rest of the kids because they had better clothes. What was more important, every day they had a nickel for candy.

When Ann matured to be a young lady, one of her schoolmates went away. When she came back home, the best-kept secret in town was that she was pregnant. She didn't come back to school but was tutored at home until she got her degree. She was the outcast of the town. She had sinned. God had punished her. Ann heard those words but never understood them. The town had very little tolerance with anything that didn't follow the strict interpretation of the Bible. The street corner politicians would say with pride, "If there is such a thing as a "Bible Belt," George's Run is the buckle."

A typical day meant being up with the sun, dressing for school (which meant putting on the same thing you had on last night), either going to school all day and afterwards going to the park by the river or else spending the whole day at the park by the river until it was time to go home for supper. After supper, the children of the town went back to the park or for a walk around town until bedtime. The next day was the same as the day that had just passed. The only thing to look forward to was tomorrow, which everyone knew would be like yesterday. If Ann went out at night, it was after a lecture from her mother about the dirty, little boys around town.

Who a girl met while she went on one of her walks was the measure of her popularity in town. If too many boys were waiting, a derogatory word was said before her name; if no one was waiting, there was an eerie silence that joined in on the conversation. The normal chatter among young girls didn't seem to affect Ann at all. She usually walked alone until her mother forbade her to do so. She would try to fit in with the other girls at school, but she always felt awkward when around them. In her mind, they were all prettier, had better clothes, and were smarter than she. The teachers were the first to notice how Ann didn't fit in, but the fact that she didn't fit in didn't seem to bother Ann at all. The teachers were more upset about it than she was. Every time a teacher would ask why she didn't join in with the other children, her response was always the same. She would look the teacher in the eye as she said, "I really don't want to. I do not want to be like them."

The teachers tried to force her to interact with the other children. If teams for a sport had to be picked, Ann was the captain. The minute she was announced as captain, a moan would rise up from the class. The selection of the team members would take place. The people who were picked for Ann's team would show their displeasure by rolling their eyes while stomping their feet as they walked to the side of the room they were to stand on. The whole scene was one that was distasteful to the students but most of all to Ann. Once when a teacher picked Ann to lead one activity, Ann refused. "Why are you doing this to me? I do not want to be the captain. Let someone else do it."

The teacher was embarrassed. She changed her mind as to whom the captain would be. The teacher appointed another student captain. The team selections were made. Regardless of the activity, Ann was always the last one picked.

By time Ann was in her second year of high school, she was labeled a loner. Her teacher asked her parents to come to school for a visit. Ann's mother went, for her father worked as a deck hand on one of the tugs. He was rarely home. The teacher expressed her concerns about how Ann didn't fit in with the rest of the children. Ann's mother tried as best she could to control her temper as she said through clenched teeth, "Mind your own business. I don't want my daughter growing up like you or the other people in this town. I want her to leave here as soon as she's old enough. You just teach her the ABC's. As long as she's good at that, mind your own business."

The teacher was physically upset by this reaction. She tried to point out why it was necessary for Ann to learn to get along with her fellow students. "What is she going to do with her life? No matter what she does, she has to interact with other people. In school we try to develop the social skills of the student as well as giving her an academic education. Her grades are good enough for her to continue her education at a university. You know, next year she will have to start deciding to which school she would like to apply."

Ann's mother rose to her feet. She pointed her finger at the teacher while speaking in a voice loud enough for everyone to hear. "I don't want you of all people telling my daughter that she has to get along with anybody. You got married. Now you're divorced. You went to college. You came back pregnant and that's why you got married. After the wedding, you had a convenient miscarriage. Just leave my kid alone. She has to come to school, but only until she's sixteen. She'll be sixteen in two months. So for the two months left, find someone else's kid to poison with that stuff you're saying. Leave my daughter alone."

Everyone was in awe of what they had just heard. The teacher was in tears. She ran from the room. One large gentleman yelled out, "It's about time someone told these goddamn know-it-all teachers to mind their own business! Good for you, lady." The large man applauded as Ann's mother triumphantly marched out of school.

As Ann left school, holding on to her mother's hand, she

thought back to the stories her mother would tell her about when she was a young girl running along the banks of the river. "I was the oldest in my family. I was named Elsie after your great-grandmother. I wasn't allowed to go to school for too long, for your grandmother thought it was a waste of time. She was afraid that I would learn a lot of silly things that would get me in trouble. She would always tell me how she would teach me what I had to know to live in our town. She would say, "The stuff they teach you in school is just to keep you from getting on with your life. There is no sense learning how someone else lived. You'll never live anywhere other than here, so there is no need for you to be bothered with what they teach in that school."

Elsie, as a young girl, would look at the river as though it was going to be her salvation. It was during one of her walks that she became a mother-to-be. The father of her children, a young boy in town, was two years older than she was. He had just gotten a job on a tugboat as a deck hand. He told Elsie he had traveled on the river many times. Elsie saw him as the knight in shining armor she had heard about in the stories at school. The boat he worked on was his silver steed. He would sweep her up into his arms to carry her from this horrid town that oppressed every fiber of her being. Their engagement was short, for their wedding had to be hurried so that they would be married before the baby came.

They had two boys a year apart. The two boys came ten years before Ann came along. Elsie became very content with her life. She was a simple soul who really didn't understand why anyone would want any other type of life. Her two sons left home as soon as the older one was eighteen. He had to be eighteen to get a job on a barge. When he turned eighteen, he had to register for the draft. He also got a job on one of the barges. He gave his registration card to his brother to use as identification so that he could get a job a year early. Other than an occasional greeting card, neither boy would contact his mother or sister at all. They would meet their father every time he came down the river to St. Louis. Ann's father would tell her all about them, but the topic quickly changed when Elsie came into the room.

Ann's recollection of the stories kept coming back to haunt her, for she didn't know whether her mother was happy with her own life or if she was sorry about her existence. The way she yelled at the teacher made Ann feel as though her mother wanted her to live her type of life. Her mother didn't want her to be like one of her teachers. As far as Ann could see, her mother's life was comparable to her teacher's life. They were both the same. They lived in the same town. They walked along the same riverbank.

Word of what had happened at school spread through town. It was the hottest topic of gossip. People altered what was said to fit their own needs. With each embellished version, the story became more noteworthy. The teacher took a week off because she was so upset by what happened, which only added to the story. The teachers in the lunchroom were divided equally on whether the teacher should have said what she did to Ann's mother.

One teacher said, "It is not our business to try to make each student fit into a mold we would like. Ann's grades were good. She posed no disciplinary problem. That is where our responsibility ends. We are not here to raise the children in our classes; that is their mothers' job."

Another offered, "If we don't try to improve our students, then who will? Ann's mother obviously has her own agenda as well as her own standards for Ann. If we as teachers don't open new doors for our students, what are we doing here? Just teaching them their ABC's?"

A third who listened to both of the arguments could not sit quiet any longer. She stood up. "Who says we're right in what we want for our students? Anyway, I think we are missing the point here. Do any of you know if anything Ann's mother said about our fellow teacher was true?" Everyone smiled as each went to his or her next class. The question was left hanging in the air until the next session of the teachers' lunchtime conference.

The principal went to see the teacher at her home. He told her, "The best thing to do is to let the whole matter rest. You will gain nothing by trying to deny anything. First of all, no one is going to believe you. If you try to sue her for defamation of character, there will have to be a trial. That will only draw more attention to you. If you say nothing, your friends will understand why you are keeping quiet. What do you care what some busybodies say? Believe me; I've been through this many times. Your silence will be the best way to go. We are not a large school, so I can't transfer Ann out of your class. I don't think it would be fair to punish Ann for what her mother said. Ann isn't a disciplinary problem, is she?'

"No."

"Well, what is the problem? She'll be sixteen in two months. Then she won't be your problem anymore. Take the rest of the week off. I'll see you on Monday." The teacher decided to take the principal's advice. The subject of Ann's future was not brought up again.

Ann became an instant celebrity. Everyone wanted to be with her. Ann became the most popular girl in school. She was picked first for every team.

The local priest heard about what happened at school, so on the following Sunday, he was on the lookout for Ann. Ann went to church every Sunday. She sat in the back row. She never spoke to anyone. At the end of mass, she would get up to leave. Usually no one other than herself knew or cared that she was there. Not so this Sunday morning. The priest made it a point to take Ann on the side. He asked her to see him after mass. Ann said she would. After mass, the two of them took a walk through the little garden that was next to the church. Like all little churchyards, this one had a fountain in the middle with a bench nearby. The priest broke the silence that hung over them. He said to Ann, "I often come here when I have a problem I want to think through." Ann looked at the priest but kept quiet. She was trying to think of why he wanted her to speak to him this day.

Nervously she said, "I have to get home. My mother doesn't like for me to walk alone with anyone. Is there something you wanted to ask me?"

The priest looked at her. He tried to smile as he replied, "Are you going to drop out of school when you're sixteen?"

Ann was shocked by the question. She thought for a moment before she replied, "I don't think my mother would want me to tell you what I'm going to do. Now if you have nothing else to say, I would like to leave."

The priest was stunned by Ann's comment. When he regained his composure, he replied, "Of course. May God be with you, my child."

Ann quickened her pace as she went home. As soon as she got in the door, she told her mother what had happened and what she did. Her mother just smiled as she said, "You did the right thing."

For the next two months, the word in school was not to bother Ann. The other students accepted her but only for a short period of time. Ann's wall started to resurrect itself, as Ann didn't know how to deal with her classmates. Her social skills had never been developed, so after a few weeks, she was left alone. The only difference was that the teachers left her alone as well.

The two months passed quickly. On Ann's sixteenth birthday, her mother made her a cake. The two of them sat down to eat it. Ann's father was working. She knew her brothers never bothered with her. It was on this day that Ann looked around the kitchen in the four-room apartment where she had always lived. This was the day that she realized for the first time that if she listened to her mother, this would be her world. At least now she left for school. If she quit school, these rooms would be her world. Ann didn't know how to explain to her mother that she didn't want to be like her. The day after her sixteenth birthday, Ann went to school.

Her teacher was shocked when she walked into class. At first the teacher didn't know what to do. The teacher excused herself from the room. She went to find the principal. He listened to his teacher who, in anticipation of what Elsie would say or do, had worked herself into a frenzy. He finally quieted her down as well as he could. He said, "She can come to school. She has done nothing wrong. The girl is here. It is our obligation to teacher her, so just teach."

The teacher, embarrassed by the experience she'd just had with the principal, went back to her room. By the time she got back to the class, it was time for the classes to change. Ann went off to the next class. The whole school by now had heard that Ann was back. The rumor was that she had sent her teacher to the principal's office.

Chapter Two

Ann was a different person after her sixteenth birthday. She began to look at her life as it was. She saw how it would surely be if she did nothing about it. She still avoided the kids at school. They did the same to her. It didn't bother Ann to have lunch alone, which upset her classmates even more. If someone were to walk over to her in the lunchroom, she was cordial and aloof at the same time. She acknowledged the person but offered nothing by way of conversation. She would answer any questions, but her answers were as abrupt as could be. One boy who approached her as a dare from the rest of his friends tried to involve her in a conversation by saying, "Hello. My name is Bob."

"Hello. My name is Ann."

Bob continued, still unsure of himself by adding, "I have gone to school with you since the first day we attended school. This is the first time I have ever spoken to you."

"I know."

"Do you always eat alone?"

"Yes."

"Do you mind if I join you?"

"No."

"I play on the basketball team. Do you come to the games?"

"No."

"We are playing this Friday. Are you going to come? I'll look for you."

"No. I don't know too much about the game. I don't think my mother would allow me to go. Excuse me, but I have to go to class. Goodbye."

Bob walked her to the doorway of the lunchroom. He watched as she walked down the hall. Everyone in the lunchroom was in awe, for no one had ever seen her have that long of a conversation with anyone. Bob triumphantly walked back to his friends. He refused to go into any details of the conversation but just smiled when asked any questions about it.

Every day on the way home from school, she walked past a grocery store. It was the same store all her friends would spend their nickel a day in. One day, there was a sign in the window, "store help wanted." Ann applied for the job. It meant working after school as well as on Saturdays in the grocery store. She would stock shelves as she cleaned up the store. She was surprised when she was hired. When she told her mother, her mother, at first, was in a state of shock. When she calmed down, she finally saw that her daughter had changed. Her mother's only advice was, "Be careful. Don't make the same mistakes I made."

Ann heard the words her mother said but did not understand what she meant. Her boss would tell her, "You have to talk to the customers. You can't be shy. If you're shy, we won't sell anything. Say 'Hello, can I help you? Is there anything else I can get for you?' No one is going to bite your head off if you smile. You're such a pretty girl. Smile."

Bob became a steady customer at the store. The owner would smile every time he came in, for he knew that Bob lived on the other side of town. The owner's only comment to Ann would be, "See? You smile, and we get a new customer." Ann just blushed.

Ann's first paycheck was the greatest thrill of her life. Her mother was so proud of her. After Ann had shown her the pay envelope, Elsie started to cry. She left the room. Ann was confused by her mother's reaction. She went into the room after her. Before Ann could say anything, her mother turned to face her as she blurted out, "I have never gotten a pay envelope in my entire life!" Ann walked away in a state of bewilderment.

The combination of the job, staying in school, and having

Bob follow her around made Ann become a different person. She had an angelic face that made her look young. As the other girls in her class were well on their way to learning all about cosmetics, Ann wore none. Her mother would always have a nasty comment to make about any woman she saw that wore make-up; this constant demeaning of other women made Ann feel that there was something sinful about wearing make-up. This feeling, along with the cost of the different lipsticks and rouges, convinced Ann that she didn't need any. Her life was starting to become very interesting without it.

Ann would spend her time between going to school, work, and church. At church, no matter which way she went, there was Father O'Neil or Bob waiting for her. Bob would be at one door and the good Father at the other. Ann became aware of her own body as she emerged from her self-inflicted isolationism. This was most evident when she went to church. She went to church by herself. Elsie wanted no part of it. Elsie never discouraged her from going but never went with her. The people around Ann before would pay her no mind, except to point to the little girl who was alone. If anyone went by her or tried to talk to her, she would put her head down as she scurried off to another part of the church. The people around her quickly accepted the fact that Ann went to church simply to go to church. They realized that she was not there to socialize.

Ann would always wear clothes that draped her. The common joke was that she had to take two steps before her clothes moved one. That changed. When Ann went to church now, she was aware of what other girls wore. She started to emulate them. In sewing class, she had learned how to sew, but since they didn't have a sewing machine at home, she never perfected what she had learned in school. In the store where she worked now, there was a sewing machine that she was allowed to use, as long as it didn't interfere with her work. Using the people she saw in church as her models, Ann started to adjust her clothes so they fit her rather than hang on her. She felt that if other people wore those types of clothes to church, there must be nothing wrong with the way they were styled or the way they fit. When she wore something new to school, it was met with a lot of snide remarks. When she wore the same outfit to church, she would receive compliments on how nice she looked. One lady who sat by her at church was very knowledgeable about sewing and would tell Ann how to correct her mistakes. At first, she felt offended by the lady's comments, but after a while, she sought her advice.

Ann was five foot, six inches tall in her flat shoes. She never wore high heels because they cost too much. Her blondish hair seemed to drape her face like a halo. One gentleman who seemed to always sit by her turned one day to tell his wife, "If I ever wanted to paint an angel, she would be my inspiration." Ann just knew that he had spoken in a loud enough voice for her to hear. She did not show any outward reaction to the comment. Her change in her style of dress caught the eye of Sister Edith.

Ann became an expert at avoiding Bob as well as Father O' Neil when leaving church, but Sister Edith was not so easy to avoid. The sister would chase after her, take her by the arm, and hold her in a corner of the church so that she could speak to her. At first, Ann didn't know what to do. She would start to pull away, but the sister would look surprised, saying, "Can't I talk to you for a moment? It seems every time I come near you, you seem to be in a big hurry. Are you trying to avoid me?"

"Yes." The sister stepped back as though Ann had slapped her. "I don't like people grabbing at me. I have nothing to say to you, so why are you always following me?"

Before the sister could answer, Bob walked up to the two ladies. "Can I walk you home?" he asked.

"I wish you would."

The sister stood in the doorway of the church as Ann, on the arm of Bob, walked away. As they walked down the street, Bob was not sure of what he should say or whether he should say anything. Finally, he got his nerve up as he asked, "Every Sunday, that nun seems to seek you out. I follow behind you, but I don't know whether or not I should interrupt. Did I do the right thing today?"

Ann stopped walking, for she didn't know how to answer Bob. After a long pause, she smiled as she responded, "Yes, you did. You can interrupt anytime. I don't know what that nun wants, but she frightens me. I would go to Father O'Neil, but he scares me worse than she does."

"I must frighten you more than anyone, for it seems you're always running from me." The young couple laughed as they continued their walk to Ann's house by way of the crowded, river path. Everyone they went by had a comment to make, for Bob was the basketball star while Ann was the knockout of the school. But at Ann's insistence, they did not hold hands. She did not show affection, nor would she let Bob show any. They acted like two strangers toward each other.

"You know, I might as well be walking by myself as walk with you."

"You're right," Ann said as she walked away.

A passing couple commented, "They're having a lovers' spat." Ann went the rest of the way home alone. Bob stood on the path in a kind of stupor. Finally, he snapped out of it and went home, trying to think up what story he would tell his friends who'd seen him on the path. He was starting to wonder if Ann was worth the effort.

Although everything about Ann changed, one thing stayed the same—her aloofness from everyone. The teachers all took notice that when she changed classes, she always walked alone. At lunchtime, she chose to sit by herself rather than with a group. If anyone approached her for any reason or they asked her a question, she would respond in a quiet courteous way as she immediately searched for some reason to leave. Her high school guidance counselor met with her to ask what her plans for the future were.

She responded, "I would like to become a nun."

The counselor was speechless. Her counselor was not too religious. The thought of a young, beautiful girl giving up her life to become a nun was in direct contrast to the counselor's ideas. "Have you really thought this through? Have you discussed your plans for the future with your parents? Maybe you should talk with your friends? There has been a marked difference in you this last year. Next year, you'll be a senior. If you want to go to college, you have to start making plans now. If money is a problem, there are plenty of scholarships offered for which I'm sure you'll qualify. I think you should talk to your priest." The counselor quickly added, "No, don't do that."

The counselor had to stop for a moment to rethink her ideas before she offered any more advice. The counselor's problem was that she had been married and divorced twice. When she had gone for professional advice, she went to one group session. She was shocked at the experiences she heard from other people. The main theme of the other attendees was that they were right in everything they did. All their partners were wrong. They were all saying the exact things she had said to herself.

Ann interrupted her thoughts by asking, "May I go now?" Ann waited for a few moments; there was no response from her counselor who was deep in thought. Ann waited a few more minutes before leaving.

The next week was Ann's seventeenth birthday. She could get her driving license. That was a problem because she didn't know how to drive. She had no one to teach her. Her family didn't have a car because her father was never home long enough at any one time. He felt it would be senseless to have one. Her mother walked to all the stores. She never even mentioned anything about driving, let alone owning a car. Her boss owned one, but Ann was afraid to ask him about driving because on more than one occasion, he had mentioned the fact that he never hired anyone with a license because they would want more money to work for him. The only person she could think of was Bob. He owned a car. As she thought about the idea of asking him, she was frightened to realize that she would be alone in the car with him. When Ann would sit in the lunchroom, she could overhear the other girls' talking about their experiences of being in a car with a boy alone. The alone part scared Ann. Her father was supposed to come home that weekend. She decided to ask him. Since there was a driver's education course being offered by the school, she would register for it. The local car dealer had donated a used car to the school to be used for the class. She felt much better about driving now that she had alternatives to the problem. The next day she signed up for the class. She waited patiently for the weekend when she could talk to her father. Somehow she couldn't bring herself to discuss driving with her mother.

For her birthday, her mother would cook her favorite dinner. For dessert, her mother would make a cake. Her father would propose a toast to the family's good fortune, and that was the extent of the party. At work, her boss gave her a bonus. Even Bob wanted to give her a gift, but Ann was ashamed to accept it. Although they had started school at the same time, Bob was older than Ann by a few months. His father had taught him how to drive. On his seventeenth birthday, he passed his driver's test. Ann knew this because when Bob could borrow the family car, he would ask to drive Ann somewhere, but she would always say "no."

"What's wrong with you? No matter what I do, you seem to get mad at me. I try to give you a gift for your birthday, and even that you don't want. What do you want?"

She responded, "Teach me how to drive?"

Bob was speechless. Finally, when what he had heard sunk

in, he responded, “Any time, any place. You have to get a permit. Do you have one?”

Ann remembered that when she had signed up for the driving class, they had told her about a permit. However, they did not tell her anything about getting one. “No, but I’ll get one. Where do I have to go for that?”

“I’ll take you after school.”

“I can’t. I have to go to work. Can’t you just tell me? Oh, never mind; when I get a permit, I’ll tell you.” Bob walked away in frustration. Ann resolved to ask the policeman who came into the store every night. He would know.

That weekend her father came home. He had forgotten it was her birthday. Her mother had reminded him, but he’d just mumbled something under his breath as he sat down to eat. After they had the cake, she told her father about her plans to get a license.

He drained the contents of his beer can and then looked at her. His only response was, “Do what-ever-the-hell you want; just don’t ask me for anything. I’m tired of just paying the bills for this house. I don’t even know why I bother coming here.”

Ann looked at her mother for guidance as to what she should do. She noticed the welt rising on her face and the discoloration of her skin where she had been unmistakably slapped. She knew that her parents had had another argument. She dropped the topic while she ate her dinner. After dinner, she went to the path to try to think about what she was going to do. Questions, for which she had no answer, started to come into her head. Next year she would be a senior, but would she still have a home? It seemed that every time her father came home, all he did was hit her mother. Her father seemed to be always around her, which made her become afraid whenever he was home. At night, Ann would prop a chair under the doorknob to her room. Could she stand another year of living like that?

“I didn’t mean to scare you off today.” Ann turned around.

She saw Bob standing behind her. She ran away. She didn't know where to run. She didn't even know why she was running. She just wanted to be left alone. Within a few minutes, she realized that, alone or not, next year she was going to be a senior. This thought scared her. She didn't know what she was going to do. She made her way to the convent. Sister Edith sat her down in one of the little rooms off of the main entrance to the convent. She just let Ann talk until it was very late. Ann fell over in exhaustion as she fell asleep. The sister helped her to a couch in the room. The sister wanted to just let her sleep.

In the morning Sister Edith walked in with a breakfast tray. The two of them sat at the little table in the room, while they had their breakfast. Every time Ann went to say something, the sister would interrupt her by saying, "Have your breakfast, go wash up, later we'll talk."

As promised, when Ann had finished eating, she had calmed down; Sister Edith sat at the table. She started to give instructions to Ann as to what she should do. "First, you have to tell your parents that you want to…" The sister stopped talking. After she paused, she added, "You have to finish that statement. Only you know what you want. No matter who tells you anything, your decision as to what you want to do with your life is the one that counts. We can help you to achieve your goal, but it has to be your goal. Your mother has made her life. We have heard many stories about your house from our other parishioners, but unless your mother comes to us, there is nothing we can do. When the police talked to her, she refused to sign a complaint against your father. The police did nothing, so nothing changed. When your father took his boys away, your mother did nothing to stop him. I don't think your mother will do anything to help you for the simple reason that there is nothing she can do. Her world is the four rooms of the apartment. She doesn't want to do anything to change her life. First off, you should contact your mother. Tell her you're all right. Afterwards, if you want to talk to me again, we will meet."

Ann got up from the table in a state of bewilderment and left the convent. The walk home took forever. She didn't know what she would say first, but like any child, she felt that if she started out with "I'm sorry," everything else would fall into place. It was Sunday morning. The people were passing her on the street on their way to church. She smiled when she was reminded that she was going the wrong way. The catcalls were all the same, "Ann, you're going the wrong way." Ann would just smile as she kept walking.

The two flights of steps that led up to her floor just seemed to drain whatever energy she had left. Unlocking the door was not necessary, since the door was slightly ajar. She pushed the door open; as she did, she knew something was wrong. The one thing her mother always insisted on was that the door be locked. Ann was going to leave but didn't know where else to go. With grit-teeth determination, she walked in. She called out, "Mom! Mom!" But there was no answer. She continued, "Dad? Dad! Is anyone home?" She walked into her mother's bedroom. She stopped in the doorway as the entire room was in shambles. Everything was broken. Things were thrown all over the room. The morning sun shining in through the windows made the blood on the floor glisten. Ann walked around the bed and saw her mother's half-nude body, lying on the floor. Her limbs were bent in an abnormal way. The back of her head was bloodied as she lay face down in a pool of blood. The pool acted as a mirror, reflecting the morning rays of sunlight. Ann turned away, for she could not stand to see the sight of her mother. She vomited as she ran from the apartment. She fell half way down the stairs. Her downstairs neighbor came out to see who was making all the noise. When she saw Ann, still sick from what she had seen, she went to her.

"Come into my house while you tell me what is the matter.

Wait. I'll get you a glass of water. Are your parents fighting again? Should I call the police?"

Ann nodded her head "yes" as she buried her face in her hands and sobbed quietly.

"Miss, are you all right? Here, inhale this. That's it. Just breathe easily. Take deep breaths. Come on now, nice deep breaths. Don't try to talk. There'll be time for that later. Nice deep breaths are what are needed now."

Off in the distance, Ann could hear two men talking. "What a scene to walk in on, that poor kid. Get everyone out of here. Put her in the ambulance. We'll talk to her at the hospital. Keep everyone out of the apartment." Ann was helped into a wheelchair. She was wheeled out to the ambulance. With the help of two men, she was placed into the back, and the doors were shut. The wail of the sirens announced the ambulance's departure. The EMT who was sitting with her wanted to give her more oxygen. Intermittently, the EMT would put smelling salts under her nose. The pungent odor made her choke. Finally, the back doors opened as she had arrived at the hospital. She was wheeled into a small room on the side, away from everything. Two people were standing in the room, a woman and a man. They both greeted her. The woman started talking first.

"My name is Detective Josephine. Take it easy now. Is there anything you want? We know it is a bad time for you, but we have to talk to you now. Can you tell us what happened?"

Ann could only shake her head "no."

"Were you home last night?" The female officer hesitated for a few moments before she continued, "If you weren't home, where were you?"

Ann stood up as she asked for a glass of water. She took a sip before telling the police where she had been all night. Why she was at the church she really didn't know, except to say that she didn't know where else she could go. She ended her statement with, "This morning I came home to tell my mother I was all right; that is…" Ann could talk no more and started to cry hysterically.

"Do you know where your father is?"

"No."

"He was home last night when you left, wasn't he?"

"Yes."

"Do you know where he is now?"

"No."

A nurse walked in to announce, "We're going to admit her for tonight. You can come back in the morning." Without waiting for a reply, the nurse gave Ann two pills to swallow. Within minutes, Ann was asleep.

The last thing Ann heard was the female officer saying, "That bitch of a nurse, we were almost done. Now we have to come back in the morning. She'll sleep the rest of the day as well as the entire night."

Ann, who was in a daze, felt herself being taken to a room. In a trance she undressed. A hospital gown was put on her as she was placed in bed. As her head fell onto the pillow, the sight of what she had witnessed came soaring back into her memory. A feeling of guilt came over her, for she wondered what would have happened if she had been home. She felt as though she had abandoned her mother. She tried to console herself by remembering that whenever her parents would fight, her mother always made her leave the house and go somewhere else. It was when she came back that she saw what punishment her father had inflicted on her mother. Her mother would be embarrassed when Ann would try to tend to her injuries.

Chapter Three

The rays of the morning sun coming through the top of the window warmed the room. Ann had a tremendous thirst. Her lips were parched. Her mouth had a God-awful taste in it. She got out of the bed to slip into the bathrobe that had been left for her at the foot of the bed. On unsteady legs, she made her way to the bathroom. As she closed the door, a nurse's head appeared. "You alright? There is an emergency cord over there if you need help." As she spoke, the nurse pointed to a red cord, hanging down from the ceiling.

When Ann came out of the bathroom, she wobbled back to her bed. She felt a hand go under her elbow to steady her. She sat on the side of the bed as she looked up to see the smiling face of Sister Edith. "I was on hospital calls this morning. I thought you could use a friend. The police called me last night. They said that they would be here this morning to talk to you. Do you want some water?"

Ann nodded her head "yes," as she tried to figure out why the police would have called Sister Edith. Her question was quickly answered.

"You told them you were with me last night? They had to verify with me that you were. I asked them to let me know when they were going to talk to you again. I thought I might be able to help comfort you."

The sister poured her a cup of water. Just as Ann started drinking it, the same two officers from the previous day came in. They were visibly annoyed that Ann was with Sister Edith. The female officer stood with Ann, while the other officer led the sister away. "We have to question the two of you separately. Now yesterday, you said your father was home when you left?"

"Yes."

"Did you have a fight with him?"

"No."

"Did he hit your mother often?" The officer waited a few minutes before she repeated the question. In a sterner tone she said, "Did you hear what I said?"

Ann lay back on her pillow but said nothing. The officer became enraged. "Why the hell would you want to protect someone like that? Did you see your father hit your mother last night?"

"No."

"Why did you leave the house? You stayed out all goddamn night?" The officer was screaming at Ann, who began to cry.

"Lower your voice, you foul-mouthed idiot. She doesn't have to talk to you. Frankly, I don't blame her. Now get out of here. Have them send another officer to talk to her—that is if she wants to talk to someone."

The nurse had entered the room. She stood by the doorway. When the detective started screaming, she walked over to Ann, who was choking as she tried to fight back tears at the same time. "Relax now. I'll get rid of this idiot. You rest easy."

The nurse turned her attention to Josephine. In a quiet but stern voice, "Get out of here. You're a disgrace to that badge you carry. Now get out before I call security to have them thrown you out. I'm the law on these floors of the hospital, not you."

The other officer came into the room. He led Josephine away. As they walked down the hall, he told her, "Their stories are the same. All you're going to do now is get the both of us in trouble. Come on. If that nurse calls the chief, we'll both be in his office." The two officers left. As they walked out the door, two security guards followed them out.

The male officer continued talking, trying to calm down Josephine, who was mumbling under her breath. "We should have arrested her for interfering in an investigation."

He disregarded what his partner was saying as he continued, "The husband isn't around. If he got on one of those riverboats, we'll never find him. The guys who work on those boats are like river rats. They go as they please. Keep in mind that we don't have a picture or a description of him. There were no pictures in the apartment. He's never been arrested. He was never in the service. The description we got from those people who saw him was…" The officer hesitated as he referred to his note pad. He found the pages he was looking for before he continued, "He's big, he's short, he's fat, he's skinny, he has light hair, he has dark hair, or he is bald altogether. He always wears a cap; he never wears a cap. The only thing everyone agrees on is that he has big hands, and he never smiles. That description matches all the deck hands I've ever seen. Come on. We have an appointment with the coroner. The autopsy is done." The two officers got in their car and went to the doctor's office that was performing the autopsies that month. Every month the job was switched from one doctor to another. This month was Doctor John. He had just been granted a license to practice medicine.

When the detectives arrived, Larry introduced himself to the doctor. Josephine walked around the office before she, too, introduced herself. Doc John stood as erect as he could. He gave his first report in a monotone. "The deceased was a woman in her early forties. She had had children by cesarean section. Both of her arms were broken. Her left leg was twisted out of its socket. The back of her head was caved in from being banged on the floor. She was not only killed but was also mutilated postmortem. The murder or murderers took their time. There is evidence that after she was dead, the culprits mutilated her body. There was a tremendous amount of blood loss. There was too much blood in the vaginal area for me to tell if she had been raped.

Josephine waited patiently for the doctor to finish his report.

When he was done, she said in a sarcastic tone, "I'm Josephine, the lead detective on this case. I, as well as my partner Larry, would like to know if a seventeen-year-old girl could have done this."

"Judging from the massive injuries and the strength required to inflict them, I doubt it."

"If you examined her, could you tell if she was in the room when the crime happened? If she took part in it?"

"Well, yes. If she were involved, she would have gotten blood in her hair or possibly under her nails. Yes, I think I can."

"Could you come with me? I want you to go to the hospital?"

The doctor nodded his head "yes."

Josephine backed out, "Larry, you go back to headquarters. See if there is anything in the evidence files that might help us. We'll meet up at the hospital. Come on. Let's hurry before that dear nurse washes the suspect or throws her clothes out."

The doctor went with Josephine. They went in his car. As soon as they got to the hospital, they went directly to Ann's room. She was still sleeping. Josephine looked at the doctor, "She doesn't have to be awake for you to examine her, does she?"

"No. I can do what I have to do without disturbing her." The doctor looked in her hair. He took some scrapings from under her nails. The door swung open as the head nurse walked in, screaming.

"Get out of here! How dare you come in to one of my patients' rooms without my permission?"

The doctor responded in a shaky voice, "I was asked by the police to examine her for..."

"Who told you that the police could do something like that? Did they show you a court order? Get out!" The nurse turned to Josephine and started to push her out of the door. "Get out of here. If you don't go right now, I will call security and have you thrown out."

Josephine was stunned and outraged by the outburst of the nurse. She took out her badge as she said, "I am a policewoman. You don't tell me what to do.'

By that time two security guards showed up. The floor nurse heard the commotion, so she had called for security by pushing the panic button. Three orderlies quickly followed the two security guards into the room. Josephine went for her gun. One of the guards took it off of her, and another one pinned her arms behind her. The guard looked at her as he tried to speak in a calm voice, "Are you crazy?" Josephine was taken outside the room. She was brought down the hall to the solarium. She put up a token struggle, for her pride more than anything else was hurt.

Doc John followed, since he didn't know what else to do. In accordance with hospital procedure, the police were called. They came on the floor. The floor nurse directed them to the solarium. The security guard turned Josephine over to the uniformed policeman, along with her gun. The guard said, "You better be careful; she is out of her mind."

The doctor added, "Do you want me to sedate her?"

The hospital administrator showed up. He told everyone to go back to his/her duties. He looked at Doc John as he asked, "Are you on staff here?"

"Well, no, sir. I was asked by the police to examine a patient here." The good doctor was visibly nervous. In that moment he saw his whole career pass before him. He envisioned having his license taken away.

"We cannot allow just anyone to wander the halls of our hospital. We must be shown a court order, allowing you to be here. Do you have one?" As he spoke, the administrator turned his attention to Josephine, who was still arguing with the two policemen who had responded to the call. The two policemen also asked her for a warrant.

"I don't need one, you idiot," she screamed back at the officer.

After a long pause, the administrator added, "Please take her out of here before she upsets the rest of the patients. Get her out of here, and we can just be done with this whole matter."

The policemen agreed and took Josephine with them. She was still yelling that she wanted to arrest the head nurse. One of the officers took her firmly by the arm, as he said, "Don't arrest anyone until you discuss it with the captain. We can always come back for her; she isn't going anywhere."

The doctor was left standing in the hallway. He was all by himself. He promptly left to return to his office.

Back in the room Ann had awakened. She was disoriented by all the commotion. The nurse sat with her to calm her down. A resident doctor came in, but he did not want to give her any more medication. "She's had enough," he said. "Doesn't she have someone to go to? Being in this hospital is going to kill her."

At that moment, Sister Edith came in. She was making the rounds of visiting patients in the hospital. When she heard about the disturbance in Ann's room, she came to see what was going on. She explained to the resident the circumstances of why Ann was there. 'If you release her, I will take her back to the convent house with me. She can stay there until this matter is cleared up."

The resident made Ann sit down, as he wanted to examine her before she was released from the hospital. Very quickly it became apparent that she was physically all right, but she had no recollection of what had happened. She remembered nothing of the previous day or why she was in the hospital. Her only concern was that she wanted someone to contact her mother to tell her she was all right.

A resident psychiatrist was called immediately to meet with Ann. Sister Edith was ordered to leave. She was told that she would be called when Ann was going to be released. Sister Edith was also asked to bring clothes for her, since the clothes Ann had been wearing when admitted were now missing. In the confusion, an orderly had burned them. When asked why, the orderly responded, "They had blood on them. I was told anything with blood on it was to be picked up with these tongs to be burned in the incinerator." As he spoke, he showed the nurse the tongs he used.

The psychiatrist, after examining Ann, concluded that she had a form of amnesia. She had built a wall around the events of the day. She could not remember anything that had happened. The psychiatrist explained, "With peace, rest, and quiet--which it seems she won't get around here--she may regain her memory. A convent house would be an ideal place for her to recover in. There is nothing physically wrong with her. It would be a good idea to give her a few menial chores to do. She should be put back into her normal routine. I will file a report with the police so they won't bother you people anymore."

Sister Edith was called and told of the psychiatrist's recommendations. With that advice, Sister Edith was allowed to take Ann home. The sister brought clothes for Ann from the many clothes that were donated to the church. It was decided to just tell Ann that her mother was sick. Her mother had asked the nuns to take care of her. The psychiatrist, who turned out to be the same psychiatrist that the police used on other cases, agreed to examine her again in a week. He also agreed to meet with police to explain his findings that he had already sent. Sister Edith added, "Keep that Detective Josephine away from here. She's nuts."

The doctor laughed as he walked away. "I'll see what I can do."

When Josephine arrived at police headquarters, she was taken directly to the chief's office. Before he could say anything, Josephine started yelling, "If I were a man, would I have been treated like this? My fellow officers didn't even back me up. I was tracking down evidence in a murder case. My own fellow officers arrested me." Josephine was trying desperately not to cry.

The chief waited for a few minutes, as he handed Josephine tissues from a box he always kept on his desk. When he was satisfied that she had calmed down enough, he spoke in a soft, deliberate tone. "You're off this case. Our psychiatrist will evaluate you before you will be allowed to carry a gun. Until he clears you, you will ride a desk. Now get out."

Josephine got up and stormed out of the office to return to her desk. Her partner, as well as everyone else in the department, stayed away from her the rest of the day. The stories as to what had happened at the hospital circulated, not only in the police station, but in the town as well. Everyone at the high school had his or her own version. Each version was a more creative tale than the truth could ever be.

Ann was given a room in the convent house. She was assigned a list of chores to do. She quietly went about them, but she spoke to no one except Sister Edith. The sister was careful not to mention anything about the incident, since she was assured by the doctor that Ann would remember the scene in her own good time. He had told the nun, "If you mention what happened too soon, she will only press it further down in her mind, building an even bigger wall around it. Nature has a way of healing itself. In this case that would be the best route to follow. Piece by piece, she will be able to deal with what she saw as well as be able to understand what happened. When she is ready, we will all learn what she is going through. Patience and understanding are needed now."

The sister stopped Bob in church that Sunday. She asked him to bring Ann's homework to the house. "Give her a little time. After a while, you can talk to her." That day never came, for Ann never spoke to anyone in the town again.

One night, after she had been in the convent for about a month, she woke up screaming. She remembered. She remembered everything. She was hysterical. The psychiatrist was summoned. He, with a member of the police force, came to the convent to take a statement from Ann. She couldn't add anything to what they already knew. The police department closed its file on Ann, as far as the matter involving her mother was concerned. The police still looked for her father, but as everyone agreed, "He melted into the river itself."

Bob brought all her homework to her, but except for taking the regional test, Ann never left the convent house. She was cut off from the world.

About a year later, Ann was transferred to Cincinnati. It was there that the nuns started to talk to her about becoming a nun. The Mother Superior told her, "You should not become a nun to hide from the world but only to do God's work. Being a nun puts you in the mainstream of life much more than any other thing you can do. You, therefore, have to be strong. You must face each challenge you'll be offered. You must accept God as you would a husband."

Ann didn't know what she wanted to do, but she knew she did not want to leave the peaceful life of an unassuming nun. For the first time, the quiet she had in the convent made her feel good about herself. She did her chores. There were weeks when she didn't have to speak to anyone. The demands her body made on her, she prayed away. The garb she wore hid her physical development from everyone. The only part of her whole psyche she could not control was her drive for knowledge. She read everything she could get her hands on. She had a special gift for numbers. She was put in charge of the house budget because she was the only one who didn't need an adding machine to add up all the numbers. She wrote all the communications to the Motherhouse for the convent itself. The Mother Superior called her into her office one day for a meeting.

"Sit down, Ann. I wanted to talk to you, for your abilities are wasted here at this convent. The church has a need for people who are skillful in the business world. We need people within our organization who can interpret the piles of paper that come in every day. The person must be able to evaluate the many financial as well as the legal problems we are faced with. I think you are such a person. I have spoken to our sister house in Bergen County, New Jersey; they have room for you there. Your studies for becoming a nun will continue, but in addition to those studies, you will be sent to different schools for different studies. If you agree, I will set up your schedule with the different churches you'll be housed at while attending school. Since you will only work for us, there will be no need for you to get a degree from any school; you'll only need to attend certain classes to acquire certain knowledge. After a while, if you wish to return to one of the schools to earn a degree, you can. Now I don't want an answer right now. I want you to think about it. We will meet in one week."

Ann got up from the meeting. She could not believe what she had just heard. It was true; she wanted more of an intellectual challenge than she was getting at the convent, but the idea of going outside of its walls terrified her. The week passed slowly. There was a great anguish in her. She wanted more, but she didn't know of what. Finally it was time for the meeting with the Mother Superior. Ann walked into the room with a determination of will, body, and mind. "I will do whatever you think I should do. I will serve in any capacity you want me to. I know that you have my best interests at heart, so just tell me where to go."

The Mother Superior got up from behind her desk, walked around it, and gave Ann a hug. The hug felt to Ann as warm as her mother's used to. The two women cried. Nothing else was said as Ann wiped her eyes with the sleeve of her habit as she walked out.

As she was walking down the hall, the Mother Superior called out, "I know God will guide your steps."

The next day Ann was sent to a convent house in Philadelphia, Pennsylvania. She was allowed to take certain classes at the Wharton School of Business. It was a thirteen-week semester in accounting, finance, and business. She was in classes with students in different years, from freshmen to seniors. It made no difference to her; she outshone them all. Two weeks into the course, they allowed her to take the first as well as the second semester accounting courses at the same time. She aced both exams.

The next thirteen-week semester was spent in Boston where she attended Harvard University. She was taking their business law classes. Again she was pushed to her intellectual limits. She still wanted more. Her fellow students were all anxious to meet this whiz kid, but Ann came to class to study. She sat away from the rest. She never spoke to anyone. She seldom spoke in class. Her tests were marked separately. Her marks were held in strictest confidence. This meant that half the school knew how she did one day after the test. The rest of the school found out the following day.

Following the same procedure as the year before, Ann found herself in Bergen County. From there, she attended Seton Hall University. The suggestion that she stay at a house closer to the campus was ignored. From Bergen County, she and three other students were taken to school. They were brought back as a group. They would all be dropped off at the cafeteria, where they had breakfast. They were picked up from the library for the trip back. They were allowed to wear an abbreviated habit that made them stick out from the rest of the students. This special attention bothered Ann, but she could not do anything about it.

Ann was allowed to work at the Office of the Archdiocese in Newark. She was quickly made the financial officer. She had no title, but everyone knew that if they wanted to know something, Ann was the one to ask. Any discussion about her moving closer to her work was answered with, "No." That would end the topic.

Ann was soon spending less time in school, for she needed to spend more time in the office. Everything went to her desk. She would sort the items out. She got the job of directing the mail to the different departments. She decided who was to do what. Every so often, cash would be sent to the administration office by mistake. Ann would open her locked drawer to put the money in. There was never more than two or three dollars in any envelope. She didn't receive money every day. Every so often, Ann would take the money out of the drawer to deposit it in the collection basket.

A new machine called a computer was starting to be used by many businesses. Everyone recognized the growth of its use. Ann was quickly named as head of the committee to see what functions it could perform for the church and how quickly its applications could be incorporated into the daily routine of the church. Ann immediately put all the mailing functions on it. Everyone applauded her abilities with this new machine. Each day found her doing more tasks with it.

Ann celebrated her twenty-fifth birthday in Bergen County. The nickname "The Baby Nun" still applied. Ann's angelic face never made her look a day over sixteen. Her body development did not stop. Her natural desires weren't so easily prayed away.

In the different schools she attended, she would never take part in idle conversations, but that did not stop her from hearing what was being said. The Monday morning laments by her fellow students as to what had occurred over the weekend were always a source of enjoyment to Ann. She found herself living vicariously through the stories she heard. She was an ardent listener, even though she never took an active part in the conversations. The other girls knew she was listening but would not try to engage her in the conversation. They would let her listen without acknowledging that she was even there. Every so often the lady who had the floor would ask, "Ann, do you have any questions yet?" or "Ann, do you want me to repeat anything?" On those occasions, Ann would just leave. On one occasion, Ann replied, "No, I like to hear how you're preparing your soul for damnation." With that response, the conversation of the group changed to what was new in the fashion world.

Ann started to view her life as that of a bonded servant that she had read about in her history classes. When she thought back to her childhood, when she had lived with her mother, her life seemed to be like that of her mother's. She started to have dreams about her mother's death, but in her dreams, her mother wasn't the one who was killed; it was she. The reality of the dream was so vivid that she woke up screaming on more than one occasion and found herself perspiring profusely.

Ann's room was the last one down the hall. She was isolated from the rest. When she screamed, no one heard her. One night she got out of bed. She just had to get out of her room. She wrapped herself in her robe as she went out her door and into the hallway. At the end of the hallway was a door that led to the back of the house. The door was always kept locked, but tonight the key had been left in the lock. Ann opened the door to walk out into the cool, night air. The sky was overcast. There was an occasional break in the clouds that let the light from the moon and stars shine through. There was no light in the courtyard. A street lamp outside the wall that surrounded the back of the convent took on a deep, mysterious, foreboding look. None of this bothered Ann as she walked around the backyard. Occasionally, she would trip over a branch or a stone, but none of that would deter her as she examined her own thoughts while, at the same time, examining the wall. There was a back door to the courtyard that had a bar across it that could be lifted so the door could be pushed opened. Ann carefully removed the bar so that she would not make any noise. She was going to venture out but remembered she only had a robe on, so she quietly replaced the cross bar as she returned to her room (or cell, as it was sometimes referred to). As Ann sat on her bed, her mind wandered to the stories she had heard from the girls at school of the area of Union City where there was a group of nightclubs. The area was only six blocks from where Ann was sitting. The thought of how the area looked started to intrigue Ann. She found herself being drawn to it.

Ann always kept a street outfit in her room. If asked about it, she would comment that she kept it there in case she had to attend a meeting outside of the church. The other people there felt uneasy about her religious attire. "Our world is not the business world. After all, that is what you're sending me to school to learn." The outfit in no way could be considered fashionable or stylish. The grayish color of the jacket and skirt projected the personality of the person wearing it. Some of the money that Ann had been handed by people as a contribution to the order was put in the top drawer of her bedside night table. She had no mirror in her room, but with her hands, she fashioned a hairstyle of sorts. As she slipped on her black loafers on this, her twenty-fifth birthday night, she was about to look at the world. Night prayers had been said hours before, so at midnight on this Friday night of her twenty-fifth year, Ann left her room. She walked through the garden, out the door, and onto the dimly lit street. She was going to see the area she had heard about only six blocks and a million miles away. This was the first time in eight years that Ann had been out alone.

The walk to the club area only took a few seconds. As she turned the last corner, she marveled to herself at how close the clubs really were. The area was just as it had been described in the stories she had heard in school. Ann was older than most of the people scurrying from one club to the other, but she looked much younger than most of them. Each group of girls that Ann passed was so busy arranging and rearranging their clothes and hair that they didn't notice Ann in her mousy, gray suit. The boys were another story. As she passed them, they didn't miss a thing. Her outfit was a little snug. Each group of boys she passed commented on the physical features that had been hidden all these years. Ann did not outwardly respond to any comment but took note of all of them. She walked past each club all the way around the entire area, which encompassed four blocks. The biggest club was triangular in shape. It was by far the largest of the group. People walked in and out of each of the clubs in the area. The biggest one had the best-sounding music. There was a five-piece group playing. Every so often, one of the members of the group would walk up to the microphone and start singing.

"Come on, honey. In or out." The words came from a large gentleman, standing by the door. There was a group of six girls behind her. Before Ann could do anything, she found herself being pushed into the club. Once inside, she saw that the large room was divided in half. On one side was a large circular bar, in the center of which was the band. Bartenders were running around the inside of the bar, trying to fill all the orders for drinks that were being shouted at them. There was an open petition that separated the bar from the other half of the room. On the side away from the bar were tables arranged around a dance floor that was jammed with people. The noise level in the entire room was deafening, as the musicians were playing loudly enough to be heard over the noise of the crowd, and the people were talking loudly enough to be heard over the music of the band. The entire scene was like a three-ring circus without a ringmaster.

Ann was pushed along through the crowd. Every so often, someone would grab her arm or some other part of her, but by the time she reacted, she was shoved further into the room. She walked over by the dance floor. She marveled at the floor that was so crowded that no one was really dancing but rather standing still and swaying to the music. Ann found herself being pushed around, as people were still trying to get on the dance floor while others tried to get off. It seemed everyone was talking at the same time, but she could not understand what was being said. She worked her way around the dance floor to the far side so that she could look back to see the crowded bar. Everyone seemed to be having a good time. She remembered one of the comments she had heard at school. One of the girls was asked why she went to a club. "You never let anyone pick you up. You always come home alone. Why do you bother going?"

"When I'm there, I come alive. Just being around all those people makes me feel as though I belong. I don't go home with anyone because I don't feel like having to fight my way out of the car. Just being there is enough excitement to last me for the week."

"Hell, that's the only reason I go," was the response from another girl.

Ann was now seeing firsthand what they were talking about. As Ann saw everyone parading around, she became aware of the total inadequacy of her own clothes. Her outfit looked horrid by comparison. Ann felt the unmistakable fangs of pride bite into her. She suddenly realized what the nuns were talking about when they said, "The hardest thing for a nun to learn is to unlearn what she was taught her whole life about pride." The nun continued, "We look a certain way. The way we look teaches us to respect our body rather than put it on display." Ann laughed to herself, for it was easy to see that none of the girls in the club, especially the ones on the dance floor, left anything to the imagination.

"Would you like to dance?"

"No, thank you."

"Would you like a drink?"

"No, thank you."

'What the hell did you come for?"

"I don't know," she responded. Ann turned to head for the door. She told herself that she didn't know why she had come. But now that she was there, she could not say that any more. She came for the same reason the girls at school came—she was in search of adventure. She also knew that she had to find someone to have that adventure with. As she was thinking, she was being shoved along the pathway between the bar and the wall. She was shoved into someone with such force that she almost knocked him off the stool he was sitting on. He spilled his drink. He turned to face her. When he saw her, the rage in his eyes calmed down. He started wiping the liquid off of himself as Ann helped him. One of the bartenders, standing nearby, quickly produced a towel. The mess was cleaned up immediately.

"Please give him another drink. I spilled that one on him."

"What about you?" the bartender asked.

"Oh, just give me the same thing." Ann shifted her weight from one foot to the other, as she wasn't sure what she should say or do. She stood by the man's side in a state of confusion. A look of bewilderment was on her face. The loud music being played, along with the constant jostling by the people passing her, further aggravated her uneasiness.

Chapter Four

"My name is Ann. I am sorry that, well, I was pushed into you. I'm sorry."

"Here are your drinks, Miss," the bartender said.

"Ann fumbled in her pockets for some money, but by that time George had paid for them. "No, I want to pay for them. Wait. I know I have money here somewhere. Oh, here it is," she said as she handed George a hand full of money. "Is that enough?"

"It's more than enough." George got up to move the stool by her so she could sit on it.

"I can't stay."

"What about your drink? I can't drink both of them."

Ann looked at George, as he stood next to her. He was a big, tall man with broad shoulders. He had brown, wavy hair that seemed to have a mind of its own as to where it was going to settle. He was trying desperately to smile, but he looked more nervous than she felt. Ann was glad he was taller than she. She always was one of the tallest girls in school. That fact had always bothered her. This was especially true when she was the last in line when the class had to line up according to height. Bob had been the only person taller than she in grammar school. The end of the line was always Ann and then Bob. Ann smiled as she said, "I think you can drink them both, as well as two more after that."

In an annoyed tone, George said, "All right. Go." George turned away from her. He went back to staring aimlessly into the room.

Ann started to walk away but stopped. She looked at George, who had turned his back on her. He was once again sitting quietly on the stool. She worked her way back to him. At first she just stood next to him. Finally she said, "May I have one of your drinks?"

George had to turn around on the stool to see who was talking. 'I don't know. Are you going to be bitchy or nice?"

"Are you going to let me sit on the stool? If you do, and you give me one of the drinks, I'll be nice."

"A drink, as well as the stool, it is."

"My name is Ann. What is yours?"

"George. I'm George. I'm lonely and alone. I am glad you took pity on me."

Ann sat on the stool, as she turned to face George. "I'm Ann. I'm alone. I have not resolved whether or not I'm lonely. But I'll tell you what we'll do; we'll talk to each other to see if we have anything in common, as long as you don't start asking a lot of questions."

"My lips are sealed. The only problem I have is how are we going to find out if we're compatible if we don't ask questions? I mean, I'm not too good at this chit-chat stuff, so you be in charge."

"This arrangement isn't going to work out because I am not one to stay here so I can scream over a band. I was hoping you would take charge of the "getting to know each other," but I do see your point. Well, okay. You ask three questions, and then I'll ask three questions. That procedure should start a conversation." Ann thought to herself, "He must think I'm weird. I feel as though I'm running a business meeting rather than being...what is it the girls at school would say? Oh, I remember—getting picked up."

Ann looked down at the bar. She saw that her hands were folded as though she were praying. She jerked as she put them down by her side. She didn't even feel as though they belonged to her. The realization that she was at a bar, talking to a man, started to make her feel very uncomfortable. Her hands were back up on the bar. She saw that they were actually trembling.

The cotton taste in her mouth added to her nervousness. She picked up the drink. She drank half of it in one gulp. The liquid refreshed her and, at the same time, made her tingle. She could feel her palms start to sweat as her face flushed. She stood up. She started to move around in time to the music, except she didn't realize that's what she was doing. "Can we get out of here?" Ann realized what she had just said, but she really didn't mean to invite George to come with her. She was asking herself if she could leave. Ann started to feel panicky as George took her by the arm and led the way out of the club. The cooling night air made her feel better but lightheaded. She had heard the girls talk about the effects drinks had on them, but Ann had never had a drink before, other than a taste of beer once in a while from the can her father had been drinking from, but that was horrible tasting. The drink she had in the bar tasted good, but this new feeling that was coming over her started to make her feel uneasy. "I better go; I mean, I have to go." As she spoke, she started walking toward the convent. When she became aware that George was walking with her, she turned toward him as she half shouted, "You can't come with me."

George didn't say a word. The expression on his face showed his shock as well as his disappointment better than he could have expressed these two feelings with words. He stood in the middle of the sidewalk as Ann started to walk away. He said nothing.

After taking a few steps, Ann walked back as she spoke, "Please don't be mad at me. I didn't realize it was so late. I'm not used to this. You can see I am very bad at making new acquaintances. I would like to try again." Ann couldn't believe she was saying the words that she heard. She had planned to walk around the clubs. Now she had been in one. In addition, a man had wanted to take her home. What had started out as an innocent plan had turned into her making a date, her first one. At twenty-five, she was going on her first date. That thought weighed on her mind. "I'll meet you right here next week at ten-thirty. By that time I'll be less of a screwball. Okay?"

George just grunted, as he watched Ann walk away. He watched until she got to the next corner. When she was at that corner, she turned around and waved good-bye. George was still in a state of shock as he waved back. He turned to walk to his car. He mumbled under his breath, "It figures; out of all the people in the club, I have to meet a nut." George resolved he had had enough excitement for one night, so he just drove home.

Ann hurried down the streets' leading back to the convent. She was pleased with herself for going but mad at herself for giving into the desires of her body. She kept thinking, "I did nothing wrong. Anyway, I don't think he even likes me. He didn't do any of the things the girls in school said the guys they meet do. She stopped as she said out loud, "He didn't try to kiss me. He didn't even hold my hand." She suddenly realized she was talking to herself. She quickened her pace because the walk back to the convent seemed much farther than she remembered when she had gone to the clubs. Finally the door to the courtyard was in sight. She went back into the courtyard. She shut the door and returned the bar to the slots that it fit in. She went in the backdoor of the convent to the safety of her room. She still had the key to the back door in her hand. She resolved she would keep it. "I'll have one made tomorrow. There is a locksmith right down the street." She undressed in the darkness but could not get the sight of all the people in the bar out of her mind. She could not get the sight of George out of her mind. "Out of all of them, he picked me." With that thought, she fell off into a sleep that came with dreams. She felt tired, but she didn't want to sleep for fear of forgetting all about the night. Finally she drifted off.

George drove home, not sure of what had happened. This meeting someone he didn't know was a new experience for him.

He couldn't remember the first stranger he ever met. In George's world, everyone knew everyone else. That was the way it was. No strangers. No new people. George had gone to the club area because, like Ann, he had heard about it. George was younger than the boys who held court on the corner every night. In fact, people said, "He was born old. He's just waiting for his age to catch up to the way he looks."

The legal drinking age was twenty-one. George looked older, but he was only seventeen. George's parents were immigrants. His parents regulated his exposure to the world very closely. His father owned a small business, so George's life from when he could remember was school or work. There was no after-school playtime. His schedule was school and work. The other people whom he went to school with developed groups that would go to all the sporting events from school, but George could not go. Everyone naturally excluded him from activities, since he was never around. In school, he would not have too much free time, since he had to get his schoolwork done during school hours. He rarely brought books home. The teachers, because of his size and disposition, saw him as an ally in keeping order in the class. As long as he took care of the noisemakers in class, he was assured a passing grade. Whether or not he learned anything was immaterial.

Some of the teachers saw that his classmates excluded George from their activities. The part that bothered them was that he didn't care. He saw no big deal in being part of some group. When he became a senior, his counselor asked what he would do with his life. George stared at him in bewilderment. He had no direction that he wanted to head in, so he would reply, "I'll see what opens up. That's when I'll make my mind up, at that time, not now."

No matter what was shown to him by way of a career, nothing interested him. Consequently, he took the easiest courses in school. He just existed as far as any social life was concerned. Since he looked so much older than his classmates, he started to spend more time with the older boys in town. He looked as old as they, but he was not ready for some of their activities. He would find himself in a group but not wanting to take part in what they were thinking of doing. The group took this aloofness as a sign of disloyalty, so they did not want him around. George's father sold his business. George found he had a lot more time on his hands. He had graduated from high school but did not even think in terms of getting a job. Rather he only thought of starting his own business. That is what he did. He started to want more out of life than just working. He started to hear words such as wife, girlfriend, or other terms of endearment. When he went to the places people his age went to, he just did not fit in. The main problem was that he didn't want to.

Being alone not only became a habit but a preferred way to live. George went where he wanted and did what he wanted. It was one night when George went to a movie that he stopped at a diner afterwards. He met an old school chum, Andy. The two boys started talking. They struck up a friendship. They decided that they would go to a local dance that was to be held at the church that Saturday night. When they arrived, there were a lot of people that George knew from school. By the end of the night, the entire group (that numbered over twenty) decided to stay in touch with each other. They would plan other activities. George put his friend, Andy, in charge. "You be in charge of staying in touch, since I'm no good at that sort of thing. When something is planned that you want to go to, you call me to give me the details."

The group was evenly divided between the sexes. Every week there was something going on: one week a local dance, another a picnic, the third a trip to New York City. The group started to break off into couples. George never complained. He would go with anyone who was left over. His attitude of not caring whom he was with created a problem, since the girls became very upset that George just didn't care whom he was with. When the other boys in the group would make a separate date with one of the girls, there was an underlying tone of "she was his girl." George would not take part in any such discussions. He would tell Andy, "It doesn't make any difference to me, so let's just enjoy each other's company. As far as I'm concerned, one girl is just like any other."

Unbeknownst to George, Andy let George's feelings be known to the rest of the group. George became an instant outcast. The problem was that George didn't know he was. He was oblivious to the fact that when the group went anywhere, they shunned him. This attitude toward George really started to bother one girl. At one house party that was being given by one of the group as a surprise birthday party for another member, liquor was being served. One girl, Mary Lou--the self-proclaimed leader of the group--was mad that George seemed to be having a good time, listening in on the other conversations. Mary Lou stood watching him. After a few drinks, she walked up to George and started screaming at him, "Don't you realize that no one here wants to be with you?"

Everyone in the room looked at her. They were in shock at her outburst. The party was in the basement of one girl's house. The basement had been finished to look just like a little nightclub. There were little tables on one side of the room with two couches up against another wall. There was a bar made out of white stone with black cement against another wall. The lighting was from recessed spotlights of different colors. A separate dimmer switch regulated each color. Mary Lou was standing under the red lights. She looked like the devil itself as she stood there, glaring down at George.

George was seated on one of the couches. He was surprised by Mary Lou's outburst. "So what?" he asked. "You want me to leave?" His response was said in a surprised tone of voice. His facial expression was one of complete surprise. He started to stand, but Mary Lou stood in front of him. She would not let him get up.

"No, you idiot. What is wrong with you? Don't you care that no one is coming by you?" Mary Lou had been the queen of her high school senior dance. She never could quite understand when everyone didn't fall all over himself, trying to meet her. To have George not care one way or the other about her was just too much for her on this evening.

Andy walked over. He could see that George was not being affected by anything Mary Lou was saying, so he interceded, "Why don't you get off his back? You don't like him. So what. He could care less, so why are you getting so mad?" Andy had been acting as the bartender for the party. To make sure the drinks were properly made, he tasted them. His test tasting had started to affect him. George had to stand up to hold on to Andy so he wouldn't topple over. He held Andy up as Andy came to his aid. "He comes to anything we want to do, I mean, to any place we want to go. He comes to all the parties. He always helps out. No matter what we ask him to do, he does it. He never complains. No one said he had to like any of you. He enjoys just being around all of us, so why don't you leave him alone?" Mary Lou, who realized that she was being a fool, became incensed. She blurted out, "What are you two—going together?" You must be queer!"

George, who was having trouble keeping Andy in an upright position, tried to push him onto a couch that was nearby. Try as he might to get past Mary Lou so that he could hold Andy, Mary Lou kept pushing herself between the two boys. Andy fell on the couch and bounced off onto the floor. Everyone started to laugh. No one came to help George pick him up and put him back on the couch. Mary Lou did not let up with her verbal onslaught.

She faced George as she continued, "Leave him there!" she

screamed. "Do you need him to defend you?"

George paid no attention to her but rather got Andy up. He sat him on the couch. George went to the sink to get a wet towel to put on Andy's face. George was doing all this, while Mary Lou kept screaming. "Who the hell do you think you are? What? Do you think you're better than the rest of us? Is that why you don't bother with any of us?"

Andy sobered up enough to try to stand again. With George's help, he stood upright. He spoke in a soft tone that was in direct opposition to Mary Lou's screaming as he replied, "He just doesn't like you. What's wrong with that?" Mary Lou started crying as she left the room. George looked at Andy as he commented, "You're a class act. Come on. I'll take you home."

"No way. I'm not leaving a perfectly good party because of that bitch. Everyone to the bar, the drinks are on me." George pulled Andy out of the house where the party was being held. He walked him around the block. Andy started to sober up as he said, "Come on. We'll go back to the house. They have some coffee there. No one at the party was old enough to drink, so bringing out the liquor had been a bad idea. By the time George, with Andy still in his arms, got back to the party, the liquor had been put away, and coffee was being served. Mary Lou was in one corner, crying. George saw to it that Andy was on the other side of the room, drinking coffee. Everyone could feel the tension between the two of them. The whole experience made George feel very uncomfortable. He vowed never to be with the group again. The night ended on a very sour note. George put Andy in the car. Thankfully, by time he got him home, Andy felt that he could go up the steps to his room without George's help.

The following week, George received a call from Mary Lou. She wanted to invite him to come with the group. They were all going to a dance that weekend. She wanted George to come. George could hear voices in the background, egging her on. George just told her "no." "I don't think I should come. I guess you're right; I just don't fit in. Skip me this time, but remember me for the next get together."

George spent the week, trying to understand why he was the way he was. Was Mary Lou right when she said he was nuts? He buried himself in his work. He had heard rumors that there was a company that wanted to buy his business. It was just talk, but like all rumors, there's usually some truth to them. By working extra long hours, George forgot about what had happened. When Saturday night came, the night of the dance that he'd said he didn't want to go to, he decided to stay home that night. After a while he became bored, so he got dressed and resolved that he was going out. He had heard stories about a group of nightclubs located in Union City in Bergen County. Tonight, he decided that he was going to see if the stories were true. He got directions from gas stations along the way. He found himself driving around the four-block area where the clubs were located. The largest one was a triangle. From all indications, it was the busiest club in the group. He parked the car and went in. As he looked around the room, he got caught up in all of the activity. He found a seat at the bar, where he could see the dance floor. George sat down on the empty stool. When the band (which was located in the middle of the bar) played, it was impossible to hear anything but the blaring saxophone. If the song was slow the dance floor was crowded. There was nothing to see that was of much interest. When it was a fast song, the girls took over. They put on a floorshow for the rest of the place. George found himself cheering with the rest of the group. He felt as though he belonged to this nameless, faceless group. It was that night that George met Ann.

Chapter Five

The week crawled by for George. He was still not sure whether or not he had a date for Saturday night. He looked back at his meeting with Ann like meeting a mirage or something like that. His outward behavior was as though he was in a fog. Whenever George did not act in his usual casual manner, his five sisters picked up on it in a second. They were suspicious that something had happened. He went to get a haircut without being told to. That added to their suspicions. They knew something was up. George even went shopping for a new shirt. When he walked in with the box, took the shirt out, and tried it on; that was proof positive that big things were going to happen.

"Big date?" one of them would ask.

George replied in his usual soft tones, "Shut up." His parents never interfered with his social life, since they realized that their son was growing up at a faster pace than the people around him. They adopted the attitude that when he was ready, he would say something. His mother relied on his sisters to keep tabs on their little brother.

Saturday arrived. He dressed in his new shirt. With his new haircut, he was set to go. As he drove over to Union City, he realized that this was his first date with a total stranger. He knew nothing about her. This fact alone started to give him some cause for alarm. He thought of all the questions he should have asked but hadn't. He started to mentally make a list of all the questions he was going to ask. The closer he got, the more questions he had. He started to question why he was going. As he drove, he resolved that she would not show up. He would spend another night in the middle of a group of people, but he would be alone. George resolved that it would be better to be alone in a crowd than to be alone with some girl he knew nothing about. He had heard many war stories from the people he knew. Some were not so pleasant. Andy always had a new adventure to tell him. The problem was that he didn't believe the stories he heard. The next corner was the corner before the one where he was to pick her up. He waited for the light to turn green. His mouth went dry. His hands gripped the wheel so tightly that he felt his hands go cold as his circulation stopped. He looked in the mirror to see if his hair was still combed, when he realized that the car behind him was flashing its lights as the driver was blowing its horn. The light had turned green. George hadn't realized it. George stepped on the gas and the car lunged forward. This was the block. There she was. He looked at his watch; they were both right on time. A thought flashed through George's mind, "Was that her? Yes. What was her name?" George pulled to the curb. He stopped. He was grateful when Ann got in. The car with blinking lights was still behind him, so George just pulled away before he said anything.

Ann started to speak as George drove off. Just the sound of her voice put George at ease. "I didn't know if you would come. I was starting to wonder what I would do if you didn't."

During the week Ann had spent a lot of time in the room where they stored the clothes that were donated to the church for the poor. She had gone through the piles, sorting them by color, style, but most of all, by size. She had assembled four beautiful outfits. In the room, they had a sewing machine that someone had donated. Ann busied herself by making small repairs to some of the items. She spent a lot of time altering the ones she wanted. She took the ironing board out to press her outfits first. Later she did some of the rest. She even found new shoes to wear with her new things. She started to wonder if she could wear high heels, for she never had worn them before. First of all, she was taller than most people without them. Second, she didn't have any need for high heels in the convent.

Tonight was her night. They hurt her feet, but she had them on. Once in the car, she took them off. As George looked over, he saw her bare feet. She said, "They're new. They hurt my feet."

"Yeah, I know. My sisters do the same thing. I have to find the shoes so they can put them back on when they get out of the car." They both laughed. That exchange of words reduced the tension in the car. George continued, "You look so beautiful that I wasn't sure if it was you, standing there. I figured I'd stop. If you got in, you were the right person. By the way, how did you know it was I? You didn't see my car the last time we were together."

"I just figured that if you stopped, you must be the one."

"You must have been very annoyed that I was the only one to stop."

"Oh no. I had three other offers. But you were the only one to lean over to open the door. Where are you going?"

"I really hadn't thought about a place to go. I was hoping you would have some ideas."

"No," she said. "I really don't. Could we just go someplace quiet that's close?"

"One close, quiet place coming up." Down the street from the club where they had met was a little jazz club that George had gone to before he met Ann. It was a dark, out-of-the-way bar. He thought that it would be a perfect place for two people to get to know each other. George could not get the nervous feeling he had to go away. He wondered if Ann felt the same way. George pulled into a parking place about a block from the club. They got out after Ann put her shoes back on. As Ann got out, she was tugging on her skirt to pull it down to the proper length. She realized that she had made it a little too snug. She wrapped her light coat around herself. The couple went into the club arm-in-arm.

On the way in, Ann pushed money into George's pocket, for the clothes weren't the only things she had allocated for her own use. "Please, I don't want you spending your money on me. I don't think I'm worth it. Please, now, don't argue with me."

"Do you mind if I make up my own mind about what you're worth?" George responded, as he looked around the room for an empty table.

"Let's not have our first argument so soon, please?" They walked over to an empty table to sit down.

"You are something else. I feel like a, I don't know what. Do you want a drink?"

"Okay, but not the one you ordered last time. I drank that. It went right to my head."

"There was nothing wrong with the drink; it was that you drank it right down. You shouldn't have done that.'

"Okay, get me what you get. This time I'll drink it slower."

George gave their order to the waitress just as the five-piece group came back to play. The song they started their set off with was a quiet, slow tune. Ann's eyes lit up as she said, "Let's dance."

"You have to take your coat off first."

Ann smiled, "You're so quick." Ann, in a grand gesture, took her coat off. She hung it over the back of the chair. The skirt /blouse combination she had on just fit her. As she walked, it seemed to have a mind of its own as to where on her body it was going to stay. Her unsteadiness on the heels was something to see. She reminded George of his sisters when they would play dress up. He laughed quietly to himself. "I forgot to ask you if you knew how to dance," she said with a twinkle in her eye.

"Me? They call me twinkle toes." They made their way onto the dance floor. As he put his arm around her, he tried to remember when he had ever danced with a stranger before. George was an accomplished dancer. With five sisters, whenever any of them wanted to dance, he was her partner.

They also had no reservation about telling him in a loud, clear voice if he was doing something wrong. As he walked out to the dance floor, he made a mental note to thank them one day.

Ann was more nervous than she had ever been in her life. Her clothes felt as though they were working their way off her. No matter how much she pulled on her skirt, she still felt it was too short. Her large bust filled the blouse to the point where she felt the buttons would pop off at any moment. After she took a quick survey of the other women in the room, she realized that she was the only one without stockings. She had found none in the donations. She really didn't have time to go buy any. She was about to dance her first dance and even her shoes weren't being of any use.

"Why don't you take them off, if they are that uncomfortable?"

Ann glared at George.

"I mean your shoes. You look like you're in agony."

Ann went back to the table and kicked them off. She ran back to George's outstretched arms. She half fell into them as she whispered, "Thank you for being so understanding. Now don't do anything too tricky. I don't know how to dance, especially in my bare feet. I also feel very uncomfortable."

"Would you rather sit down?"

"No." Ann did not want to sit out one dance, even though she didn't know what she was doing. She found that dancing with a man was exhilarating. George patiently led her through all the steps, for he too found that dancing with a stranger in her bare feet was exciting.

When they finally found themselves back at the table, Ann excused herself to go freshen up. George took his first sip of his drink. By now the ice had all melted. The drink tasted horrible, but he didn't mind. He laughed at himself for having any doubts about coming because she was a wonderful person to be with. Ann at last came back. As she sat down, she was just beaming.

She took a small sip of her drink. Her facial expression said it all. She put it down, "You actually enjoy this?"

"It gets to you. After a while, you really don't care how it tastes."

"I believe that." Ann reached across the table to turn George's arm so she could see his watch. The smile left her face as she announced, "We have to leave."

George could not hide the disappointment or the anger he felt. He didn't have to speak. His shocked, angry look spoke louder than any words he could say. He got up to help her find her shoes. He stood patiently by, holding her coat as she put her shoes on. In an eerie silence, they left the club. In the car, the atmosphere was not any better. George drove to the designated corner in silence. He pulled to the curb. Ann turned to face him. "I realize you're annoyed at me, but I do have to go. Will I see you next week? I'll make sure I can stay out later. She leaned over to kiss him.

"Are you going to pat me on the head next?" George asked in a strained voice.

"Next week, same time." With those words, Ann got out of the car. She put her hand in her pocket to make sure she had her key as she left. George watched as she went down the street. He was going to follow her but decided against it. He drove home, not knowing what he felt. Anger? Love? Frustration? He ran out of choices. During the week he would find Andy. He had to relate his experience to him. Andy knew everything. The rest of the drive home was done with an uneasy feeling that maybe getting involved with this girl was not the right thing to do.

The week started out like all others with George going to work. He was trying to forget Ann. He became more engrossed with trying to make a living. Business was not good. The question of whether or not he should stay in business was starting to weigh on his mind. The rumor that a company wanted to buy him out was heard more often. A lot of people where asking him if it was true.

Up to that time, no one had contacted George about a sale. That night, which was a Wednesday, he still had not forgotten Ann. That thought alone drove him to forget about everything except her. After dinner he left his house. He started to walk in no particular direction. He was so deep in thought that when he realized where he was, he was in the shopping area of his town. His thoughts so preoccupied him that he walked right into a girl, almost knocking her over. In his usual manner, he mumbled something about being sorry. The girl started talking to him. The words sounded like they were coming from a far distance. George was about to walk away when in a loud, clear tone he heard, "Are you alive?"

George turned to face the direction of the voice. He recognized the speaker's voice and responded, "Mary Lou. It's you. I'm so sorry. Are you hurt? You Ok? I wasn't even looking where I was walking. I'm sorry. Come on; let me help you, please?"

Mary Lou resisted as George took some of her packages.

"I'm parked on the next street. I thought you hit me on purpose because of what I said the last time we were together."

"What did you say?" George asked in a surprise tone.

"At the party. Don't you remember? What is wrong with you? Why are you walking around in such a daze? Where is your car?"

"Home, it's home. I just felt like taking a walk. I didn't realize that I walked this far." Mary Lou was walking ahead as George followed behind her.

"Something must really be bothering you. Here's my car. Do you want a lift home before you walk into someone or something else?"

"No. I'd rather just put your things in the car. "George started to walk away but stopped and hesitantly turned to face her again. In a sheepish tone he said, "Will you walk a little with me."

Mary Lou was surprised by George's request. His asking her anything was out of character. In fact, those were the most words she had ever heard George say to anyone, let alone her. They knew each other but certainly were not on a friendly basis. "What do you want to talk to me about? A girl? Sure, it must be about a girl. Nothing else could get you to look the way you do. I don't believe it. You're having women problems? George, are you keeping something from me? Are you really leading two lives?" Her comments were all said in a sarcastic tone.

George realized that his idea of talking to her was stupid. He turned away and started to walk again.

"Wait. This I got to hear."

"Not if you're going to...Oh, never mind."

"Wait," Mary Lou yelled as she hurriedly put her packages in the car. She quickly locked it. In two strides, she was next to George, putting her arm in his. They walked toward the park that was next to the shopping area. There was a section of rides for the kids. The night was pleasant, so the area was crowded. Once they were past it, Mary Lou asked as her arm was in his, "Are you going to talk to me?"

"Well, I met this girl." After that introduction, George hesitated as he swallowed hard. He felt tense, yet relaxed, as he was walking with Mary Lou. Before he realized it, he had told her the whole story of how he had met Ann. He described their date. When he was done, he ended with, "I don't know why, but I can't get her out of my mind. What makes it worse is that I know nothing about her. When I'm with her, I don't want to be any other place. I've got to tell you, it is a scary, new experience for me."

Mary Lou had been listening very intently. "You mean you were sitting in a bar, and she came over to you and dumped a drink on you in order to meet you? That's a new one on me. She must have really wanted to meet you."

"No, it was an accident. Anyway, I think it was. When you say it like that, I don't know." George's voice expressed the confusion he was feeling inside.

"Well, if she wanted to meet you, how else could she? She didn't have any way of doing it, did she? For her to be in the bar by herself, she must be older than you are. Is she?"

What followed next was a list of questions to which George's answers were, "I don't know," or every so often, "I don't think so."

Finally Mary Lou asked, "Do you have her phone number?"

"No. I never asked her for it. Should I have?"

"Well, yes, if you want to see her again. Is she pretty? I mean, you must know that!" Mary Lou's tone had a sarcastic ring to it. Mary Lou had a way of being very attentive as she lingered on every word that was said. In a matter of seconds, her tone changed to one of a condescending bitch. George thought she had switched personalities with someone else.

George stopped to ponder the question for a minute before he replied, "Well, yes. I mean, she's a lot like you, only bigger." George started to make a gesture with his hands. He saw the reaction on Mary Lou's face, as he realized what he was doing. He put his hands down by his side as he turned beet red. "I really don't know. All girls are pretty to me."

Mary Lou started to laugh as George followed her back to her car. When they arrived, George was about to go when Mary Lou added, "Where are you going now?"

"Home, I guess."

"Do you want to go to a party at my school? It's a mixer. I think the diversion will do you some good. Anyway, you have nothing else to do until Saturday night." By the expression on George's face, she knew he didn't know what she was talking about. In an annoyed tone, she added, "A mixer is a party where everyone comes. They bring someone so that everybody at the party can get to meet him/her. No one is with anyone; we just all sort of hang out together. Come on. You'll probably love it. On the way, you can tell me about this mysterious girl that has you walking around in a daze. Come on; get in."

George nodded "yes" as he got in the car. As soon as they were on the way, Mary Lou started with her analysis of George's problem. "She could be married, and that is why she didn't give you her phone number."

"You never gave me yours. Does that mean you're married?" George responded.

"I never give my phone number out unless I want to. Anyway the boy is supposed to ask for it. I wouldn't give just anyone my number. In your case, I never figured you wanted it." George was surprised by Mary Lou's apparent annoyance at his question. "She could have a child she doesn't want you to know about."

George was taken aback by that comment. "A kid?"

"Yes. She has a kid. She may want to know you better before she tells you about it. You don't have to be married to have children. Your friend Andy is going out with a married woman."

"He is?"

"He's your friend. You didn't know that?"

"No. I don't ask him whom he goes out with. When something is going on, he calls me, and I go with him. I really don't care."

"Did you go over your problem with him?"

"No."

"Well, why did you ask me? You certainly know him better than you know me, don't you?"

"Not really. I've known you longer. Anyway, you're smarter than he is." Mary Lou didn't respond but parked the car in the parking area. She got out of the car. George followed behind her.

"We'll stay an hour only. I have homework to do. Now

everyone here is your age. They are all nice people. Try not to get in trouble." They walked into the large room where the party was being held. A group of girls Mary Lou knew called her over to their group. They were all wondering what she was doing with George. George didn't look like he belonged. Mary Lou introduced him to everyone. When George left to get her a soda, she explained to her friends, "He just looks that way. He's really a nice person."

George got the sodas and walked back to where Mary Lou was standing. The mixing process had begun, for George had to walk in between people to get to her with her soda. After making his delivery, George withdrew to the far side of the room, out of everyone's way. A girl walked up to him with a nametag on her hat that said "Party Hostess." "Hi, I'm Janet. Who are you?"

George looked at her. She was shorter than he was. She had her hair done up on top of her head. She wore a hat that reminded him of a dunce cap. It made her look even taller. Her beaming smile just distracted George from seeing anything else about her. "You're supposed to be mixing, you know, meeting people. You're supposed to be acting like you're having a good time. You look like you're about to kill someone or are bored to death. Have you known Mary Lou long? Do you come to this school? I haven't seen you around before. Do you come days or nights? Do you live on campus, or do you commute?"

The questions were coming faster than George could answer them. He just shook his head "yes" or "no" at the appropriate time. He was really trying to remember the questions so he would be ready for Ann when next they met.

Suddenly he heard his name called in a panicked voice. He looked up to see Mary Lou, waving frantically to him. She was beckoning him to come to her. He responded by pushing his way through the people as he went across the floor. Janet was following right behind. George heard Janet say, "Oh, those two idiots are at it again. I don't know who invited them, or why they came. No matter where they are, they always start trouble. They ruin the night for everyone."

A little circle had formed around the two boys, as they squared off against each other. They were exchanging threats when George arrived. George walked into the circle right between them. He looked at one boy and then the other. They both made a lot of remarks, but neither one did anything? George said nothing but just kept looking at the both of them. After a few moments, they separated. They went their separate ways. Janet leaped up to kiss George as she yelled, "My hero!"

George replied, "Are you going to pat me on the head next?"

Janet looked at him with a queer look on her face. Mary Lou laughed as she announced, "We have to go. I've got a lot of homework." Mary Lou left, with George following behind her. When they got to the door, Mary Lou looked at him. "Well?"

"Well, what?"

"Did you get any of their phone numbers to call them?"

"Please. One girl at a time is driving me nuts. Imagine if I tried two. No, I didn't. Don't get mad. I just didn't."

"You know I just thought about what you said before. Why do you think I'm smarter than Andy? You hardly ever talk to me."

George was surprised at how quickly she changed the topic. "Well, I hear you. Or don't you think I'm listening when you talk? More importantly, why did you call me over to what was going on in there?"

"Oh, those two jerks always start trouble. I told them that if they started anything at our sorority party, I would have someone throw them both out. They made a comment that they would like to see the guy who would try. I just smiled at them. That was when I called you. I figured they wouldn't start anything with you there. See it worked."

"Did it bother you at all that I might have been killed?"

"Oh, George, don't be such a baby. Anyway, you weren't, so let's not discuss it. Now, have you resolved what you're going to ask what's-her-name? Why don't you bring her to one of our parties? I'll find out all about her for you. You know, the more I think about it, I think that's a great idea. I know everyone would love to meet your girlfriend. What's her name?"

"Ann. Her name is Ann. Oh, yes, that's a great idea, but first I'm going to ask her all the questions Janet asked me. Janet knew my life's story in two minutes."

"Did you ask for her number?" Mary Lou hesitated. "You insulted her by not asking for her phone number? Yes, sir, George. You sure know how to impress people." The rest of the trip home, Mary Lou chuckled to herself, while George was pondering the order of the questions he was going to ask Ann when next they met. Tonight was Wednesday. He had two more nights to go.

When they arrived, in front of George's house, he got out. He thanked Mary Lou for listening to him. "Oh, and thank you for taking me to the party. I hope I'm not the topic of conversation when you're with the girls."

"George, I would never do that. Here is my number. Call me to tell me how you make out Saturday night." At that, Mary Lou handed George a card with her name and her telephone number on it. She waited until he stepped away from the car and then sped off into the night. George went inside the house.

As soon as George stepped into the house, his mother immediately commented, "That's nice. At least she drove you home." George didn't say a word. This Saturday was his twentieth birthday. He had not heard of any plans for a party, so he had assumed there would be none. Even if there were, it would be over with in plenty of time for him to make his date. "His date." The words took on a special meaning now that he knew what to ask.

Chapter Six

Saturday night finally came. Her phone number—that was what he was going to ask for first.

Saturday night, after dinner at home, a small cake was produced, and a single chorus of "Happy Birthday" was sung. After cutting the cake, he was off. He was at the corner early, so he decided to drive around a little, on the chance he would see Ann walking.

After making the third trip around the block, there she was. The cool September night had her hurrying along. When she got to the corner, George pulled right up. He leaned over and opened the door, as he said, "Your chariot awaits you."

Ann got in. She loosened her coat, exposing her dress. When George really looked at her, she had on a long, loosely fitted dress. It was the kind of dress that his sister wore when she was pregnant. He was so intent on looking at Ann that the car behind him started to blow its horn for him to move. George complied. He pulled away from the curb very slowly. All George could think of was Mary Lou's warning from Wednesday night.

"Are you alright? You better watch the road. You can look at me later." The last phrase brought a chuckle from her. George didn't outwardly act at all. "We can go to that place we went last week. It was really nice there. Is that all right with you?"

"Sure. To the club we shall go. You know, I was thinking. I don't have your phone number. What if something happened to you? What if you couldn't make it? How would you tell me?"

"You're right. You should give me your number. Wait until I get out a pen." She opened her coat pocket from which she took out a stub of a pencil. She tore a piece of paper from a newspaper George had in the car as she said, "What is it?"

George gave her his number.

They drove to the club where they had been the previous week. They walked into the club, while George was still thinking about her phone number. He was annoyed that he had asked the question, but she had gotten his number. He resolved that when they got inside, he would ask her again. They went to the same table they had sat at the previous week. The waitress remembered them. She brought them over the same two drinks they had ordered before. Ann took her coat off to put it over the back of the chair. George could see the entire long, loose-fitting dress she had on. She had a belt around her waist, but George figured that she would open that up when she got bigger. "Come on. Let's dance," she said.

George, without verbally responding, got up. He went to the dance floor with her. She put her arms around him as George cringed.

"Is something wrong?" she asked, as she stepped back from him.

"Oh, no, it's just that when you touch me, you make me tingle." She smiled while George congratulated himself on thinking of something to say so quickly.

After what seemed an eternity, they went back to the table. When they were comfortable, it was time for the band to go on their break. Ann turned to George, "I know very little about you. I spilled a drink on you and now, here we are. There must be something more than that about George."

In the next few minutes, Ann asked him all the same questions Janet had asked him. When she was through talking, George was about to speak, but before he could say anything, the band came back onto the stage. Ann took him by the hand as she led him back to the dance floor. As George held her, he could feel her long, slender body, but somehow it had no effect on him, for all he could envision was her talking him into going to a motel and afterwards, saying the baby was his. He could now appreciate the phrase, "Every man's worst nightmare."

The longer they danced, the less George thought about the nightmare. He started to think more about living through it. His inexperience at such matters was starting to take its toll, for he didn't know what he was going to do next. He realized he had never even kissed her. That didn't bother him, for kissing someone he didn't even know was not the sort of thing he really wanted to do. The thought of kissing a married woman who was out cheating on her husband started to bother him. Kissing a pregnant woman who wasn't married was even more of a turn off. Spending time with her would make him the prime candidate for being some kid's father, and this started to make George more nervous. By now, Ann had rested her head on George's chest. Their two bodies became one. He could feel that she didn't have any undergarments on. The worst part was that George didn't give a damn about why she was with him. "Let's get out of here and go somewhere else," he managed to say in a hoarse voice.

"Okay, but I can't stay that long. There is one down the road from here. We can go there." Ann had done her research as to a safe place to go. She had heard stories in school from people in the church. The young girls had a way of talking loudly enough for her to hear when they were talking about something that she should not hear. Her Mother Superior would tell her, "It's a game people play. They think we've been raised in a vacuum."

When George heard her reply, he really became nervous. What a way to spend his twentieth birthday, screwing up the rest of his life.

They left the club to drive to the motel down the street. It was a local place that specialized in short stays. George got a room. Within a few minutes, they were both in bed. He was right. She didn't have anything on under the loosely fitted dress. No more nervousness or inhibitions. George kept thinking, whatever happens is going to happen. He kept telling himself he could handle any problems. He wasn't so sure he could, but so what. She was worth it, whether she was pregnant, married, or both.

The night ended in silence. When they got to the corner, Ann leaned over to give George a long, hard, lingering kiss. She exited the car, turned to him, and said, "Same time next week?" George nodded "yes" as he drove home on a cloud. His life had just changed. He didn't want to leave the person who had just changed it. He didn't know what he was feeling, but he knew he had never felt that way before.

The next morning, being Sunday, he could not bring himself to go to church. Somehow, going to church today would be sacrilegious. He stayed in bed as long as he could, for somehow he didn't feel right on this first day of the rest of his life. He now understood the comments that going to bed with someone was one thing; going with someone you cared for was an entirely different experience. What an experience it had been! He knew it was going to be a long week until he saw her again.

"George, there's a call for you." To receive a phone call at home was a strange circumstance. Not many homes had phones in the 50s. Those that did limited their use to emergency calls only. In addition, George hated talking on the phone. When he received a call, his conversation was very short. If it wasn't a business call, a simple "hello" or a response like, "Okay, I'll meet you in an hour" was typical for him; it was strange indeed to him to get a call. This call was not only personal, but also from a girl. The phone was located in a downstairs entranceway to the house. It was a private area so George, after saying "hello," waited for his mother to leave the room. It was Mary Lou.

"How was your date?"

"Great. When next we meet, I'll tell you all about it."

"What are you doing? I'm having some friends over on Friday. I thought if you weren't doing anything, you'd come too. Do you know where Andy is? Find him and bring him with you. Friday night at seven, okay? Janet will be here."

"All right. I'll try to find the dear boy." George went upstairs to get changed. He decided to visit the haunts where Andy usually went. Andy loved to bowl. He was not really any good at it, but he loved the game. He belonged to three leagues, so it was a good bet that he was at the bowling alley.

As George was leaving, his mother asked, "Are you going to meet…" She left the sentence hanging in the air. George thought to himself how boring life would be if he lived in a house where no one cared what he did. Not so here. Everyone was on George's case. Once he got mad about the nosy questions until he compared his home life to that of Andy's. He decided he liked his much better.

He replied to his mother, "As soon as I know, I'll let you know; until that time, you got me."

As George expected, Andy was at the lanes, bowling pot games. As usual, he was losing. A pot game was when a group of bowlers would pool their money. The highest score won. When George walked in, the others involved let out a low moan to show their displeasure. When George arrived, he would always yell at all of them for taking Andy's money. "You know he can't beat any of you, yet you let him in. What kind of friends are you?"

It was George's size as well as his personality that stopped anyone from doing anything about his speech. Once, one person had decided to shut George up. The onslaught was short, since he had waited until George wasn't looking. He hit him as hard as he could. When he saw that George wasn't even affected by his punch, a strange sort of look came over his face. Everyone else just started yelling, "Come on, George! He didn't mean it." George didn't do or say anything. He calmly walked away, as he mumbled under his breath what an idiot he was.

Andy saw George coming. Before George could say a word,

Andy yelled, "It's my money."

"I have resolved that you're an idiot. Lose. The only reason I'm here is because Mary Lou wants us to come to a party on Friday night; just say "yes" or "no." I don't want to hear a speech."

"Okay, we'll go."

"I'll pick you up at seven." George left the lanes to a standing ovation.

Friday came. George was ready. He had spent the day at his lawyer's office, for his business was going to be sold. The thought of getting out of business had a bittersweet taste in his mouth. For the first time in his life, he would be unemployed. The mere thought of not having to go to work was a great feeling. The reality of that day was also that George would have to find a job sooner or later, for he was only twenty. That would be in the future. Tonight, he was going to Mary Lou's party. Tomorrow, he would be with Ann. How could he ask for anything better than that?"

Andy was waiting downstairs on the sidewalk for George. He was very annoyed because it was Friday night, payday, and he was already broke. His parents wouldn't give him a dime because they did not approve of his gambling. Andy got in the car. After explaining his financial circumstances to George, they proceeded to the party. George advanced him the necessary funds. In fact, when Andy had gotten into the car, his foot had kicked a roll of money into sight. It had been under the seat. George realized that the past Saturday night Ann had not given him any money. Now he knew why. George put the money in his pocket. He just said that he had dropped it.

Mary Lou lived about ten minutes from Andy in a more affluent area of town. Her father was an engineer for some company. He did not like the thought of his daughter's going out with anyone except a college graduate or student. He definitely didn't like Andy because he thought Andy was one step up from a bum. He let his feelings be known, no matter who was around. Once he had been at the bowling lanes and had told his feelings to George. George was annoyed but said nothing because he agreed with him.

George pulled up in front of Mary Lou's house. It was a one-family house with a low hedge around it. In the back yard was a patio. That was where the party was. The girls had decorated the area. The invitees, who numbered about twenty, were all there. George and Andy was the last to arrive. Mary Lou came over to both of them. She immediately started introducing them to everyone. Other than Janet and Mary Lou, George didn't really know anyone else. Andy knew everyone. Within a few minutes, Andy was absorbed into the group. George went to the side to his usual spot. The music was tuned up another notch. Finger sandwiches were served with a punch/soda combination.

"My father will not allow any liquor to be served." Mary Lou's announcement was greeted with mixed reviews. George stayed to the side, as was his nature, for try as he might, he could not get used to a crowd. Janet came to his rescue.

"You just disappeared the other night. Did you come with Mary Lou? You didn't have your own car? That was really nice of you to break those two idiots apart before they ruined the evening for the rest of us. Mary Lou tells me that you didn't go to school but instead went into your own business. She said she met you through Andy, but you aren't really good friends with Andy, are you? It was just that he was the only one you knew. Are you ever going to go to school again? I think that's wonderful that you tried doing something else by yourself. What made you do it? What kind of business is it? Was your family involved in it with you, or were you in it alone? I really thought I would see you again before you left. Did you have a nice time? Mary Lou said you did. She said that you were sorry that you didn't ask me for my phone number; I'm sure it was just the fact that facing down those two jerks upset you. That was really nice of you to do that, or they would have spoiled the evening for everyone. She said she had to leave so soon because she had a lot of homework to do. Do you want a soda?"

"Yes." George was glad for the reprieve. He resolved to bring Janet the next time he met with Ann. She would find out all about her for him.

Andy was on the other side of the room. When he saw George he came over to him. "I see you're with Janet. Are you two hitting it off pretty well? Why don't you take her; I'll get Mary Lou, and we'll leave?"

"Andy, it's Mary Lou's house party, remember? I don't think she can leave. Anyway, this Janet is talking my ears off. She doesn't shut up. I can't get a word in edgewise. At the rate she's going, she is going to talk me right through our three children. She went to get us sodas. When she comes back, say you have to go some place, and you don't have a car, so I have to take you."

Just as George got done talking, Janet was back. "Here's your soda. They ran out of soda out here; that's what took so long. I had to go inside to get more. That soda was hot, so I had to get ice to put in it. They are running out of ice. Someone will have to go get some."

Andy had an insidious smile on his face as he said, "Why, Janet, why don't you take George? I'll go tell Mary Lou that George will take you. I don't have my car with me."

"That's great. Come on, George. You don't mind, do you?" Janet pulled on George's arm. "Wait. I have to get something."

"Not at all. In fact I would love to." As Janet went somewhere to get something, George grabbed Andy. "I ought to kill you."

"Why? Everyone is saying how much you have changed. You smile more! You talk more! You're becoming an all-around nice guy. Mary Lou said she ran into you. You two had a long talk. See? She is taking credit for turning you into a nice guy. They'll probably give you the award for being the nicest guy at the party. I know that going for the ice will push you over the top. You got my vote."

"I'm ready." Janet stood on the side, waiting for George.

Someone yelled out, "Come back before the ice melts."

George led the way as Janet followed. Their leaving the party together became the topic for everyone. Andy pointed out, "They're going for ice."

Someone replied, "I know what he'll use to chop it up." Everyone laughed as they went about, continuing their conversations.

As soon as they pulled away, Janet started up. "I don't know where we can go. There is a store down the street that may sell it, or else we can go to the supermarket. That's only three blocks away. How much ice should I get? Three bags should be enough. Yes, we'll get three bags. You know how to get to the store, don't you? If you pull to the front, I'll run in; that way, it won't take long. I can get a cart since I don't think I can carry three bags."

"You can if you shove one in your big mouth."

"What did you say, George?"

"I'll take them out of the cart when you come out. Here's some money."

"Mary Lou's father gave me some." George pulled in front of the store. Janet bounded out of the car, while George sat patiently waiting. He started to think about Andy with Mary Lou's father back at the party; that should be fun. Janet was back in a second. George got out to load the ice into the back of the car. He headed the car back towards Mary Lou's house.

Janet squirmed around on the seat so that she was sitting right next to George. She leaned over as she said, "We better hurry back because they will be waiting for the ice."

"We better get back before Mary Lou's father has a battle

with Andy."

"What did you say?"

George smiled. "I agree with you. I would not want to bring back hot ice."

"Oh, you're just saying that. I never knew you were so witty. At the sorority party, you stood in the corner. It was as though you were afraid that we would bite your head off. When we have another one, I'll let you know. I'll tell Mary Lou so she can tell you, or when you call me, I'll tell you when the next party is."

George pulled in front of the house and got out of the car. He took the ice in. As he had expected, Andy was fighting with Mary Lou's father. They were just starting up. George went right over to the two of them and quickly handed one of the bags of ice to Andy. "Come on. Let's put the ice away." They walked into the house to put the ice in the freezer that was inside the back door.

Andy was seething. "That guy gets to me. I've met him three or four times. Every time, he has something nasty to say to me. I always try to be nice, but that jerk has got a comment to make about what I do or what my future will be if I don't get a degree in something. Who the hell is he to tell me what to do? I was all set to tell him to mind his own business when you came in. Just because we're in his house doesn't mean he can talk to me like that. His daughter called us to come; we didn't call her. He should take his dear daughter…"

"Andy, don't be stupid. It is his house. It is his daughter. He's giving you good advice. He's concerned about whom his daughter goes out with. What's so bad about that? Look, if you feel uncomfortable, let's just go. It's getting late. I have to get up early tomorrow. I think the business is going to be sold. If it is, I'll have a lot of things to do to clean up the place and get out. Come on. We'll just go say good-night."

As they came back into the backyard, Mary Lou was crying.

George, with Andy by his side, went over to her. He told her that they had to leave. She looked up as she said, "I'm sorry about what my father said."

Andy was all set to say something nasty when George kicked him. Andy replied, "Don't be silly. He is your father. He wants the best for you. What's wrong with that?"

Mary Lou looked at Andy before she stared at George. She knew Andy didn't think of saying that himself. George, as well as Andy, kissed her good night. They started toward the door. "Oh, I have to go, too. Could you give me a ride?" Janet's voice was unmistakable as it went right through George's head.

"Why, we would be honored. I have to get home first. Would it be all right if George drops me off first?"

"Sure, that will be fine." The threesome left.

The drive to Andy's house was done in silence. George thought to himself, she's probably charging her batteries.

Andy got out of the car. The closing of the door was Janet's signal to start up. "It is nice of you to give me a ride. One of the girls picked me up at my aunt's house. I had to go there with my mother. I came right from there to Mary Lou's house. Did you come from home? You live by Andy, don't you? I'm sorry I am making you go to his house first because now you'll have to take me to the other side of town where I live. You know where I live?"

"No. I've never been there."

"Well, it's very easy." Janet kept a running commentary about the streets as well as the houses on the way to her house. Finally they were there. As soon as the car stopped, George got out of the car to walk her to her door. At the same time, another car pulled up. It was her mother. She was just coming home from her sister's house. Janet made the necessary introductions. George turned to leave, but Janet's mother insisted he come in for a cup of coffee for being so nice as to drive her daughter home.

Through clenched teeth, George agreed, but first he had to shut the car off. Being with Janet was one thing; being with Janet as well as her mother was listening to Janet in stereo. Between the two of them, there was never any silence. By the time George got done listening to one and tried to respond to her battery of questions, the other one started. Finally he said, "I really have to go. I have a busy few weeks coming up. Thank you, but I have to leave."

Janet added," George is selling his business." Before her mother picked up on that statement, George headed for the door. Her mother's parting words were, "I'm sorry you didn't get to meet Janet's father. Maybe the next time you come."

George was out the door. Janet handed him a card with her phone number as well as her address on it. On the back, she had written her school schedule. "Thank you again for the ride home."

"It was my pleasure." George got into the solitude of his car. It had been quite an evening. Andy had gotten into an argument with Mary Lou's father, Mary Lou was crying at her own party, and I got all Janet's vital information. He laughed to himself as he thought, "Who could ask for anything more!"

The thought of his business being sold was the next thing on his mind. He started to think about all the things he would have to do before he would be out. The reality of changing his life from being an entrepreneur to being a worker started to scare him. Having to take orders was going to be a new experience. On the other hand, he would not have to worry about meeting payroll every week. He would be able to take a vacation. The thought of being able to stay home if he felt like it brought a smile to his face. A job was definitely going to be a new, exciting experience.

Traffic on the road to his home was the next problem to overcome. He wanted to get to sleep, for the next day was Saturday. Tomorrow night was Saturday night! Sleep would help the time pass. The morning was just another hurdle to overcome. Saturday seemed to drag. He went to work, since he had to get started getting things ready for the impending sale. No matter how hard he worked, somehow the clock worked against him. The hands just didn't seem to move. Finally it was time to go home.

Chapter Seven

It was Saturday night. It was time to go see Ann. George rehearsed all day the questions he was going to ask. He memorized them in sequential order, according to importance. "Who is she" was going to be the first one. He was not going to be swayed from his quest. George pulled up to the corner, armed with his list of questions. There was his honey, waiting. The autumn air had a chill in it. He felt sorry that she was standing on a windy corner. He thought to himself, this is a perfect lead-in to the first question: why do we have to meet on a street corner?

As he pulled away from the curb, she slid over to him. She rubbed up against him. "It's getting cold. I put this light jacket on, but I should have realized that it wouldn't be heavy enough for the night air."

"Well, why don't I pick you up at your house?" George was so proud of himself for working that comment into the conversation as painlessly as he did.

Ann ignored his question as she said, "So tell me, how was your week? You seem more relaxed this week than I've ever seen you. Could we just go for a ride? I have heard about the road next to the Hudson River. If you follow that, it goes to Bear Mountain. Do you know how to get there?"

"Yes." George had to turn the car around, since he was going in the opposite direction from the river. He got the car pointed in the right direction as he drove toward Bear Mountain.

"They have a lodge up there where we can get a light snack. I know it is late, but it should still be open, shouldn't it?" Ann busied herself by taking off her coat. She sat back, as she relaxed in the seat next to him. Her outfit looked like the one she'd had on the previous Saturday night.

"I don't know. I haven't been there in years." As George spoke, he was trying to remember if he had ever been there. He knew he'd never driven there but concluded that there would be signs. Now back to his questions. "What do you do all week?"

"I keep track of the time until we'll be together."

"Do you mind being serious for a few minutes? I really don't know anything about you."

"Well, if it bothers you, let's see. I look at a pile of paper that other people have looked at before me. When I'm done, a lot of other people look at the same papers after me. Would the world end if I didn't look at the paper? No. Would the world end if other people didn't look at it? No. I am just a little clog in a great big wheel that would turn with or without me. I have a hard time trying to justify my existence. I feel there should be more to this thing called life, but I am starting to wonder what. I sit back to try to resolve what is good in my life. That's when I think of you. Now does that answer your question? How would you like to buy me a present? There is a store open over there. Let's go."

"It's eleven o'clock at night; that store isn't going to be open. The only place stores are open is New York City on Forty-Second street."

Ann started jumping all over the seat. "Let's go. I have heard about it, but I have never been there. You don't have to buy me anything. Let's just go, please?"

"You sound like a little kid. Ok." George had to turn the car around again to head south toward the Lincoln Tunnel. The roads weren't crowded, so the drive didn't take that long. As they drove there, Ann kept up a constant chatter about the New York City skyline. She abruptly turned the topic to George. "What about your life?" she asked. She kept asking him about what he wanted out of his time on Earth. When she used that phrase, a chill ran down George's spine. Ann, with her calm, insistent manner, soon had George telling her all about the things he wanted. He told her about his whole family, as well as the time they spent together. George kept thinking to himself that the Janet bug must have bitten her. The only difference was that Ann sounded much more mature. George was going to ask her how old she was but decided not to. He just knew from her mannerisms and her vocabulary that she was older than he was. So what?

"Just by listening to you, I can tell you love your family very much. Is that the kind of life you want?" Ann had put her arm around George's arm, making steering the car difficult.

"Well, yes, I think I would like to live the way I have gotten used to. Why not? I always felt very fortunate that I had a family around me. They were always very close to me. Don't you want those things?"

George had to concentrate on driving. The traffic at the tunnel was heavy. While he had to maneuver his car, he remembered that Ann had never answered his question about what sort of life she wanted. The horns started to blow as he got into one of the lanes. He had to concentrate as he drove through the tunnel. One tunnel was shut down, so they had two-way traffic in the tunnel George was in. Driving took his full attention. When he exited the tunnel, he parked the car in a parking lot by Times Square. They got out to walk. That was a bad idea. In New Jersey it was a little windy and a bit cool, but in New York, it was very windy and extremely cold. George saw an empty checker cab. He hailed it to stop. They got into it. George told the driver, "Just drive around for a half hour. We just want to see the stores."

Checker cabs were roomier than a regular cab. They cost more to ride in, but they were still hard to find. After they were in, the driver turned around in the seat. As he looked at them he said, "Okay, but I'm telling you now, you two start fooling around on the back seat, I'll call a cop."

Ann was embarrassed by his comment. George became enraged as he yelled, "Look, idiot, just drive the goddamn cab. Keep your filthy mouth shut."

Ann grabbed George's arm, "Please, George. I thought we were just going for a ride."

George, in a low tone, replied, "I'm sorry. Yes, we are." The cab pulled out into traffic as George started to point out the sights, as well as the sounds of Time Square. He soon realized he really didn't know that many. His trips into the city were few. When he did come, he was never that interested in it.

The cab driver heard him stammer, so he took over the sightseeing responsibilities. Within a few seconds, he was giving a detailed description of the buildings with the stores as he whizzed by them. An hour flew by. When he brought them back to where he had picked them up, he only charged them for a half hour. He apologized for his comment. "You know, after a while, this driving a cab gets you nuts. Here's my card. Call me if you want to do this again. I think I enjoyed it as much as you two did."

George paid him and gave him a generous tip. Ann grabbed George's arm as they hurried back to the car for the ride home. Ann was just ecstatic about seeing the city. She relived the cab ride all the way home. When they got to the corner, it was almost two o'clock. Ann leaned over to kiss George good-bye. As she did she said, "I had a wonderful night. I will thank you more properly when next we meet, but for now, thank you. Just one question, do you always get like that when you're mad? You don't hide your emotions. The night I met you, I thought you were going to hit me. Tonight, I thought you were going to take that man's head off. Don't answer," she shouted. "I'll see you next week." Ann got out of the car and hurried back to her home.

The other nuns were starting to wonder why she would fall asleep during mass or go to her room right afterwards to pray for a few hours. Ann never gave them any explanation. She knew she would be tomorrow's topic, but so what? She'd had a great time.

With a promise of better things to come, George went home and wasn't sorry at all, that he hadn't gotten his questions answered. George would have been satisfied with not getting any answers except that there was no getting away from his upbringing; something was wrong. Sunday, he would call Andy. Andy would have the answers. Anyway, George had to tell someone about the terrific girl he had met. The only one he could think of was Andy.

On Sunday mornings George usually would go to his place of business to do odd jobs so that on Monday mornings, he was ready for anything. He had forgotten that this Sunday was going to be busier than ever. The negotiations to sell were almost concluded. He had to clear all of his things out within thirty days. This meant selling a lot of items. He had to get everything ready for sale. Sunday morning roared in on him, as both his parents were on his back to get moving. It was a long, hard day. There was definitely no time for any thoughts but those that related to work. By Sunday night, George went right to bed, for he knew Monday would be even worse.

Monday came bounding on him for the thirty-day period had been cut to one week. He was happy, for he had had it with being the boss. His thoughts of just having a job started to appeal to him even more. His activity level was brought up a notch. The one good thing about it was a lot more got done than he had ever anticipated. Working at a feverish pitch, he could see that he would be all done by that Friday. Done. The mere thought of waking up and not having to go to work was motivation enough to push him. He was right, for by Friday evening, everything major had been finished. He went to bed, wanting a full night's restful sleep--the only one he'd had all week.

Saturday was spent cleaning up a few loose ends as well as reviewing the final sale contract. George was proud of himself that he had gotten everything done. The last thing to do would be done with the help of his accountant and attorney. He had made an appointment with them for Monday morning at ten.

No more work. Now it was Saturday night. George had a lot on his mind. Ann was most definitely included. When George put his copy of the contract in the glove compartment of his car, a roll of money fell out. He remembered she hadn't given him any when they went to New York. The previous week the money was under the seat; this week it was in the glove compartment. Both times, George put the money in an envelope he had in the trunk of the car. He resolved he would ask her why she was giving him money. Tonight he would find out—maybe. He put the contract in the compartment. As he did so, he resolved not to think any more about it. Ann would be waiting.

The October night was colder than usual, so George hurried, for he didn't want to be late. Driving to meet her gave him time to review his question list, but thinking of her and their anticipated activity pushed all questions right out of his mind. He made the last turn and spied her at the curb. The wind had picked up. She was arching her back against the wind. A car with two men in it had stopped near her. The men in the car were trying to talk to her, as George pulled up behind them. When Ann saw him, she ran to his car.

As she got in the car, she was out of breath. While gasping for air, she said, "Go. Please, just go."

George stopped the car. "What happened back there?"

"Nothing," she said, as she continued to gasp for air. A smiled worked its way across her face as she added, "And nothing is going to happen here if you don't calm down. Now just go."

George pulled away. Without a word being said, he headed for the motel. "I don't want to argue with you, but how long is this street corner thing going to go on? I really don't understand you. The trouble is that I want to. I've known you for over a month. I just get to see you for a few hours after the world goes to sleep. I feel that I'm doing something wrong. I don't know why."

"You know we're doing something wrong. The only question in your mind is, how wrong? Is that it?" Ann had a strange look on her face as she spoke. George resolved to save any more questions until they were in the room. He realized he hadn't asked her if she wanted to go; he'd just gone.

George pulled into the motel lot. He registered for a room. Tonight, he got the room for all the wrong reasons. He was determined to find out just who Ann was. The quiet, uninterrupted time in the motel room would be the best place to do that. When he got back into the car, he saw Ann reading his copy of the contract. They got out of the car to go into the room. Ann put the contract down on a table. She came to George, but before she could say or do anything, George asked, "Now, no more hedging. Who are you? Why are we meeting on a corner like I-don't-know-what?"

Ann stepped back and took off her coat. She hung it up in the closet. She had on the same long dress that she had worn the first time they came to the motel. She went over to the little desk-type table that was in the room and sat down as she turned on the lamp over it. She picked up the contract. She started to do an analysis of it from a legal, accounting, and tax point of view. When she was done, George, who had sat on the bed, was staring at her in amazement. Ann looked at him, for she could see that she had mesmerized him.

"If I knew you could do that, I would have never hired those two numb-nuts."

"Now don't ask me any more questions tonight. Let us just enjoy each other. I'm afraid that if this discussion continues, it will spoil the evening."

George was able to say, "I agree." That was how the evening ended as far as any unanswered questions went. The last thing George remembered was Ann's saying as she got out of the car, "Next week, we can meet on Wednesday night, for a while, if you want."

"Of course," George said. "By that time, I'll have a surprise to show you." On that note, Ann got out of the car and waited for George to leave before she started for home.

The following day, when George was cleaning out his car, he found a large roll of bills under the seat again. He tried to put it with the rest of the money, but it wouldn't fit in the envelope. He had kept all of the money together in a large manila envelope in the trunk of his car. He put it there under the floor mat in his trunk, resolving that he would count it tomorrow. Until that time, he felt it was safe where it was. He finished cleaning his car out. He put the tools he carried around with him in the garage. No cars were ever kept in the garage; it was more of a workroom than a garage. The room was complete with a workbench and a complete set of tools to do any type of job, regardless of what it was. The prize spot in the garage was saved for a fifty-gallon drum of motor oil. George's father had resolved a long time ago that gas stations charged too much for oil changes. All the necessary equipment for changing the oil in a car had a prominent place in the garage.

Chapter Eight

Sunday morning, George got up as usual, but for the first time, he didn't have to go to work. No work. The two words sounded strange at first, but as he realized it was true, he got up with a new vigor. He came downstairs into the kitchen. He announced he would take everyone out for a Sunday brunch he had read about. It was advertised as a champagne brunch at one of the local restaurants. It was something new they were trying. Much to his dismay, no one wanted to go. Instead, it was decided that one night he could take them out for dinner. Somehow, George just could not let this Sunday morning go by without some sort of celebration. He downed a quick cup of coffee, went back upstairs, and finished getting dressed. He went to Andy's house. He went up into his room to throw him out of bed.

Andy was trying to focus on what was happening to him as he said, "Oh, man, leave me alone. I had a rough night last night. Why are you here? You always go to work on Sunday mornings."

"Not today. Come on. We'll go out for brunch—my treat. If you say "no," I'll add up all the money you owe me. Now get up."

"You know, it's only eight-thirty. Who goes for brunch at eight-thirty?"

"Okay, we'll go for breakfast. That's always good. Come on. Get up. The day is wasting."

"Okay, we'll all go. I told Mary Lou I would go to church with her this morning. We were out last night. She made me promise I would go with her. Here's her number. Call her. Tell her you're coming. She'll love that. Oh, tell her we're going out for brunch afterwards. I know she'll love that."

George had never told Andy about the time he met with Mary Lou or anything of their conversation. George called her. He told her about the plans. Mary Lou was more interested in hearing about George's latest date with his mystery woman. George had to promise that as soon as they got rid of everybody, he would bring her up to date. She too asked, "How come you're not working?"

"I'm free," was the only explanation George would give.

"I'm going to invite Janet."

"I don't care whom or what you bring. We'll go to eleven o'clock mass."

"There is none. Ten-thirty or twelve."

"It's eight-thirty now. Brunch starts at twelve, so ten-thirty it is."

"We're going to brunch?"

"Yes. I'll make reservations for four. I'll see you at ten." George hung up with Mary Lou, as he waited impatiently for Andy to go through the long, arduous task of getting dressed. While he waited, George had a cup of coffee with Andy's parents. He listened to their complaints about their son. Finally, Andy appeared. He looked like he was still sleeping. His mother started complaining about him as soon as he entered the room. Her complaints acted as an accompanying music to the march the two of them made as they left for their impromptu dates.

Mary Lou was all primed for church. She was waiting by the door. Janet didn't live but ten minutes from her. The church was somewhere in between their two homes. Mary Lou took command as soon as she got in the car. She directed George to go to Janet's house. Janet was also waiting at her door. When she was in the car, they were off to church.

Mary Lou expressed a concern about what time they would arrive, but they were on time when they got to church. A parking place was quickly found. The foursome walked up the front steps as they entered the filled church. George walked in the door. Suddenly he remembered all the teachings he had learned at church. He wondered if it was a good place to be. Everyone was praying and confessing his/her sins. George figured he could sneak his in, when God wasn't looking. George was so intent in his meditation that when Andy genuflected before he entered the pew, George almost fell over him. They sat down. Andy poked him as he said, "Pay attention. We're in church. You almost killed me."

George did not reply for he was deep into the praying process. The mass seemed to fly by. When it was over, the foursome walked down the aisle to get out. Between Janet and Mary Lou, it seemed as though they knew everyone in church. The lines of people George and Andy were introduced to seem endless. The line included the priest, Father Somebody. "I feel like I'm being put on display," George commented, when they were finally outside.

His three friends just looked at him as they made their way to the car. The group got in. With a copy of the ad about the brunch that promised ten percent off if presented, they made their way to the restaurant. Mary Lou was holding court, while Janet was trying desperately to take over. Other than George's saying which direction to drive or giving an occasional comment, Andy, as well as George, was completely upstaged. When they arrived at the restaurant, the attendant took the car while the group entered.

The restaurant was set up with a large buffet table with everything on it in the middle of the room. The food all looked good. There was a wide variety. Off to the rear of the room was a dessert table with coffee and an assortment of desserts. Janet was finally able to speak, "This place is incredible. Look at that table; I think it is going to break. My father took us to a buffet, but it was nothing like this one."

Everyone in the room was elegantly attired. They all looked much older than George's group. Mary Lou made the best observation, "This place must be expensive. That is why it looks so good. Most of those people are all older than we."

Everyone laughed, as the youngest group was shown to a table. The main attraction of the brunch was that they served champagne. The waiter poured the liquid as soon as everyone was seated. George couldn't help himself as he proposed a toast to Mary Lou, who had regained control of the conversation: "To our matriarch."

Andy looked up. "Matriarch?"

Janet added, "The head lady."

Mary Lou didn't respond verbally, for she didn't have to. The group made a single line as they started toward the table. George took Janet by the arm. He led her to the left side of the table, while Mary Lou and Andy went to the right. As they started around, George heard his name being called. "George. George, come over here."

The man doing the yelling was Jules. Jules owned a large company. He knew all about George. He had seen George get his start in business. He watched as he made a mild success of it. When he had heard that the business was sold, he had called George. He wanted George to come to work for him. George said he would let him know. Jules, as well as his group, were well started into the champagne course of the brunch. The third bottle had been opened. They showed no sign of slowing down. Jules kept saying, "Drink. The food will be here."

As soon as George and Janet got to the table, they were handed champagne glasses, while another man filled them. Jules pointed out, "Easy. He's not old enough to drink. I got underwear older than he." The table applauded his comment; the pourer of the champagne took the filled glasses that he had given Janet. George watched as the two glasses were replaced with two others' containing just a little liquor in them. Jules again took over, "To George and to his beautiful girlfriend. May he be smart enough to come work for me and smart enough to invite me to the wedding."

Jules' wife got annoyed. "Jules, be still. You're embarrassing them. Go enjoy yourselves. Don't listen to this old fool."

Jules added, "Yeah, go ahead. You go with your friends. You are all my guests."

George thanked everyone and went back to the buffet table with Janet. Janet was still in shock. She went around the entire table in silence. On the way back to their table, George asked, "Are you all right? I never remember your being quiet for so long."

"That man seems to think a lot of you. Is that diamond ring on his pinky real? Does he really want you to work for him?" George was glad that Janet was back; he had to admit that he liked this Janet much better than the silent one. George left her question unanswered.

The group enjoyed the brunch. They went to Jules' table to thank him, as well as his wife, for treating them. Before Jules could say anything, his wife interceded, "He was glad to do it. Now go away before he starts up again."

George led his procession as they left. He dropped everyone off and headed for home. The amount of food, the champagne, along with the previous night's activity had started to take their toll. He went home to sleep.

Ann's Sunday didn't go as well. She had to be awakened so she would not miss Morning Prayer in the church. As a rule, breakfast was served after mass; that allowed time for socializing between the parishioners as well as the nuns. Today was different, for today was parents' day. The parish school was inundated with parents who came to visit their children's classrooms. The Mother Superior of the Order, who was also the principal of the school, asked Ann to act as one of the hostesses for the coffee hour. Ann hated doing things like that but found herself saying "yes" because she didn't have enough nerve to say "no."

Ann was an immediate attraction, since she was much prettier than the other nuns. The habit they all wore did not detract from her beaming, angelic, infectious smile. The parents of one little girl were being led over to Sister Ann. Ann knew the girl from one occasion when she had helped out in the schoolyard. The girl had scrapped her knee. Ann took care of her. She even made up a "brave star" for her because she didn't cry. The child dragged her parents over to meet her. When the little girl's father saw Ann, he froze. He remembered her from the bar. She was the one in the mousy gray suit, who had spilled the drink all over the customer. She was the one who insisted on paying, even though she didn't have any money. When their eyes met, they locked on each other. Their immediate recognition of each other was a source of embarrassment for both of them. Ann turned red. The bartender's wife pinched him. "You're embarrassing the nun. Stop staring at her."

He replied, "Where am I ever going to see an angel like her again?"

Ann left the school. She went to her room to sit on her bed as she cried. She couldn't help herself. She suddenly realized that the bar was in her area. She would undoubtedly meet other people at church functions who frequented it. The thought had never occurred to her before. She was always involved in the affairs of the Newark church instead of her own. When one of the other nuns came to her room to see what was wrong, Ann said nothing. She put her head under the pillow as she continued to cry. She stayed in her room for the rest of the day and night. The Mother Superior had a tray of food sent to her room. Ann vowed right there that she had to make up her mind as to what she was going to do. Most of all, she was debating what she was going to do about George. She had to see him to tell him of her problem. She had to be honest with him. She resolved that, no matter what, she had to be truthful to him, as well as to herself. She opened the secret compartment of her drawer to take out his phone number. She would call to tell him everything. She would do it tomorrow. She'd call him the next day from work. No, I'll take tomorrow to think about what I want to do. I'll call him Tuesday or Wednesday. No, I told him I would see him on Wednesday, so I'll tell him everything then. Once she resolved her plan, she could rest easy. She put the phone number back into the secret compartment. She climbed into bed and went to sleep.

On Monday morning, George was punctual for the big meeting he'd scheduled with his lawyer and accountant. He tried to remember everything Ann had said so that he could mention all of her concerns. Both the lawyer and the accountant were impressed with George's critique of the contact. His lawyer said, "You should consider continuing your education if you can analyze this contract like that without having any training. Where did you find out about deferred payments as a tax consideration?"

George did not answer but rather continued with his concerns. The meeting went very well. At the end, all the people left. George felt good about his contributions to the meeting. He made a mental note to thank Ann for her help. He remembered he had no way of contacting her until Wednesday night. He resolved that his arrangement with her had to change. Here he was, wanting to be with her at an important time in his life, and he couldn't even call her to thank her. Her mysteriousness really annoyed him for the first time. What made it worse was his memory of Mary Lou's words of wisdom—married, maybe a mother. George was infuriated with himself for not being more demanding the last time he'd been with her. He'd never had any of his questions answered. He also remembered (when last he was with her) why his anger went away. His thoughts about her as she stood in front of him at their last meeting in the motel made him realize that his current situation wasn't that bad.

When George left the meeting, he had his father drive him to the car dealership, for he had purchased a brand-new car—a white Chevy convertible with a turquoise interior. The car was something else. The dealer had promised that it would be ready Monday afternoon. His father knew George had bought a new car, but when he saw that it was a convertible, he was impressed. He was so impressed that he drove it home with the roof down as George finished doing the paperwork with the dealer. After signing all of the papers, George had to drive his father's car home. His father's car defied description. It ran; that is about the best that could be said about it.

When George was done at the dealer, driving home only made him become more unsatisfied with his arrangement with Ann. Who was he going to show his new car off to? Somehow just showing his family wasn't enough. The only other person was Janet. Janet was at school. She had made sure George had her schedule in his pocket when they left each other on Sunday. George took it out of his wallet and looked at his watch; he was relieved to see he had plenty of time to go home to get his new car from his father so he could show it to Janet. When George got home, he took everything out of his old car to put it in the new one, including the money. He was going to give his old car to one of his sisters.

On that Monday, after Ann came home from work, she was changing in her room for dinner. She was summoned to the Mother Superior's office. When she walked in, she could see by the group of people in the room that there was a problem. An elderly priest, whom she didn't know, started talking about a large sum of money that had been donated to the church. He explained, "It was over ten thousand dollars. I put it in the top drawer of my desk until I could get it to the bank. I was busy at the time it was given to me; that is why I didn't bring it in right away. I called the police. They told me to make a list of everyone who had access to the area. There were only three people in that day. "He stopped talking as he pointed his finger at Ann and said, "You were one of them."

Ann said nothing but stood staring at the other people in the room. It seemed all eyes were on her. She tried shifting her weight from one foot to the other. Her nervousness got the attention of one of the detectives. He said, "Would you like to say something, sister?"

"Yes," Ann responded. "Who are you? Who are these other people? May I sit down?"

The Mother Superior was taken aback by the brashness of Ann's statement. The Mother Superior introduced the priest and the three detectives to her, while one of the other detectives got a chair for Ann.

"Who was the man that gave you the money?" The question Ann asked was directed at no one in particular. Everyone started to talk at once to answer her. The detective who had spoken before raised his voice above the rest as he said, "That is not important. The question you are being asked is were you in the archdiocese office on Saturday morning?"

"Of course I was. I am there every Saturday, but you must have known that." Ann's belligerent tone caught the detective off guard.

"If you don't mind, I will ask the questions," he snapped back.

"Well, I do mind. I do not like being questioned without my knowing why. Whoever heard of someone giving that much money to the church without demanding a receipt so that they could use it for a deduction? I can tell you how many—none. What could the good Father have been doing that was more important than depositing a large sum like that in the safe or the night depository at the bank? We certainly have enough bags floating around the place for just that purpose. Before I answer any more questions, I would like to know the answer to mine."

The detective was really annoyed at Ann's statement. Ann

sat in the chair. She refused to speak anymore. The detective looked at the Mother Superior, and they both started talking to her, but all Ann would say was, "I don't believe there was anything taken. I will not answer any more questions unless I have an attorney present. That is my right, you know. Surely, Mr. Detective, they taught you that at detective school."

The detective was livid. Ann got up as she added; "Now, if I am not under arrest, I wish to leave." No one responded, so Ann walked to the door, looked back when she heard no one say anything, and left.

Once she was out of the office, the detective said, "You know, of course, she's right. I can bring her downtown to question her there, but the newspapers will have a field day if I do."

The Mother Superior gave the detective a quick background of Ann. She explained that Ann knew quite a lot about the law, as well as the inner workings of the church. "If we press the issue about the money, I am afraid that her questions would do more harm than good, even if we were to get all the money back. The public trust must be maintained. Of course, I will have to ask the Archbishop his thoughts, but I don't think he will disagree."

The door opened as another detective walked in. He went over to the head detective. He handed him the phone number that he found in the secret drawer in Ann's room. "I'm having it traced now. I did not touch anything. I made sure that I left the room the way it was."

"Do you know whom this number belongs to?" the detective asked the Mother Superior.

"No."

"Can we talk to the other nuns?"

"Of course. One at a time or all together?"

"I will speak to them together if you don't mind; the rest of you, leave. I think we will scare the hell out of them. Oh, I'm sorry; I think we will scare them if they see all of us. You guys drive the good priest back to his church. I'll meet you in headquarters when I'm done here."

The Mother Superior summoned the nuns to an anteroom. The detective started asking them all questions about Ann. As a result of his questions, one by one the nuns started talking about Ann's late-night walks into the garden on Saturday nights. One added, "I went out looking for her. When I saw that the rear door to the yard did not have the bar across it, I just went back to my room." A hush fell over the room.

The Mother Superior was hurt that she knew nothing about what was going on until that very moment. She flushed with anger. "Call Sister Ann back here."

The nun who went to get Ann came back to announce, "She will not come. She will not say anything else with the detective in the room, unless she has an attorney present."

The detective looked at the Mother Superior, who just shook her head in disbelief. "This has nothing to do with me any longer," he said. "It seems you have to work this out with her. I'll find out who this number belongs to, but other than that, there is nothing else I can do, without causing a big stir, which I don't think you want me to do."

"I will talk to her alone. I will get back to you." As soon as the detective left, the Mother Superior called all the nuns together again. She expressed her disappointment that they did not tell her of these walks before tonight. One by one, each nun started to tell what she had observed, as well as what some of them had heard from people in the church who lived in the area. Pretty soon, the Mother Superior pieced together the fact that Ann was seeing someone on her walks. Whoever it was would pick her up on a certain street corner after the Saturday night prayers were said. One nun added, "She asked me to switch our nightly duties so she could be free this Wednesday night."

The Mother Superior told all of the nuns to say nothing. She called the detective about what she had learned and asked him to say or do nothing. She asked him to be at the rectory by ten o'clock on Wednesday night. He agreed.

Chapter Nine

Janet had made sure that George had her complete schedule when last they met. George found the right building. He was on time, for when he pulled up, Janet was coming out of class. She saw George and came running over. She was pleased to see him. With him as a guide, they inspected the car. George started to compare the way Janet was acting to how he envisioned Ann would react. He was suddenly very annoyed with himself because whatever way Janet was acting might be a little less sophisticated than the way Ann would act. He stopped for a moment as he realized that Janet was here, and Ann was someplace else.

Janet got in and George drove to her car. He followed her home. The two of them went out for dinner. Try as he might, George felt horrible about being with her. Janet was interpreting George's being with her as a sign of George's affection rather than the fact that George didn't have anyone else to be with. Not realizing that his aloofness was that obvious, George was shocked when Janet, in a very somber tone, said, "If I bore you that much, take me home. Why did you come to the school for me if you didn't want to be with me?"

"It is not you, it is me. I told you I was selling my business. I am now…what? I don't know. I should be doing something, yet I don't know what. One minute I feel as though there is a great big world out there, waiting for me; and, the next, all there is a big, black hole, waiting to swallow me up."

Those words transformed Janet from a very irate girl into a very compassionate, somber, young woman. The transformation was amazing.

"Every feels like that at one time or another. You need to talk to someone." Janet hesitated as she thought for a moment before she added, "Go see Jules. He seems like a smart man. He acts as though he likes you. Ask his advice. I am positive he'll help you come to the right decision. I really don't know what to tell you, for my life has always planned for me—college after high school. Go talk to him. What can you lose? I wish I could help you out—I really do—but, well, I truly can't help you." When Janet was finished talking, she took George's hand. The two of them sat at the table in the corner of the restaurant in silence. In a split second, two young people had matured, and both of them didn't know how to handle this new feeling. It was a very dramatic moment for both of them. George didn't know what to do next. His last speech had drained him of his creativity for the day.

"Would you mind if I took you home? I'm not really good company right now. I do not want my problem to affect our relationship. I guess I have to resolve my own life before I make any other plans." The last part of his statement had Janet's attention.

She sat up in the seat, squeezed George's hand, as she replied, "If I can help, you know you can call on me."

George paid the bill. They went to his car. George started to speak but thought better of it. He took Janet home. Silence was the third person in the car. Silence dominated the conversation all the way home. When George pulled in front of Janet's house, her parents had just come back from their nightly walk. They wanted George to come inside, but George said "no." He wanted to leave. Janet put a pleading look on her face, so George agreed.

The house was a one-family structure that was modestly decorated. Janet set at the table in the dining room, while George went with her father to sit in the living. An archway connected the two rooms. George could see the progress Janet and her mother were making.

Janet's father started a conversation with, "Janet tells us you had your own business?"

George moved around in the chair, for he felt this was going to be a man-to-man talk. He really didn't want to hear one. In a mechanical tone, he responded, "Yes."

"Have you decided what you're going to do now that you have sold it?"

"No."

"Well, what do you think you would like to do?"

"I don't know." George was trying hard not to lose his patience. He hated being interrogated like this.

"Well, I always wanted to start a business of my own, but somehow I never had the time or the money at the same time to do it."

"A lot of people tell me that." When George finished responding, he felt embarrassed for the way his answer must have sounded. He didn't know what to do. He didn't want to continue the conversation, but he didn't know how to end it without hurting the man's feelings. He got up to walk towards Janet, who was listening to her father talking to George. She knew George was not enjoying it.

"Sit here, George," her mother said as she pulled out a chair for him to sit on. She, too, could tell George was not enjoying his stay. Janet sat to his left. Her parents sat across the table from them. The scene reminded George of the seating arrangement at the negotiating table in his lawyer's office.

Janet was cutting the cake that her mother had baked, and her mother was pouring the coffee. Janet's father was all set to start talking, as George asked where the bathroom was. Janet pointed and George left the table. It was obvious to everyone that George didn't feel like being questioned again by anyone. Janet's father looked at his daughter and wife, "I was only trying to make conversation and offer him my help if I could."

Janet looked at her father and said, "Dad, not everyone likes advice. Anyway George seems to be doing alright without any outside advice."

When he returned to the room, George was determined to avoid being questioned, while at the same time, he felt silly for feeling that way. He realized Janet's parents were interested in whom their daughter was going out with. George smiled to himself as he envisioned the same scene if he ever brought Janet home to his house. He sat down, determined to dominate the scene. The only problem he had was that he didn't know what to say.

As a strange sort of silence loomed, Janet's parents each took a turn, asking him a long list of questions about himself and his family. When that topic was exhausted, they asked again about his plans for the future. George tried to answer them but found he didn't really know any of the answers. School and work was what he knew. When school had ended, he'd only had work. Now that the working part of his life was ended, there was nothing. A void was created where none had existed before. He felt the cold wind of uncertainty. It made him shudder, as he sat in the chair with three sets of eyes on him. George had had enough. He had to leave.

He stood up as he said, "I am sorry; I do not have all the answers you wish. I just don't know what I want right now. I am going to take a little time to figure my future out." George looked at Janet's father as he continued, "I doubt if I'll ever work for someone else because I don't think I could. But who knows? Now if you're done questioning me, I would like to leave." George could feel that he was doing a poor job of hiding his anger at being questioned like that.

Janet's parents were stunned by his directness. George went to the door to leave. He turned and thanked them for their hospitality, as he walked out the door. Janet grabbed his arm. George turned to face her as he was saying, "I'm sorry, but I can't take being treated like that. I know they mean well but, right now, I just can't deal with all those questions. Please apologize to them for me. I just have to go. I'll see you again when I know who George is and what George wants. Goodbye." George walked out of the house and got in his car. He drove away. Janet returned to the silent, dining room to help her mother clean up. The topic of George was dropped.

As George was driving home, he felt alone and frightened. The honking of horns brought him back to the reality of driving. Suddenly he remembered that when he had cleaned out his car, he had put everything in the trunk of his new car. Whenever Ann had left money in the car, George had put it in an envelope in his glove compartment, but the last wad of bills wouldn't fit, so George had put it in the trunk of his old car under the floor mat. When he had transferred everything to the new car, he had taken a small box and put everything in it. Surprisingly, the box was full. George could see it was a lot of money but put off counting it, for he felt something was definitely wrong. With a grim determination, George decided now was the time to face reality. He went home to start to put his life in order.

The first thing he did was to bring the box to his room. He dumped it on the bed. It was shocking to him to see that a lot of the bills he thought were singles were, in fact, hundreds. He separated the bills into piles by denominations. He started to count. Twelve thousand, one hundred and eighty-one dollars was the final tally. That was more than three times what his car cost. George sat on the bed and stared at the money in amazement. He heard one of his sisters coming, so he put all of the bills back in the box. He couldn't believe that Ann had given him that much money. She had never said a word about it. He was more amazed that he did not realize until that moment that there was that much there. He put the box in his drawer. He decided that he would definitely go see Jules the next morning. George tried to envision where she could have gotten all that money but, more importantly, what he should do about it. Tomorrow he would ask Jules. Sleep finally helped George pass the night.

"Keep it!" Jules yelled. "Some girl gives you two thousand dollars. You want to know what to do with it? Spend it. You said you wanted to go away to think about what you should do. Well, now you have financing for the trip. Look, kid, assume she stole the money. No one is going to believe you didn't know about it. I saw you pull up in a new car. You paid for it with clean money, didn't you?" Before George could answer, Jules continued, "Leave. Go to Florida." While Jules was talking, he wrote down the name of a friend of his that ran a hotel in Miami Beach. "Go see him. I'll call him. I'll tell him you're coming. Leave now. The longer you hang around, the more likely the police will want to question you. What are you going to say? I knew nothing of it? Leave. When you come back, there will be plenty of time to answer any questions anyone might have. I have a friend of mine on the police force. I'll ask him to find out what he can. What was that girl's name? Janet? It was Janet, wasn't it?"

"No, not that girl. This is another girl I'm seeing. Her name is Ann. She's from Bergen County somewhere. I've never been to her house…" George kept talking. Before he knew it, he had told Jules everything about Ann. George did not leave out any details, except the true amount of the money he had received. When he was done, he sat in the chair, facing Jules with his head bowed.

"Leave. Go now. Forget this girl until you come back." Jules got up from his chair and walked around his desk; he handed George the piece of paper on which he had written his friend's name.

"I have to go home to pack," George said.

"Don't go home. I've seen your clothes. Believe me, it is time for new ones. Go ahead and go. Call me to let me know how things are going. I'll see you when you get back."

George thanked him as he left. When he got into his car, he

could not bring himself to just leave, so he went home to tell his mother he was going. He wanted to pick up the money, since he had left it in his room. On the drive home, he wondered what Jules would have said if he had told him there was over twelve thousand dollars instead of only two thousand. When George got home, he quickly packed his bags. He said goodbye to his parents, who were the only two home at that time of the day, and left.

He couldn't bring himself to leave without saying goodbye to Ann. He had to find out what she had done. It was Tuesday afternoon. He was supposed to see her the next night—Wednesday. George resolved he would go to New York to stay for the night. He drove into the city to get a room for the night. The time seemed to drag until he was able to see Ann again.

He spent the day walking around the city. The city can be a wondrous place, except when you're trying to make time pass quickly. The lights took forever to change. The people walked so slowly, as they pushed and shoved him around the streets. The city didn't seem to come alive but rather roared down on those within its grasp. The normal fast pace describes everything but the passage of time. Time moves in an almost unbelievable slow motion. Every step that George took was an exertion of effort that drained his waning strength. He finally just stood on a street corner and shook himself out of the fearful trance he was in. The people walking by took little notice as they shoved him into the street. At last it was time to go face the reality of what he had gotten himself into. George got into his car for the drive to Union City.

By the time George got in the area, he had resolved in his mind what he would say. First, he would demand to know where the money came from and, secondarily, why was she giving it to him. His mind went blank. He stopped the car. He pulled to the curb to gather his thoughts. What was the next thing he should know? George was about a block away from where he usually picked her up. He could see the corner. He saw a car pull up. Ann got out. The car she got out of moved about two hundred feet from her and parked. Another car, which was behind the first, let two men out. The two men stood within fifty feet of Ann, as they tried not to be conspicuous. One went close to a bus stop, as though he was waiting for a bus. The other man walked across the street to look in a store's window. He positioned himself so that he could see across the street, yet it appeared as though the window had his complete attention. George watched all this, as it became painfully clear that some sort of trap was being set. He knew he was the prey. He waited for a few minutes. Neither car nor any of the men on the street moved. Ann stood where she normally would wait. She just looked around. George realized that she wouldn't know his car, since she had never seen it before. He remembered that he had never told her he was getting a new one. A car pulled up to Ann. She went to it, as though she knew the person driving. Everyone converged on the car. The trap had been sprung; only, the wrong person was caught. The man was taken out of his car and was patted down. He stood up against the car with his arms stretched across the roof while he was frisked by another one of the group. George pulled away from the curb. He drove down the street in a stream of traffic. His palms were so sweaty that it was hard for him to hold the wheel. George drove directly to the turnpike and headed south. He doubled-checked to see that he had the piece of paper that Jules had given him. He headed for Miami Beach, Florida. George was so wound up from his experience that he drove the whole fifteen hundred miles to Miami Beach, stopping only for gas and a large cup of coffee.

The scene George had just witnessed had started earlier that evening, when the Mother Superior told Ann to be in her office at ten o'clock on Wednesday night because they were going somewhere. Ann quickly surmised what was going to happen and where they were going. At first, she resolved not to go, but the more she thought about it, the more she believed that not going wouldn't end anything. She went to her secret drawer to get George's number. She immediately saw that someone had tampered with it. She was going to call George to tell him not to come. She memorized the number and threw the paper away. Wednesday, she called George's home, but his mother told her that he had gone away. Ann hung up in the middle of the questions his mother started asking her. Ann's next plan was to go to the corner. If George pulled up, she would just tell him to leave. She would make believe she didn't know him. She knew that idea wouldn't work either, for she rationalized that by now the police would have his name as well as an address. A description of his car would be easy. Ann decided that she would not go because she didn't want to get George involved any more than she had already. Just as quickly, she remembered that every night (while she was waiting for George), some car would pull up to offer her a ride. Tonight she would act as though the person in the car that stopped was the person she was to meet. By the time the police figured out that she was lying, George would see the commotion. She was hoping that he would be smart enough to leave. She could always call him another time.

At ten o'clock on Wednesday night, the Mother Superior called Ann to her office. At ten-thirty, the Mother Superior and Ann got into the detective's car. He drove to the corner, where she usually met George. At first, Ann refused to get out of the car. It wasn't until the Mother Superior pushed her out that she did. She stood on the corner as she'd been told. As she had predicted, a car pulled up that she knew wasn't George's. She went over to it, as though she knew the driver. The scene that followed was what George had observed from a block away. What George saw was enough to have him start his mad dash for the safety of Florida.

The drive down was just a blur of super highways with

detours through back roads as parts of the highway were under construction. The detours led him through the different states, but he could not distinguish one from the other. Night became day and day became night. The miles whizzed by unless he had to proceed slowly on one of the detour routes.

The Florida welcome area was indeed a welcomed sight. The free orange juice they gave renewed his strength for the long trip down the state and into Miami Beach. The last causeway bridge was finally crossed. He was passing a long row of hotels. George double-checked the address. At last the hotel was in front of him.

In comparison to the ones nearby, it was the oldest--well maintained but old. There was a small, circular driveway in the front under the supervision of a large doorman whose main job was to keep the area clear for registering guests. When he arrived, George told him whom he was there to see. The doorman had him pull his car to the side of the front entrance. George had to leave the keys while he went inside to see the man whose name was on the piece of paper he had gotten from Jules.

Chapter Ten

When does the story end? How does anyone know that the story about two people is over? Even though they are apart, as long as either one of them has any conscious thought about the other, the story goes on. The intensity of the relationship may grow or wane, but there is still a flame flickering. Memories never die; they are always present, even if subdued. The only sure way to kill a memory would have to be when the two people are both dead.

George's drive to Florida had come to an end, but he was still trying to figure out what had happened to him. The first time he meets a stranger, he has a torrid, love affair. Was what he felt for Ann love? Does anyone know when he is in love? Does anyone know everything about the one he thinks he's in love with? Where did the money come from? Was it safe under the floor mat in the trunk of his car? The questions kept repeating in George's mind. The constant flow of questions with a lack of answers had contributed to his ability to stay awake for the whole trip.

While George was waiting, he looked around the interior of the hotel that looked as though it had just been redone. The lobby was crowded with guests who were waiting to go to dinner, while others were waiting for the bus to go to the dog track. It seemed everyone was going somewhere, except George. He had just arrived at the hotel. Jules' friend Sal came up behind George, "I was wondering when you would arrive?"

Sal gave George a warm greeting, but after looking at George, he told him to put his car in the back of the hotel garage. "I'll see you tomorrow when you look human again."

Sal summoned a young man. He gave him instructions about George. The young man went with George to his car and got in, as he waited for George to thank Sal. The two, young men pulled away to go to the garage. The young man showed George where to park. George got out. They covered the car with a canvas that was kept for just such an occasion. As they walked away, the man said, "We reserve this spot for visiting dignitaries. Who are you?"

George didn't answer, for the lack of sleep was taking its toll. George got his bags out of the car. He was shown to a room where his young guardian bid him goodnight. The young man walked away, mumbling to himself about George's refusal to offer any information about himself.

Back in New Jersey, Ann was dismissed from her church position. She was sent back to Cincinnati. As soon as she got there, they transferred her back to George's Run. Sister Edith had been put in charge of her rehabilitation. Ann withdrew into a shell of silence. Sister Edith realized that withdrawing into her own little world was not the best thing for Ann to do. Sister Edith made it a point to seek out a woman whom she had gone to school with and who lived down the street from the church. Her name was Norma. After Sunday mass, Sister Edith introduced Ann to Norma. The three of them went for a walk. After a few minutes, the good sister remembered she had to do something. She left Norma with Ann to talk about old times.

"I know we never really got along that well when you lived here, but Sister Edith said you could use a friend outside of the church. She asked me to volunteer."

Norma was a married woman with two children. She lived down the street from Ann when Ann had lived in town. She knew the whole story of what had happened. She had the good sense to keep quiet about it. She had gotten married as soon as she had graduated from high school. Her husband was studying for his skipper license so that one day he could have his own tug. Until that time came, he worked as a deck hand on one of the tugs.

* * *

At the end of his second month with Sal, George still felt very uncomfortable working at his job. Monique would tease him with, "It's your stupid middle-class, first-generation morality. If you're that uncomfortable, leave. Sal will call one of his buddies in a different state. You can move around the country. That way, you'll get to see the country. The longer you're at this business, the easier it gets."

"I sure hope you're wrong about its getting easier. I would rather dig ditches than do this." George took Monique's advice. The next morning he went to see Sal. Sal was very understanding.

"Look, kid. Do me a favor. A friend of mine is having a big group for a three-day convention at his hotel in New Orleans. Go there to help him out. You'll be out of here. You can move around and see different things while, at the same time, picking up some loose change."

George agreed. George went to his car to take off the canvas. He realized that from the day he had gotten to the hotel, he had never used the car. He started it up. He felt a hand on his shoulder. He turned and stared into Monique's smiling face.

"It still runs? Come on; I'll help you clean it up."

With his friend Monique, they cleaned it. While Monique worked in her skintight shorts, she stated, "I don't believe I'm doing this. I'm not designed for housework. This is going to cost you dinner tonight at the Fontainebleau."

"Only if you wear your red dress," George responded, as he wiped an imaginary spot off the car.

Monique stood up and shook her hips as she said, "You'll have to wear your white dinner jacket. We are going out on a date?" They both smiled at each other. Monique added, "It will be my first one since I've met you."

"A date, not an appointment. What's the difference?"

George responded, as he again wiped off the imaginary spot.

Monique laughingly responded, "On a date, you get to kiss me goodnight." That night George went to pick Monique up, carrying a bouquet of flowers and a box of candy. The new couple pulled up to the Fontainebleau in George's white convertible with a turquoise interior. That night, they did all the things the other tourists did, including dancing in the moonlight by the pool bar.

"You know, I owe you a lot. When I first met you, I was going through a personal hell. Well, you know what I mean."

"Some day, you'll tell me the story, but not tonight. After all, this is our first date." The rest of the night was spent without further discussion of George's problems. Everyone admired the elegantly dressed couple.

The next morning George bid Monique goodbye, loaded his car, and headed for the hotel in New Orleans. He checked to see that he still had the money in the trunk of his car. Although he thought it was safe there, he knew he would have to deal with it sooner or later.

The drive from Miami to New Orleans was an easy one. For the first time since George had left home, he felt at ease. His only problem was that thoughts of Ann started to dominate his nights. The first day's drive to New Orleans was up the west coast of Florida. On Route 10, he went across the Florida panhandle to Mobile, Alabama, where he spent the night. The next day he went through Mississippi into New Orleans. The whole trip took two days. George, during that time, resolved that when he got to the Big Easy (as New Orleans is referred to) he would call Jules to see what had happened with Ann.

The hotel in New Orleans was located right off of Bourbon Street—also known as the Strip. The jazz clubs were greatly outnumbered by the burlesque clubs. As soon as George arrived, the manager of the hotel immediately introduced him to everyone.

"Sal tells me you're very good. You must be, for I never heard him say anything good about anyone. You get the same deal here. The strip clubs will give you the same cut. Here is a list of the girls with the addresses of where they work. They will give you the same deal as the clubs. The cops won't bother you. If they do, just show them this card, and they'll leave you alone. If you're having trouble with one of the marks, don't be afraid to call the nearest cop; he will get you out of the situation. Oh, I don't want you rolling any of the marks."

After his abrupt speech was delivered in a tone unbecoming a manager of a hotel, the large, balding man left. One of the bellboys who everyone called Curly showed George where he would be staying while in the hotel. Curly, who was a great deal older than George, said nothing as they walked to the room assigned to George. It was located in the back of the hotel, next to the kitchen. The room was very large and comfortable, but it was noisy as one of its common walls divided the room from the kitchen. As Curly left, he turned and said, "If any of us give you a good steer, we expect a cut."

George was left alone in his room. He quickly unpacked because he wanted to call Jules. While he was in Florida, with Monique's help, George had assembled a wardrobe of some note. A phone was located in one of the private suites. George asked the operator to place the call. "Just give me the charges."

The operator was stunned by his request.

"You must be the new guy. No one pays for his calls. We just let Baldy moan." George assumed she was referring to the manager.

She put the call through. The next voice George heard was Jules. "Sal called me. He told me you're doing a great job. I'm busy now. I can't talk long, so give me a call next week. But since you did call, just let me tell you that it is still hot up here. I called about that thing you were interested in. There was a big mess found when they moved the furniture. It seemed the more they looked, the bigger the mess. The two was more like twelve. They threw the whole mess out. They returned everything to the factory from where it came. I have to go. Call me next week. I'm trying to find out if the owners are going to look around for any other suppliers. I'll talk to you." The phone went dead.

George went back to his room. He had heard what Jules said, but there was a lot more that George wanted to ask. He remembered that Ann had told him she came from a town named after him in Ohio. George's only thought was that he had to go to George's Run one of these days. His thoughts were rudely interrupted by the bellowing voice of a rather large, Black lady. "Where are you? George—is that your name? You're the new man, George?" The door to his room was pushed opened. It banged against the wall. "Come on. The first of the group is going to be here in a couple of hours. I have to have your jacket ready."

George followed the woman to a sewing room down the hall. The woman had a strange gait. She seemed to lope along, rather than walk. George found out later she had been born with a defect in her hip. She amazed everyone that she could walk at all. Within a few minutes, she had a jacket on him. On the breast pocket, there was an emblem. In the design was a number that so fitted in with the design that unless someone pointed it out, the casual looker wouldn't even know it was there; however, to the trained eye it was easily distinguishable. "You're twenty-seven," she said. She maneuvered George or the jacket until she was happy with the way it looked. "Come back in an hour. I'll have it ready."

George left to go back to his room to plan his activities. He intended to put his business acumen into full use with what he had learned in Florida from Monique. He went to the office. The youngest lady in the office was very accommodating. George had her make up a business card for him out of paper the size of a dollar bill. On it was George's name, as well as the phone number where he could be reached. "You're on this weekend?"

"Yes."

"Will you work with me to help me out?"

"What do you want me to do?" she asked.

"Take the calls. When I call you, you give them to me. Also, I want you to make some calls for me. Will you do that?"

"Yes, that is what I'm supposed to do."

"Good. Oh, what is your name?"

"Jean."

"Okay, Jean, I'll call you in a little while to get the cards."

"You don't have to do that; just wear this pager. I'll beep you when I want you." The other ladies in the office laughed at the last remark. Jean blushed. George was already out the door by that time.

The guests were going to start to arrive at one o'clock on Friday afternoon. The convention lasted until Sunday night. The group was comprised of flower growers from around the country. There would be talks all day Saturday. A big dinner dance on Saturday night in the grand ballroom was planned. The hotel was full, as were the three hotels nearby. The hotel George was at was the headquarters for all activities. George's official title, as printed on the regular business cards that the hotel ran off for him, read "Social Coordinator." George's cards that he'd had Jean make up for him read, "If you want IT, call me."

The visiting group's organizer was an uptight lady who wore thin-rimmed glasses that hung on the end of her nose. Her facial expression behind the glasses warned everyone that she was all business. She was a very demanding person. She didn't ask for something; instead, she would make a speech about the way things should be done. Then she'd ask, "Why isn't it done that way at this hotel?"

George told Curly, "You keep her away from me." As the

guests started to arrive, Jean gave him his finished business cards. George gave some to Curly with the instructions that every man was to get one. George called Monique for help in finding where everything was in New Orleans. Within twenty minutes, George received a call from one of Monique's girlfriends, Adele. She told him where to get whatever he wanted. She lived locally and had a very commanding voice. After George introduced himself, she responded, "Monique told me all about you. Get a pen and paper. You ready?"

"Wait," George responded, as he made himself comfortable at a desk. With pen in hand and a pad in front of him, he added, "I'm ready."

Her commanding voice came out of the phone, "The local dice game is held right around the corner from the hotel." She gave George the address and the contact person. She added, "They don't take calls from strangers. Go there, if you have to. I will call them and will tell them call you, but I don't know if they will. The house of ill repute to use is located three miles out of town. The operator has cars' circling the area. All the drivers have pagers on them. Each pick-up location in town has a number. All you have to do is call and say your number, which is twenty-one. The first car to come will give you a listing of other pick-up points around town. A car will be at that place to pick your people up. If you need me, just call; I'll handle the in-hotel appointments."

George hung up and within a few minutes, he received a call from the crap-game operator. "Hello. You're George? You're a friend of Adele? She told me you're good people. You're a friend of Monique and Sal from Miami?"

"Yes. They sent me here. Sal told me to call you good people."

As soon as George mentioned Sal's name, a deal was struck. The voice on the phone said, "You get a ten tok, kid."

"What is a tok?" George asked.

"A tok is your cut." The phone went dead.

George soon found out that tok was the word used by all of the clubs in the French Quarter. It was a code word; only those who were involved knew what was going on. The number in the design was the one who was to get the tok. George was assured that there was honor among the street operators. One owner told him, "Don't worry. No one is going to cheat you. We are all in the business of getting the tourists to spend. You do your part; we'll do ours."

From the time the people started to arrive, until Monday morning when the last one left, George was in constant motion. Jean, with Curl's help, kept George busy with making contacts for the conventioneers. Every attendee was given a lapel pin by Curly with a copy of George's emblem on it. They were told to wear them so everyone in town would know where they were from and would take good care of them. Curly also handed out cards with the emblem on it as well. "If anyone doesn't treat you right, give them a card."

George kept the crap game fully stocked with fresh pigeons. The whorehouse did a banner business. George organized a dinner trip into the New Orleans bayou country for a group of forty-five people. He hired the bus with a local entertainer to act as the host. George got a tok from the bus company, the restaurant, the driver, and the comedian, as well as some of the husbands who didn't want to go. George sent the bus group on their own excursion.

A visit to a local lady's shop was needed to have a Sunday morning fashion show in the hotel. That was a twenty percent tok.

Adele, Monique's friend, never left the hotel. George had her in the penthouse suite. He had the maid keep the room clean as well as stocked with champagne and strawberries. Of course, there was an extra charge for that. "When am I going to see you?" Adele asked George.

"After every trick. Twenty-five tok, or you're out of here," was George's immediate response.

Adele hesitated before her booming voice came over the phone again. "Monique warned me I wouldn't be able to offer you anything in trade."

"Good. Now we understand each other." With those words, George hung up and was off and running, for he was always wanted somewhere. His pager/beeper never stopped.

Jean was not used to such activity, but when George gave her a three-hundred-dollar bonus, she was always on call, twenty-four hours a day. She too never left the hotel. She made or received all the calls for George to the outsiders. Everyone demanded George's services. One club owner raised George's tok from the usual ten to twenty percent. George immediately spread the word about the hot, new club in town. He made it the "must see" spot in town. The bellhops from the other hotels all showed up at George's door, looking for a piece of the action. George accommodated everyone. Jean got a new job to do. She was now George's bookkeeper, as well as his telephone operator. Jean was as old as George but very naive. She did his bidding, but really didn't know what was going on.

The trip to the bayou country was great. George kept the one-man-band/comic on to give a show on Sunday night, while some of the people were waiting to leave. That was a fifty tok. Even the local priest gave ten tok for the people that George sent to his church. George made them all wear a special piece of red ribbon so that they would be assured of a good seat. He provided a ride to the church. After church, there was a short, sightseeing trip around town. The bus ride was a fifteen tok. Because of the convention's being in town, the money came rolling in. Monday morning after the last conventioneer left, George went to his room, vowing not to wake up for a week.

The manager of the hotel heard a few stories about what was going on but kept in the background, as everyone seemed to be having a good time. The organizer of the convention gave George a tip that George refused. "I could get fired if I take that. The tip was only fifty dollars, a mere pittance compared to his three-day take. The organizer went to the manager, and she was overflowing with compliments about the job George had done. The tip was raised to a hundred dollars. The manager insisted George take it.

By Tuesday, George had received all of his toks from everyone. He started handing out bonuses to everyone involved. Curly was in awe of what he received. "I never made this much money in my life." George tried to smile, as he realized that he gave him too much. Jean was in tears. George gave her a little extra with a promise to take her to dinner the next night. His large, Black lady friend was surprised beyond belief when she was on his list as well. When George kissed her for taking care of him (as well as his room) while he was there, the woman cried.

Wednesday morning, the complaints started to come in. It seemed that very few people attended the talks. Their absence was directly attributed to George's overzealous attitude toward finding entertainment for the attendees. The stories abounded about how much money was lost at the crap game. There were many stories about what went on in the hotel and the activities at some place three miles out of town. The complaints, at first, were a trickle but, all of a sudden, the dam broke. The manager was flooded with calls, complaining about George's activities. One of the owners of the hotel had been very friendly with one of the attendee's wife. She overheard a conversation between her husband and her friend's husband about their activities. The woman suddenly realized why she had never seen her husband. When she found out he never went to any of the exhibits or seminars, she was outraged. A quick survey of the other wives answered all of her questions. She now knew why there were very few men on the bus trip to the bayous.

Wednesday morning, George called Jules to find out what was happening. As soon as the telephone operator answered, George knew something was wrong.

"George, hold while I switch your call to his home."

Jules' wife answered the phone. It was easy to hear the sorrow in her voice as she said, "George, he's gone. You know he thought the world of you. He had a heart attack Monday night. He never regained consciousness."

After George heard those words, he dropped the phone. He just stared into space. He sat in a chair, trying to understand what he had just heard. The tears started to well in his eyes as the full weight of what he had just heard sank in. Dead. George was going to call Sal, but somehow he just couldn't. There was a knock at his door. Mechanically, George said, "Come in."

Jean walked in the door. She was on her break. She came down to tell him his phone was off the hook. One look at George, and Jean started to cry, too. "Oh, George, what happened?"

"I just found out that I've lost probably the closest thing to a friend I had." Jean put her arms around him, as she tried to console him. "What a sight I must make, a big jerk like me crying on your shoulder."

"You're not so big that you can't cry on someone's shoulder, so why not let it be mine? Who knows? I may become the next closest thing to a friend."

The door swung open as the manager came busting into the room. "You son-of-a-bitch! You ruined me. Everybody is calling me to tell me another story about what you did." While the manager was screaming, George got up. He put Jean outside of the room. He closed the door and turned to look at the manager, who had a reputation for being a very rough and tough person. There were many stories about how he would take someone by the scruff of the neck to throw him out the back door of the hotel. After the news he had just heard, the manager with his attitude was just what George didn't need. The manager turned a chalk white as George grabbed him. He was hitting George, but to no avail. The blows just bounced off, since George was in a different world--one not affected by any physical pain. The manager started to turn white, as George was choking him. Jean came back into the room. She grabbed George's arms and pleaded with him to let the manager go. George did. In a quiet deliberate voice, he said, "Get out of this hotel until I leave. If I see you, no one else will." George threw him out of the room. Jean was hysterical. The manager had a hard time catching his breath. The large Black lady who had made George's jacket walked over to the manager to help him up. She walked with him as he went down the hall to the back door to go outside until he was breathing normally again. Curly was standing on the side. He laughingly said. "Do you think that big jerk is going to try to throw George out?" With his arm around the Black lady, he just laughed.

George turned to face Jean. "I'm sorry; I just couldn't take him today."

Jean stopped crying as she started to pack George's clothes. "Come on. You can stay at my house until you decide what you're going to do. We have an extra room. I know my mother won't mind. I've told her all about you. I know she would love to meet you. Come on, before the manager calls the police."

George packed his clothes. With Jean at his side, Curly helped take George to his car. He waited while Jean went inside to get her things. When she came out, she showed him how to get to her house. "Oh, here is your pay check. The manager gave it to me to give to you."

"He didn't say anything else?"

"No, nothing." George knew she was lying, but so what?

The drive to Jean's house took about a half-hour. Jean drove her car as George followed. Her mother was working in the front yard, attending to her flowerbeds. The house was a picture perfect, one story, wood-framed building with a white picket fence around it. The front yard extended about fifty feet in from the curb. There was a driveway on the side of the house that led to a one-car garage about fifty feet from the house. The backyard was thirty-five acres of part woods, part swamp. Jean told him to park his car in the driveway so it would be easier for him to bring his things inside. You get settled. I'll see you after work. Jean left before George could say anything. Jean's mother was a small, frail woman. Her physical stature was nothing like her personality. She was a peppy, effervescent type of person. She made George feel right at home with her greeting, "I know you must feel awkward being here with me. Don't be. I promise I am as nice a person as you'll ever meet. I won't treat you like a son if you promise not to call me mom or treat me like an old lady. Agreed?"

"What should I address you as?"

"Maude. It's not my name, but I love it. You call me Maude; that way I'll always know when you're calling me."

Just meeting Maude lifted George out of his doldrums. "Well, my new friend Maude, you get changed. I am taking you to lunch right after I make a phone call. Where is a phone?"

"You can use ours if you want."

"I'd rather not. There must be a store nearby that has one."

"Down the street on the right, there is a pay phone you can use."

"Do you need anything? Milk? You can use milk."

Maude laughed as she replied, "Milk with bread, the two staples of life."

Maude went to get changed while George went to the store. He called Sal. The conversation started with, "Were you going to kill him? The manager called me, still shaking. What happened? Oh never mind. Have you calmed down now?"

"Jules died. The manager just came into my room, screaming, at the wrong time. I had just found out that Jules died. I can't believe that he is dead. His wife told me when I called him today. Sal, are you there?"

"Yeah, I'm here. He was supposed to come down to see me next week for a few days. Dead. From what?" Sal asked, as he choked back his tears.

George waited a few minutes before he responded, "A heart attack. He just keeled over. That was it. I left the hotel. I am staying in a rooming house. I wanted to call you before I did anything else. Any suggestions?"

"The last time I spoke to Jules, he said that the thing at home is still a little warm. Why don't you go to Mexico? I'll call my friend at the Del Prado Hotel in Mexico City. I know he can always use someone. You'll go there for a little while. I'll call some of my friends in Jersey to find out how things are. Get a map of Mexico so you don't get lost. If he can't use you, you'll take a vacation. What's so bad about that? I heard you made a killing in Orleans, so you're not hurting for cash, are you?"

"No, I'm fine. I'll leave in a few days. I'll call you when I get there. The Del Prado Hotel? Whom do I ask for?"

The manager, José." Sal responded. "Everybody down there is called José. He'll take care of you. I'll call to tell him you'll be there next Wednesday; that will give you plenty of time. Good luck."

George drove back to the house. Maude was waiting for him on the front porch. She looked great. She had changed into a flowery dress that seemed to fly as she walked. The dress' bold print made it stand out. The three-quarter sleeves seem to fit her thin arms perfectly. Her beaming smile was just what the dress needed to make the whole scene perfect. "I want you to know that this is the first time I ever went out with a gigolo. Will I be expected to pay you by the hour or the occasion?'

"Since this is the first time I've been out with a lady, I will look upon it as a free, introductory offer. I wish you wouldn't refer to me as a gigolo. Think of me more as an engagement. It sounds classier. Anyway, what makes you think I'm a gigolo?"

"Jeanie told me what you do. You were the first one the hotel ever hired."

George laughed as he drove back toward the city. As he was driving, he couldn't help but compare the way he had acted today to the way he would have acted before being with Monique in Miami Beach. He didn't know whether or not he liked the new George better. George drove right to the restaurant, The Court of Two Sisters, in New Orleans.

As the valet took the car, Maude said, "This is the first time I've ever been here. No, it's the second time, but it's the first time with an engagement."

Armed with his new experiences, George ordered the entire meal, including two types of wine. Again he smiled to himself, for prior to Miami, he would have not come to this restaurant. He would have not known what to order. One thing he resolved was that he liked the new George better than the old one. At least the new one could go to a classy restaurant. He knew what he was ordering. More importantly, he knew how to dress for the occasion. The sport jackets that Monique had made him buy were outstanding.

George stayed with Janet in her mother's house for two days. Both days, he acted as their escort around the City of New Orleans and the surrounding areas. All the club owners were sorry to hear he was leaving. Everyone in town knew about his encounter with the manager. Wherever he went, he was congratulated for the manager incident. George announced he was leaving the next day. When he left, the departure scene was tearful, but George answered all of their questions with, "I have things I want to do in my life. I will not be able to do them here. You are wonderful people. I will always be thankful for knowing both of you, but I must return to New York now. I will contact both of you when I arrive there." George kissed both of them goodbye, and he put money in both of their hands as he left. He got in the car, and he drove off, thinking about what a low person he had sunk to. He had just lied to two wonderful people but felt it was better that way, since he didn't think he could live with the fact that he had slept with his girlfriend by night, and her mother by day. The drive along the lonely roads of Texas on the way to Brownsville was the best place to purge his mind as well as his soul.

Mexico. The name itself made George feel uneasy. He had to drive from New Orleans through Texas to get to Mexico. George resolved to stop in Texas at a bank, since he didn't want to carry all the cash he had with him. With the money Ann had given him, plus the money he had made in New Orleans, he had over twenty thousand dollars in the trunk of his car. He resolved that he would open an account in the bank. The more he thought about it, the less he liked that idea—too easy to trace. A safe deposit box would be the answer. Someone may be able to trace that he got one but not what was in it.

The first thing he did when he arrived in Brownsville, the town on the Mexican/Texas border, was to go to the largest bank he could find. He rented a safe deposit box. He put in the twenty thousand dollars. He got two thousand dollars of traveler's checks. Once that was done, he headed for the border. His route would take him to the town of San Luis Potosi for his first, overnight stay. The next night he spent in San Juan Del Rio. The morning of the third day of travel in Mexico, he was at the Del Prado Hotel in Mexico City. He checked in. He spent the rest of the day, walking around the city. Meeting José would be his next project.

George got a local map to drive out to the pyramids. They were located on the far side of the city. Just driving though the city with the roof of his car down was an experience worth having. His convertible was the only one in Mexico. Wherever he drove, people came over to get a better look. He didn't get out of his car but made a mental note as to what he wanted to see again.

He drove back to the hotel. He allowed the valet to park his car. He went to his room to rest from his drive through Mexico. That evening, he went to a local restaurant for dinner before getting to bed early so he could rest up for his meeting with Jose.

Chapter Eleven

The brightness of the sun woke George from a very restful sleep. The dinner the night before, complete with margaritas, had done wonders for him. He showered before he went to the hotel restaurant, where a buffet breakfast was being served. The hotel had three restaurants. Each morning, breakfast was served in a different one.

A gentleman walked over as he signaled for a cup of coffee. He sat down. Just from the size of the ring on his hand, George knew this must be José. "Sal called me. I understand Jules died. He was a good man to know as well as to be with. I understand you were very close to him. I am sorry for your loss. Sal tells me that you would like an engagement in my hotel. We get a higher class of tourist here than at the other two hotels you worked at. I do not allow any toks. Don't think you can pull what you did in New Orleans here. If a client gives you a tip, you can accept it. If you touch a client, you're out. I'll have someone move your stuff to your room. Someone will contact you about a shirt. It is too hot here to always wear a jacket. Watch what you are drinking. Remember you are in a ten-thousand-foot-high city. Just walk around today. Tomorrow, I'll send you around with one of the drivers. He'll show you where to go for different things. Always take our cars whenever you go anywhere. The guests feel safer, and we can charge them more on their bill. Any questions?"

"No questions yet, but if you don't mind I'd rather take that ride today. I'll go nuts, trying to hang around and doing nothing all day; I did that yesterday."

José thought for a minute. He nodded his head "yes." Go get measured first. A car will be waiting for you downstairs at the front door in an hour. I usually have breakfast at seven."

George responded, "Great. So do I."

As José left, a man came over to escort George to his new room. He went past the sewing room, as it was referred to, where George was to be measured. George followed along obediently. When his duties were done, he went to the front door to introduce himself to the doorman. He found that was not necessary, for the whole hotel knew who he was and what he was. The doorman waved as a car pulled up. It was an American sedan. George got in the back, and he was off on his sightseeing trip. The driver kept a running commentary of all the buildings they went by and pointed out the parks and nightclubs in the area. At the end of a three-hour trip, George was standing in front of the pyramids of Mexico. He had just driven by them the previous day, but today he got out to walk around. He was in awe of them. It looked like a scene from a movie. He could envision where the chariots would come in. The entire area was just unbelievable. Since he had arrived in one of the hotel cars, everyone thought George was a guest of the hotel. He was inundated with street vendors.

"They think you're a rich American; that is why they are bothering you." The speaker was a beautiful, black-haired, Mexican girl. She was George's age—his real age, not as old as he looked. Her nails were meticulously done. Her clothes were of the finest quality. George had Monique to thank for showing what telltale signs to look for in a woman. Her shoes had a high shine on them that made them look out of place in the dust bowl that surrounded the pyramid site. She had a slender build. Her black hair matched her piercing, black eyes that seemed to burn a hole right through him. "Are you done looking at me? If so, what is your estimate as to how long it will take you to talk me into going to bed?"

A phrase like that would have floored the George who had existed before Monique, but the new George thought for a moment before he replied, "You're the kind of girl whom I would not even think about going to bed with. I know if I did, I would never want to leave you. You would be the mother of my children. Anyway, how do you know I'm not a rich American who came down here to sow my wild seeds?"

"Because your name is George. You work for my father."

George fought his instinct to be shocked by the comment; he walked around her as he said, "Well, I think we better have a long conversation about your father. Now will I have to call him "Dad" right away? That would bother me. You know I would get mixed up: Dad or Boss."

"Hi, I'm Maria." As she spoke, her eyes lit up. She extended her hand to shake George's.

"Hi. I'm George. I can see we're going to have many arguments about how many children we're going to have. What are you doing here, following me?"

"No, I'm here with my art class. I go to the University of Mexico."

Maria immediately saw George's surprised look. "We do have schools here, you know. We wear shoes as well. We haven't worn pelts for some time. I can even count past ten without taking my shoes off. We're a civilized country now. Didn't you know that, Mr. George?"

"That was unfair. I'm a guest in your country; that comment was unfair. Rather than being mean to me, why don't you take me on a tour of your school? I'm tired of riding around with Pedro over here."

"Will you put the roof down on your car?" The question was asked with a playful tone in her voice.

"Will you promise not to hit me in front of everyone?"

"Yes. I'll tell him to take you back to the hotel. I'll meet you there at three. You don't have to take a siesta, do you?"

"No. I would not want to miss the tour."

George went back to the hotel. He rested as he waited for Maria to show up. She had changed into a flowery flair skirt with a ruffled off-the-shoulder top. With her black hair, she looked like a Mexican dancer in one of the posters that advertise, "Come to Mexico."

The rest of the day, as well as half of the night, was spent visiting the University of Mexico as well as all of her friends' houses. One of the parents insisted that they stay for dinner. The father of her friend was amazed that George enjoyed the hot peppers as much as he did. Maria whispered to George, "You are certainly making a favorable impression on our host. He can't believe you're eating the hot peppers with him."

"How am I doing with you?"

"I'll let you know later."

Their host insisted upon showing George the garden with his stables. George was amazed at the elegance of the ranch. Halfway through the tour, Maria told George, "My uncle just loves you. He told me that he would adopt a girl so you could become his son-in-law."

"I thought you told me he was the father of one of your friends?"

"I lied. He's my uncle, my father's younger brother. He raises bulls for the ring."

George couldn't hide his surprise as he said, "Are you serious?"

"Yes. The bulls have to come from somewhere. They have to be bred to have strong hearts. They must charge in a straight line."

"You mean they have to not mind being killed," George responded.

"Yes, that too. Do you want to go to his ranch? It is one hundred miles or one hundred eighty kilometers from Mexico City."

"Just let me know when. But I'm telling you, if you're lying to me, I'll make you walk back."

A smiled flashed across her face as she said, "If not, you

will buy me a gift from Taxco—that is where the silver mines are located."

"You got a deal."

"Wait here while I go tell him. We'll leave Friday afternoon. I get out of school by twelve. We'll leave at that time."

George waited while Maria spoke to her uncle. When she came back, Maria was all smiles. "Okay, we are set for Friday. I told him you would stay over.'

"What about you?" I asked.

"Oh, I'll stay over too, but my aunt runs a strict house. You won't even see me after the sun goes down."

"Well, that's wonderful; I can spend the night with the bulls."

The couple returned to the hotel. Her father was waiting on the front steps. He started yelling at her. He just looked at George, but his look said it all. He was so upset that he was only speaking Spanish. Somehow all curse words sound the same. Maria went into the hotel crying. George had already had his bags packed by the maid. Three men put his bags into the car. One of the men said, "Go. If you stay, there will be big problems. I don't think you want that, so just go."

George left. He went to another hotel in town. The next morning he called home. His mother was in tears. "I only had one boy. You're not coming home? You had enough vacation. Come home." George agreed he would. He spent the next three days, riding around the area and taking in all the sights. One morning, he went to the Chevy dealer in Mexico City for a scheduled check-up. He was pleasantly surprised when the dealer honored the American service agreement. The service didn't cost him anything. He went to Taxco to visit the fine shops that were there. They were having a sale on silver bracelets, two for one. He bought two with the intent of giving one to one of his sisters and the other one to Ann when he saw her. The shop next store to the silver shop sold Mexican skirts.

They were very decorative with a lot of beadwork on them. He bought four for his sisters.

The following morning he went to the university. No matter where he went, his car always drew a crowd. Today was no exception. He kept repeating the words Maria and Del Prado Hotel. One girl came over to him. She explained she was Maria's friend. "If you go to the stadium, I will bring Maria to you." George went where he had been told. In about half an hour, Maria came. She was wearing sunglasses, but he could still see where she had been beaten.

"My God, what happened?"

"My father got a call from his brother. When he heard that we were going to my uncle's ranch, he went crazy. We're in Mexico, not the States. I will go with you if you want, but I can't see you in Mexico anymore."

George thought back to all the things that Monique had taught him, but somehow nothing seemed to fit this situation. George took a deep breath as he said, "Maria, I would be lying if I told you anything but the truth. Your life is here. Mine is in America. We are both young. We both have our lives to live. I realize that, and I think you do, too." George remembered the bracelet in the car. Ann would have to wait for hers. This was an emergency. "I did not want you to forget me, so I bought the gift I was supposed to buy you. When you look at it, please have a fond memory of me." George went to his car to get the bracelet out. He gave it to Maria. Maria was in tears. George walked away and got in his car to leave. He didn't know why he had given her the bracelet, except that it appeased his conscience for getting involved with her. He was annoyed with himself, for he had come to Mexico to work, not to act like a stupid tourist. He had just made a date to go out with one of the locals.

George drove back on the same road he came in on; only this time he spent an extra day in each town. He went to a cockfight on Saturday night. The marketplace was the only place to be on Sunday morning. After he left the village, he began driving home. Just driving through the countryside was like stepping back in history. It was beautiful, except the people were very poor. One of the hotel managers warned him about stopping on the road for anything. "There are many bad people from here to the border. You are big and strong, but you are only one."

George took the warning very seriously. He did not stop except in the towns. He crossed the border back into Brownsville. His first stop was at the bank. He took out his package and found a post office. He mailed it to himself at his home. Riding with that much cash was too much of a risk to take. He called his mother and told her to expect a package. "Just put it on the side until I get home." She was glad to hear from him and glad to hear he was back in the States. Mexico to her was just a poor, foreign country.

George drove from Texas up to Ohio. He stopped often to sightsee along the way. The time he took also allowed him to reexamine whether or not he wanted to go to Ohio. He called Sal. From him he heard that the church had dropped the whole matter. "Ann was kicked out of the order." George was stunned. He screamed into the phone, "What church? What order? What are you talking about?"

Sal gasped. "You didn't know she was a nun? The girl you were going out with, Ann, is a nun. You didn't know that? George, I'm sorry I'm the one to tell you, but she's a nun. The church doesn't want any bad press, so they just dropped the whole thing. I'm sorry, kid. Look at the bright side; you can go home now. You don't have to worry about anything."

George was speechless. He hung up the phone, still not believing what he had just heard. He stood in a motel off the beaten path for a full day, trying to understand what had happened to him. A nun. Those two words rang through his head like a bell, tolling out bad news. A nun. He finally just got in his car and drove home. No matter what he did, the car just didn't want to go where he was steering. It was as though it had a mind of its own. George's Run was his next stop.

There were no hotels in George's Run. The nearest motel was in Steubenville about five miles away. George drove to the motel for the night. He asked the clerk where George's Run was, as there was no sign for it, or at least he hadn't seen any as he drove up Route 7. The clerk, who was a heavyset girl, smiled as she announced, "Of course I do. I was raised there. I know everyone. Who are you looking for? No one just comes to George's Run."

"I was looking for a girl who lived there. Her name is Ann."

As soon as George said Ann's name, the smile disappeared from the girl's face. "Oh, Ann." The clerk took a long, hard look at George as she added, "It figures."

She gave George the key to his room. She didn't say another word. George went to his room to lie down, for it had been a long day. About an hour later, there was a knock at the door. George got up to see who was there. Just as he was about to open the door, he smelled a perfume. He knew it was Ann on the other side of the closed door. He opened it without asking who it was, for he knew it was she. He wanted very much to be with her, nun or no nun. So what? He was with her. As he stood there in the open doorway, he smiled as he saw he was right; it was Ann.

"I never thought I would see you again. There is so much I want to tell you." As Ann spoke, she came into the room. She stood in front of George, who had buried his face in his hands. He could not stop the tears that were welling in his eyes. He was ashamed to be seen like that. He went to the bed to sit on it, trying to compose himself. Ann sat next to him. She leaned over as she whispered in his ear, "I know I've hurt you, but I didn't know what else to do. That night I was forced to stand on that corner. When a car stopped, I went to it. I told the police, as well as my Mother Superior, that the man in it was you."

George was choking back the tears as he said: "I was on the opposite corner in my new car. How could you possibly know I was there? That I saw all that?"

"I don't know, but I knew you did. I don't know how I knew. Is that so important right now? There is a lot about me that I never told you. I went to meet you that night to tell you everything about me."

George excused himself and went into the bathroom to wash his tear-stained face. When he returned, he sat on the bed next to Ann again.

Ann held his hand as she continued, "When I left this town, I thought I wanted to become a nun. I was supposed to take my final vows. I didn't know if I should. I went out that night. God had me meet you. Right from the first night, I knew that my feelings for you would have never allowed me to be a good nun. I could not have forsaken all others for the church. From our first meeting, you became a part of my life that I would never want to do without. I didn't know how to tell you I was a nun. I didn't know how to tell the church that I wanted to be with you. When the first nun, Sister Edith, spoke to me about becoming a nun, she told me I should not become one to escape or to hide from life. I had convinced myself that I wasn't doing that. I really wanted to devote myself to God and His work. I met you and that changed. I thought that with time, all our problems would work themselves out, but that wasn't happening. When the bartender, the one who served us the night I spilled the drink on you, recognized me in the church that is when everything started to go wrong."

"What bartender? What are you talking about?" As George sat on the bed, he started to regain control of himself. The words he was hearing from Ann were hitting him as an additional punishment. George was thinking to himself, Sal said she robbed the church. She's saying that she was spotted with me and that was the problem. She hasn't even mentioned the money. Is this Ann? Am I ever going to know who or what she is? Do I want to?

It is necessary at this point to put in an explanation of what had really happened in Union City. The Mother Superior became incensed with Ann's reluctance to say anything about George or the money that was missing. The Mother Superior, unbeknownst to anyone, called a friend of hers who was a psychiatrist. The two women had gone to school together. They had kept in touch throughout both of their careers. The Mother Superior wanted her friend to hypnotize Ann to find out the answers to her questions. The Mother Superior found her friend's card. She called the doctor to tell her what she wanted. At first, the doctor was reluctant to do it, but after the Mother Superior assured her that whatever was learned would not go further than the doctor's office, the doctor agreed. After calling, she left the card on her desk.

"Don't bring her here. Don't tell her who or what I am. I'll come to the convent house Tuesday night. We will meet there. I'll order some drugs from the drug store for you to give to her to make her relax; that will make things go easier for her. Understand, though, you might hear things you don't want to hear."

The Mother Superior agreed and said she understood; the two women hung up. The Mother Superior made a note of the date and time the doctor would be there. On the chosen day, she put the drugs into Ann's after-dinner tea and waited for them to take effect. The rest of the nuns knew something was going on, for she made them all leave the dining room right after tea. The Mother helped Ann to a couch in her room and made her lie down when Ann complained about being light-headed. Ann sensed something was wrong. She spied the doctor's card with that day's date on it. When the Mother Superior went to get her a glass of water, Ann put the card in her pocket.

The Mother Superior came back into the room and handed the glass of liquid to Ann. After Ann drank the liquid, the Mother Superior said in a reassuring tone, "Here, my child, lie down on the couch for a while to see if it passes. Within a few minutes, Ann was in a daze that made it hard to distinguish day from night or light from dark. She started to slip out of consciousness. The last clear thing she remembered was someone's saying, "Relax. Look at this light. You are going to fall fast asleep. Look at the light."

When the doctor was assured Ann was asleep, she started the video/tape recorder she had brought with her. She referenced the date. She referred to the patient as Sister X. The doctor started asking the list of questions the Mother Superior had prepared. The doctor began, "What is your name?"

"Ann."

"Were you born in George's Run, Ohio?"

"Yes."

The questions continued. They had been designed to bring Ann chronologically through her life. When she came to her seventeenth birthday, she suddenly sat up on the couch and started screaming, "Don't touch her! Please don't hit, mama! I'll do what you want; just don't hit her!"

The doctor and the Mother Superior were shocked by Ann's outburst. The Mother Superior told her friend about how Ann's mother was murdered. They never knew who did it, but everyone thought it was her father. He was never caught. The doctor continued with the questions. "Tell us, Ann, what happened? Why was your father going to hit your mother?"

"After we had dinner, we ate the cake that my mother had baked. My father went into his room to get me a big surprise he had for me. When he came out, he was nude. He started chasing me. My mother tried to stop him. He started hitting her. My mother kept telling me to run; I didn't want to, but my mother kept yelling for me to go. She yelled for me to go to the church. She kept screaming, "Go to the church!" I ran out of the house. When I came back, Mama was dead in the middle of all that blood."

Ann was sweating profusely. The doctor made her lie down and gave her a shot of something to calm her down. The doctor looked at the Mother Superior, who also was in a state of shock. The doctor said, "Still want to hear about the money?"

The Mother Superior replied, "The hell with the money. Will she sleep now?"

"Yes."

"Will she remember what we did here tonight?"

The doctor replied, "She may remember the incident, but I doubt if she'll remember anything of what happened here tonight. I mean, the incident is still in her mind, but tonight won't be. Just let her sleep here for the night. In the morning, she may have a headache but give her two aspirins. That should take care of it. In a day or two, she'll be as good as new."

The Mother Superior thanked her friend as they parted company. The doctor took the video/tape recording with her when she left. That night, the Mother Superior did all the paper work necessary to have Ann transferred. The next day was Wednesday; that was the night Ann was made to stand on the corner to wait for George. That was the last night she was in Bergen County. The next morning was Thursday. Ann was put on a plane to Cincinnati, Ohio.

Ann never remembered the doctor or the session with her. Ann accepted her transfer as a chance to find herself. At the moment, she was thankful George was with her. What had happened was in the past. She took George's arm and put it around her. She started talking to him in such a low voice that at times he didn't hear what she was saying. "You remember the first night I met you? We were in that bar the night I knocked over the drink onto you? Well, the bartender who served us the replacement drink goes to the church where I was stationed. I helped out on the playground one Sunday. His daughter hurt her arm. I bandaged it for her. On the day that the parents were to come to open house, the little girl introduced me to her parents. Her father was the bartender. He created such a scene that day that I ran out of the room. The Mother Superior wanted to know whom I had been with; she wanted to meet you. When I said I wouldn't take her to you, she became very nasty. I didn't know what to do. The other nuns all knew I was coming to see you. They all turned on me, too. I left Bergen County to come back home. I thought once I was in my own town that I would find the answers to all my questions; after that, I would find you again. By that time I hoped that we could build a life together. When I came here, Sister Edith helped me get a job, teaching in the school. When I had joined the church, they sent me to many schools to learn all about financial law. They wanted me to become an expert in financial matters for the church; that is how I knew all about that contract you showed me. Did you ever sell your business? Even though I went to all the schools they wanted me to go to, I never got a degree in anything. Sister Edith helped get the local university to let me attend their school. I don't have to attend a lot of classes. They send me homework; I do it. I submit it back. They tell me it will take only a year. I'll only be twenty-seven."

"Twenty-seven? You'll only be twenty-seven? I'm only twenty-one. Twenty-seven?" George just could not believe what he just heard. He had been raised to believe that the man should be older than the girl he was going to marry. With thoughts of the word "marry," he broke out into a cold sweat. He thought to himself, "Marry? Monique warned me about this. Monique talked about getting personal with engagements. Ann isn't an engagement, George said to himself. So what if she is older than I am? I look older than she does. Who says that the man has to be older than the woman? What's the difference? My family will accept whomever I bring home. If I love her, they will too. They will, or they can go to hell."

Ann had stopped getting undressed when George said he was twenty-one. She looked at him and could see he was having a terrible time accepting the fact that she was older than he. She put her clothes on again. She started talking in a very somber tone, "When we had that long talk about ourselves, you wanted all of the traditional things in life. You want a stable home, children, and a wife who stayed home to take care of the house. At first, I didn't think I could do those things. For me, there has to be more than that in life. The church, it seemed, offered me more. When I decided to become a nun, I went for an operation so that I couldn't ever have children. After I met you, I knew that was the wrong thing to do. If you love me the way I think you do, please do me one favor. Leave. Leave now! Go back to your family. Think through the things we have just discussed. Realize what you'll be getting into. Let's meet again in a year. Then, when we meet, there will be no secrets. We can see if we want to try again and if we think we can build a life together."

Ann left. George was still in a state of shock. He got dressed as he ran out of the motel, looking for her. He saw her walking down the street. He ran after her. When he got to her, he spun her around. He waited until she stopped crying. Within a few minutes, she had composed herself. They started to walk together. Ann, in a quivering voice, said, "George, I have your number. I think you should leave. I will call you after we have both had a chance to think about what we're doing."

George was about to respond when he heard, "Hi, Ann. I thought it was you, walking. Oh, hello. I'm Norma, Ann's friend. I saw your car. You're from New Jersey?" As she spoke, she walked backwards. George and Ann couldn't get around her.

Ann looked at George. In an apologetic voice, she said, "George, this is my friend, Norma. We teach school together."

Norma took control of the conversation. She talked non-stop as the threesome walked to the end of the road. He started walking back. George wasn't paying attention to what Norma was saying but couldn't help but compare her to Janet. Norma had the same voice, mannerisms, and gestures. Looking at Norma, Ann, by comparison looked very old. The lines under her eyes, which George had never seen before, became more pronounced. All of her features suddenly took on a whole new look. George could not believe how much she had aged right before his eyes. When they got back to the motel, he interrupted Norma's incessant chatter. He had to get away from the two of them. "Can I drive you home?"

Norma responded, "No, I have my car." Norma finally could sense that staying with George while he was with Ann was not a good idea. She knew George wanted to leave.

George walked them to the car. At that moment, what Ann had said about leaving seemed like a good idea. To a twenty-one-year-old, twenty-seven seems like a big difference. No children! To be married to an old lady? Ann's advice seemed like the right thing to do. George turned to face both women and said; "I will leave you two ladies now, for I have a long drive tomorrow. He leaned over and kissed Ann goodbye on the cheek. He shook Norma's hand. "It was a pleasure meeting you." George went back to his room. He rested for the drive home, which he started at the crack of dawn.

All the way home, George couldn't believe that not once had Ann mentioned the money or how she had gotten it. George could not believe she was six years older than he was. He laughed as he said out loud, "I must really look as old as everyone tells me I do. I wonder how old Maria's father thought I was. From now on, when I meet someone new, I'm going to say, "Hi, I'm George. I'm 21. How old are you?" Is this the end of the story? It could well be, but it isn't.

The drive back from Ohio was a straight line on the bumpy,

smelly turnpike. There was an endless line of trucks that made passing them a game of nerves. The drive lasted all day, but somehow it didn't seem far, for George had a lot on his mind. Aside from Ann, he had the rest of his life to plan. The twenty thousand was in a package at home. He still didn't know what he was going to do with that. There was no more Jules to guide him. All these thoughts helped pass the time away until, at last, he made the last turn into the driveway of his house.

Chapter Twelve

"Home is where your heart is" may be a cliché, but it is nevertheless very true. George was home. The drive had taken a full day, but he was home. He knew there was no way that he would leave his family for Ann or for anyone else. Well, maybe, but not the way he felt as he pulled into the yard of his home. Home--just the sound of the word made George feel like a whole person again. The first thought that came to his mind was what he was going to do with the money in the package. Jules was dead. That thought kept plaguing him. He really didn't know whom he could talk to. My lawyer, George thought. His lawyer had known him since he first went into business. He'd set up the incorporation papers. He'll give me an answer. George resolved he would go see him the next day. Right now the more pressing problem was how he was going to explain to his sisters why he didn't get them all the same thing.

That night George called Andy to seek his advice on the Ann matter. He met with Andy at the bowling lanes--where he was engaged in his favorite pastime—losing money to the lane hustlers. Andy walked over to George, and after the usual greetings, borrowed some money from him and sent him to pick up Mary Lou, with whom he'd had a date a half hour before. "Go get her; the three of us will go for coffee. I promised I'd pick her up at Janet's house. You remember where Janet lives, don't you?"

"Well, yes, I do. But I really wanted to talk to you—alone."

Andy could see that George was really hurting, so he quit the games, and the two of them went into the bar. Andy looked at him; five minutes later, George had told him the whole story. George looked relieved when he was done. Of course, George didn't go into the money part but limited his story to Ann's being a nun and their difference in age. The nun/age factors were enough to deal with.

"Are you nuts? What are you going to do when she pats you on the head and says, 'Come on, sonny, time for biddy-bye'? Go get Mary Lou and Janet; we'll go for a drink or something. You better stop going places by yourself; you're getting wackier than before. Don't tell me now. You can tell the three of us about your trip to Mexico and wherever else you went. She wasn't with you, was she? You are nuts. Go get the girls."

George left, for he could see that from Andy's point of view, he was not going to persuade him that maybe Ann wasn't such a bad thing. He'd wanted Andy's opinion. He got it. Just because it wasn't what he wanted to hear didn't make it wrong. George continued driving to Janet's house. He received a nicer greeting from Janet's mother than he thought he would. The two girls were happy to see him. Mary Lou added, "I assume Andy sent you for me because he is bowling?"

George responded, "No, I wanted some time to be alone with you. After all, you are my advisor, you know."

"Well, we're not going to be alone, since Janet just went to get changed to come with us. My phone number's the same. You can call me later. We'll get together."

"Why?" Janet added. She had heard the last part of Mary Lou's speech. The question was never answered. The group said goodnight to Janet's mother, as the three of them got in George's car to go to the lanes to pick up Andy. Later at the diner, everyone listened in awe as George related his experiences. He left out the part about Maria, as well as the part of his being an escort. His story was more like hearing a travel brochure.

Janet was sitting on the edge of the chair as she asked, "Why did you go so suddenly?"

George left Janet's question unanswered. George suggested they leave, since he was still tired from his drive from Ohio.

George took everyone home, but the last thing Janet said as she got out of the car was, "I wouldn't want you to call Mary Lou too late." Janet got out and made an extra effort to make sure that the door was tightly closed.

The next morning George received a call from his lawyer. "Why don't you come here? We'll have lunch today? Pick me up at twelve-thirty at my office. I want to discuss something with you." George agreed.

He couldn't believe his good fortune. How did he know I was home? Someone called him. I never told him I was leaving, so why wouldn't he think I was home? The coincidence was too great. Things like that just don't happen. At twelve-thirty, George drove over to Lenny's office. Lenny came out. He motioned for George to park his car in the lot in the back of the building as he said, "Come upstairs to my office." George complied with the command and parked his car and walked up the back steps to Lenny's office.

When he entered Lenny's office, he saw that Lenny had two placemats with sandwiches set up on them on the conference table.

"How was your trip? You look none the worse for wear." As the two men sat down, a secretary came in with a glass of water for Lenny and a can of soda for George. She left. As soon as she was out of the room, Lenny started, "Your mother was very worried about you. I assured her you had a good head on your shoulders and that you wouldn't do anything stupid. But now that you're home, what are you going to do next? Not many people your age have done or seen the things you have." Lenny kept talking; George just tuned him out. He knew he had to do something, but he didn't feel like listening to him. Who the hell did he think he was? Now George knew how this nosy bastard knew he was home.

"Be a lawyer."

George's head snapped up when he heard those words. In

shock George responded, "A lawyer? That takes ten years. I don't want to spend the next ten years in school. Anyway, I don't think I passed lunch when I was in high school. What college would let me in?"

"If I get you into one, will you go? It doesn't take ten years. You can go summers; you'll be done in six. I have represented many people in my professional life; if you can't make it, we'll have to rewrite the books. Go. What can you lose? The worst that can happen is that you'll be six years older and you won't be a lawyer. Listen to your lawyer. Go. I'll make some calls you'll get in. You just go. The school is in Rutherford." As he spoke, he handed George a brochure of the school. "You just go. Orientation is tomorrow, so be there in the gym at nine o'clock. The registration desk will have all your paperwork waiting for you. If you run into trouble, just call me. Now get out. I have paying clients coming in. George got up from the table and left in a daze. He got in his car for the drive home. On the way he thought, School. No not school, college. I have nothing in common with the other students. So what I never gave a damn about them before. I'll go.

George drove home, still wondering if he was dreaming or not. This school thing was not what he'd had in mind. Also, he had never gotten a chance to ask what he should do with the money. George decided he would rent another safe deposit box. He still had travelers checks left over from his trip, but he felt that going to school was going to be an expensive situation. He decided he would try it. What could he lose--some time? He suddenly felt very old as he thought about the fact that his classmates were going to be younger than he was. He would be the Ann of the class. That thought alone brought a smile to his face. He looked at the clock and decided to go pick up Mary Lou, since he still wanted to talk to her. She was the most levelheaded person he knew.

He called her. As soon as she heard his voice, she invited

him over her house. "Come right now; I was just going to take a tea break."

As soon as George got there, she sat him down in the parlor. She came in with his tea, as well as cookies she had baked. She set everything down on a little table next to the chair.

George told her about his lawyer's idea. She responded, "School? That's a great idea. You would be very foolish if you didn't take full advantage of going." Mary Lou's enthusiastic acceptance of the school idea made George feel a lot better about going. "But you didn't come here to tell me about going to school. They were alone and sitting in the parlor of her house, while her mother kept finding reasons to come in. Every time she did, George would keep quiet until she left or until she asked some stupid question, after which she would finally leave.

George started telling Mary Lou about Ann, but when he got to the part about her being a nun, Mary Lou could not restrain herself any longer. The age difference didn't bother Mary Lou; the nun thing did. She spilled her tea as she said, "How could you ever trust her? I mean, that is not the kind of thing you lie about. George, she wasn't truthful to you from the beginning! Where do you think your relationship is going to go from here?"

"Mary Lou, can you come here a moment?" Her mother's voice was enough to bring George back to reality. He had to resolve this Ann thing by himself.

"Mary Lou," her mother said again, only this time with a little more urgency to it.

"You better go. We'll talk again." With that, George got up to leave the house.

Mary Lou went into the kitchen where her mother was. As she walked into the room, her mother held out the phone to her. It was Janet. Mary Lou glared at her mother, "Couldn't you have taken a message? You could have told her I'd call her back?"

"What should I have told her? That you were too busy to come to the phone because you were talking to her boyfriend?"

"George is not her boyfriend. We just all know each other," Mary Lou responded in an annoyed tone.

George got up early for today was going to be the first day of school. He reminded himself--college, not school. Somehow the two words had a different ring to them. George presented himself at the registration desk; at first, no one could find his papers. A very studious lady came over, and in a condescending tone announced, "Oh, him. He's a special case." She disappeared in a few minutes and came back with his forms already filled out. "Here you are," she said as she handed George all of his class cards. "Here is a map of the campus. I have marked your classroom buildings in red. When you go to the class, give the card to the teacher; he or she will instruct you as to what books you'll need. I also marked the location of the book store for you." When she was done talking, she let out a sigh as she spun around on her heels. She left by saying, "Tomorrow, you have off. The day after will become the first day of the rest of your life."

That night when George got home, there was a call from a police detective from Newark. He called the number he was given. The detective asked if he would come to the police station. There were some questions they wanted to ask him. George went at the appointed hour. He was seated in a small room when two detectives came in. They started asking him questions about Ann. To their surprise, George answered every one of them without hesitation or reservation.

"When you were going out with Ann, did you know she was a nun?"

"No."

"Would it have made any difference to you?"

"I don't know."

"Did she give you money?"

"Yes."

"How much?"

"I don't know. I didn't count it. She asked me to pay for everything because she didn't feel I should spend my money on her."

"Do women usually pay for you? They give you money to take them out?"

Monique's words came to mind, "The customer always pays." George's response surprised the detective by both its speed and content, "The women always pay, or I don't go."

"What the hell are you? A Gigolo?"

"I would rather use the word 'escort,' but yes. I've worked as an escort throughout the southern states as well as Mexico. I have now returned to New Jersey. Tomorrow, I'm starting college because I don't like being an escort. Now, if you don't mind, I would like to go, for tomorrow is going to be the first day of the rest of my life."

"You're not going anywhere, are you?"

"Only to school." George got up and walked toward the door. One of the detectives said, "You think you're pretty slick with the escort story, don't you?"

George turned to face the two men with a sincere conviction in his voice and added, "I told you the truth. I don't like being called a liar."

One of them asked, "Well, do you think I would be good at it?"

"Not with that attitude, you won't." George left to the accompaniment of the two detectives' mumbling. George couldn't figure out how they knew he was home. He put the whole matter out of his mind now that he was a college student.

The next two weeks flew by. Besides reading everything he was supposed to, learning to listen in class, and studying; George was having serious doubts as to his ability to do this college thing. He received word in one of his classes that the president of the school wanted to see him when class was over. A low buzz went through the classroom. As George had expected, he was the oldest student in the daytime classes. It seemed everyone had been warned about bothering with him. George found himself always alone. When he had lunch, no one sat at the same table he did. When he went to the library, as soon as he sat at one of the tables, everyone found some reason to get up. Although this isolation was apparent to everyone, George didn't even know it was happening. He did his work and went about his studies, oblivious to the fact that he was by himself.

At the end of the class George went to the president's office. The president was on the phone as George walked in. He was a little shorter than George. He had a stocky build. He was starting to lose his hair. Instead of trying to hide the fact he was going bald, he combed his hair straight back, which emphasized the fact that his hairline was rapidly receding. When George walked in, he nodded towards a chair, indicating for George to sit down. He finished his call. He paid full attention to George.

"How are you doing?"

"Ok I guess."

"Are you getting along with the other students? I mean you are the oldest one in all your classes; sometimes that can cause a problem."

George could not hide the puzzled look on his face, as he didn't know what the baldheaded guy was talking about. Finally George said, "I don't bother them, I guess, so they don't bother me."

"Yes, I know. Well, if you don't want to intermingle with them, I guess that is your business. I asked you here to make sure you understand that I let you in, but I will not do anything to keep you in. So far, your instructors inform me that you seem capable of doing the work required, so this is the last time I'm going to inquire. You're on your own. You either keep up or you're out."

"Don't worry about me," George responded.

"That's all I wanted to hear," the president said.

"Okay," George responded, as he stood up to leave. The two men shook hands as George left. The meeting was as cold a meeting as two people could have, but George didn't care. His teachers said he was doing well. He was still in.

George's time in school started to fly by.

During his first semester, he concentrated on his accounting studies. He had enough money to go to school full time and not have to work for the first three years. He took summer courses, which allowed him to be done sooner. He was really surprised when he met people with whom he had done business. When he told them he'd gone back to school, they were surprised yet happy that he had. Recognizing that money is usually a problem, they offered him loans, opportunities to make "some fast money," or a part-time job. They would end these offers with, "Make sure you stay in school. I always wanted to go, but I didn't. Don't be stupid like me; you go. Make sure you finish."

Mary Lou was always around to help him any way she could. On occasion, Janet pitched in to help, too. They both would type papers for him and help him understand what he was reading. All thoughts of Ann started to vanish from his mind. Her name no longer came up in any conversations he had with Mary Lou or Andy. Janet was always excluded from those discussions.

The days became years. College became law school. He lost contact with Andy and Mary Lou. He saw Janet once, but they both recognized there was nothing between them. They drifted apart as it became apparent that they didn't share the same dreams. After his third year, he got a job at night. He went to school during the days. His schedule left little time to socialize.

After graduation from college, he worked days and went to law school at night. His lawyer was wrong about the time element; it took George seven years, not six, to become a lawyer. George went from working for an accounting company to working for a privately held company. His drive to be his own boss was overwhelming, so he opened his own accounting law office. He became very successful very fast. His meteor rise took its toll. One day George got up and wasn't even sure who or where he was. That afternoon, George went to see a doctor.

The doctor took every kind of test imaginable; when he was done, he sat George down and said, "You are no doubt the strongest man I have ever met. That is the only reason you're not dead." George stiffened as he sat in the chair. George didn't know what to expect, but he hadn't expected that.

The doctor continued, "You are not suffering from anything physical malady, so I can't give you a pill or a shot, but I can tell you that if you don't learn to relax, you'll start to get more symptoms than I have names for. Relax. When was the last time you took a vacation? I mean a time by yourself to just contemplate your navel? Well, I can assure you that you better. Go fishing. That's good. Or better yet, go get a boat. Just driving the damn thing will keep your mind off of everything else, and you'll soon learn to fear the water more than anything else."

George got up, thanked the doctor, and left. At first he was going to disregard what the doctor had said, but when he discovered he had passed the street he lived on, he rethought the advice he had received. The next afternoon, with the aid of one of his sisters, he bought a twenty-three-foot, center-console boat. He quickly read all the books about boating that everyone gave him. He wrote away to the Army Corp of Engineers. He received maps of all the rivers in the eastern half of the United States. He bought a series of boating books that showed all the marinas around the same area. Armed with his nautical library carefully wrapped in a plastic bag, on a clear October morning, he headed his boat toward Florida. He had no idea, at the time that his trip would take him down to Florida. From there, he went across the Gulf of Mexico to Mobile Bay and came up the new canal to the Ohio River and directly to George's Run. He didn't make the trip all in one period of time; he broke it up so that he would travel for a week, find a marina to leave his boat, and then go home and work a couple of weeks before he would leave to go back to his boat. Once there, he would continue his trip for another week. If he really liked a place, he would spend a few days before continuing his voyage. When he got to Ohio, somehow, the boat would not go past George's Run. George reluctantly pulled to the public dock and tied the boat up. It was at that time that he recognized that he was at his destination. He knew from the beginning that this was where he'd wanted to go, and that was why he'd gotten all the books with the maps in them.

A policeman patrolling the area saw George docking and came over to help him. "This river has a very strong current. Make sure you have four mooring lines, or you'll find your boat in St. Louis," was the advice offered by the officer.

George thanked him as he started to look around for a phone to call a cab.

"You have a place to stay?" the officer asked.

"No. Can you help me out or at least tell me how I can get a cab?"

"You are a stranger in town. What made you stop? Something broke?" The last part of his comment brought a smile to the ruddy-faced officer.

"Yeah, me. I suddenly felt very tired, so rather than push myself, I decided to stop."

"Good for you. Come on, the least I can do is help a smart man like you find a bed. We have a small hotel or a bed and breakfast right down the street; I know the lady can use the money."

"A bed and breakfast it is." George got into the police car with his one bag. The police officer was right; the house was one block from the river. As he pulled up, he saw a woman tending her flowers in the front yard. The scene reminded George of the first time he had met Jean's mother, Maude.

"I have a customer for you. Do you have room?" The officer's yell frightened the woman, but she quickly recovered.

"Yes. Oh, yes."

George got out, and the officer smiled, saying, "See you. I'll check on your boat before I go off duty. You go to sleep. You look like hell." With that farewell, the officer left George with his hostess.

The lady was an elderly woman whose husband had died. She was trying desperately to hold on to her house. Her three children had moved away, rarely calling or coming to visit her. She started to really get into the story of her life when George interrupted her with, "Hold those stories for when we go out tonight for dinner. That way we'll have something to talk about. Right now, I would like to take a shower and a nap. I'll see you later." Before the lady could say anything else, George shut the door. George realized he was tired when even the thoughts and memories of Ann could not keep him awake.

When he woke, he and his hostess went to a nearby restaurant, which was nothing more than a storefront with some tables. They were the only customers. They chatted through dinner. George walked her home, for she was tired; the two glasses of wine that the owner had given them had started to take their toll. George went toward the railroad tracks and down by the water to check on his boat. Somehow George knew he wouldn't feel comfortable anywhere in town except by the water and his boat. They were reality. The town was nothing like Ann had told him. It must have been her dream. There was no little park, with a path running along the river, where everyone went at night. She must have made that town up in her mind. The buildings that were here were a generating plant on one end of the area and a steel mill on the other. The barges were there since they brought the coal to the two factories. The train ran next to the river. There was some space between the riverbank and the train track; maybe that was the little park to which Ann had referred. He remembered that when he'd been in the town last, he'd never come out of the motel. The road leading home went north from Steubenville. George doubted whether he'd ever been in George's Run before tonight.

George checked the lines on the boat as he started to walk to Main Street, which he believed to be the only street in town. It was in town he finally felt at ease. The long boat trip was worth it. He was near her again.

George began to realize there was no beginning or ending to his story, but it was rather like a tune that just kept playing in his mind. It began, it paused, it continued; the end might never come or it might be around the next corner. He tried to remember when he had last seen Ann. To his dismay, his last meeting with her was so vivid in his mind that he thought it was yesterday instead of two schools plus a hundred years ago.

Chapter Thirteen

George sat on a bench in front of the closed, general store for most of the night. The people who walked by nodded toward him as if they knew him. It seemed a blink of the eye since the time that George had last been there. That was twenty-five years ago. Twenty-five years! The words sounded strange to his ears. Twenty-five years is a lifetime, yet it seems like… George hesitated, for he felt ridiculous for thinking that it felt like yesterday.

"Well, I never thought I'd see you sitting on a bench in our town. How long has it been?"

George knew it was Norma who was speaking. Silently, he had said a prayer that it was Ann talking, but he pushed his prayer aside and took the disappointment out of his voice and off his face. He smiled and got up. He hugged Norma as he was saying, "Hello."

"You can kiss me. So what is a little gossip? Anyway, who cares? When I heard there was a boat from New Jersey here, I knew it was you. I just knew it. When word got to me that there was a large, scary man sitting on the bench by the store, I was positive it was you. Don't be surprised if our deputy dog comes around. Everyone in town is wondering who you are, as well as why you are here. So let me guess. Ann was here, as you know. She married a local yokel; within six months, she threw him out. She was teaching with me at the parochial school while she went to college to get a degree and…are you ready for this...she continued her education and became an attorney. She left about fifteen years ago to go to work for the State of New York in some important, judicial job. On her last trip home, she told me she wasn't coming back anymore; it was too painful. That was ten years ago. She wrote me two letters; I haven't heard from her since. So to answer your questions: no, I haven't seen her, except as last mentioned; no, I haven't heard from her, and finally no, I don't know where she is." Anything else? If there is, there is only one place still open nearby, but it will cost you a cup of coffee. They may still have pie, but I can't swear to that or that if they do have any left, it will be any good."

George got up as Norma took his arm and led the way to her car to drive to the local coffee shop. She kept up a running commentary about Ann, but finally she stopped. "This is painful for you, isn't it? Did you know Sister Edith? She died two years ago."

When Norma paused to see George's reaction to the Sister Edith news, George was finally able to say, "Well, what about you? You have told me about everyone except the most important one."

"Me? How nice of you to ask. I had two children who left this town as soon as the youngest one was eighteen; they had talked me into co-signing a loan for them. I never hear from them unless they need money. I am just about finished paying the first loan off. My husband left two years before the kids. The romance of the call of the river was too much for him. One day I heard from someone—not that he told me—that he had a job on a barge that was going to who-knows-where. He didn't contact me again until three years ago. I was served with divorce papers that said that if I paid him $5,000 right away, he would never bother me again, and I could get a divorce. The lawyer and the settlement cost me $6,500. I'm almost done paying that bill off, too. So, all in all, I am a free woman who isn't wanted by her children or her husband or anyone else in this town.

I can't leave because I would lose my seniority, so I still teach; in five more years, or something like that, I can retire. Now I ask you, isn't that something to look forward to? Damn, the store is closed. If you're not tired, we can go to my house;

I'll make you some. I do have cake, and it is good. Oh, you're not tired. You had a long nap this afternoon." She looked at George and added, "It's a small town. The boarding house you're staying in is around the corner from my house; your hostess is a good friend of mine. Come on, I'll show you where Ann lived before she went into the church."

They drove to a different part of town, got out, and walked to the top of a hill. When they stopped walking, George suddenly realized that this was not the same area. "This isn't George's Run. Where are we?" There was an urgency that wasn't in George's voice before.

"This is Mingo Junction, the next town up. The area known as George's Run is only that area back where you were. The towns around here are Mingo Junction, George's Run, and Brilliant is the next town over. How's that for the names of towns?"

When they got to Ann's house, Norma paused and said, "She lived on the second floor with her mother, father and two brothers. Did you know Ann had two brothers?" The house Norma pointed to was on the side of the hill above the church school. The house was a two-story house, overlooking the church; from the front porch, you could see the church and railroad and even the Ohio River. The church with the school was on the next street over. The street after the church had other homes on it, and the street after that was a main road. On the other side of the main road was the railroad, next to which was the Ohio River. George was amazed at the actual location of the house church. It was not at all the way Ann had described it.

"Why did she tell me she lived in George's Run?" George asked as they got back in the car and were driving toward Norma's house.

"I don't know," Norma responded. "Maybe she just wanted to forget all about this place and what happened here." They parked the car and walked toward Norma's house. Norma kept up a running commentary about the houses they passed and the people who lived in them. "Didn't Ann ever tell you any of this good stuff?"

"No. Ann never told me anything about herself. Every time I asked her anything, she would change the topic. Anything you tell me will be news to me."

A smile came over Norma's face. She knew she had a willing listener. "Her brothers left when she was young; they never came back. When the murder occurred…"

"What murder?" George shouted out.

"She didn't tell you her mother was murdered? Everyone thinks it was her father that did it, but it was never proven because he was never found. Her mother was beaten to death. The only person who was at the funeral was Ann. I wanted to go, but my mother wouldn't let me. I went anyway. The priest, Sister Edith, and Ann were at the burial site. Her sons didn't even come home for it. I really can't make fun of anyone because I don't think anyone will be around for me either. What about you, George, will you come back for my burial?"

George and Norma continued their walk until they were in front of Norma's house. It looked like all the other houses on the block, a one-story wooden structure with four rooms. Each room was the same size with the bathroom squeezed between the master bedroom and the other two rooms. One room was set up as a sewing room; the other as a dining room. "If you want to watch television, we have to sit in my bedroom. Now I ask you, is that an invitation or what?"

George just smiled and said, "I want to thank you for the tour and information. It's funny, but I learned more information from you about Ann than she ever told me."

"I know. She told me that she was afraid to tell you too much for fear of losing you. She said you were the kind of person who wanted a lot more stability to your life than she could ever give you. In addition, there was her inability to have children; she probably didn't want to burden you with her problems. You know they accused her of stealing money from the church? But they were afraid to say too much, since she knew too much about who was taking from the building fund. Of course, that was just gossip. No one knows for sure. This man who moved here from where she was stationed said it, but who knows? A little town has nothing but gossip. In Ann, we had it all: murder, robbery, a mysterious lover, you. At one point, she thinks they drugged her to find out what happened. The Mother Superior gave her something to make her sleep. She didn't know what happened; within a week she was transferred to Cincinnati. Before she left, she had to go to the Mother Superior's office; she found an appointment card with a date and time on it that coincided with the night she thought she was drugged. She took it, but she could never find anything out. I told her to give me the card, and I would send it to a cousin of mine who is—or I should say was—a doctor. But the only thing he did was call me to tell me that anything that was said to the doctor was a patient/doctor thing, and he wouldn't be able to do anything. Wait. I bet I still have the card. I am known as a notorious pack rat. I'll give it to you. This way you'll have something to remember this trip and her by."

George just looked up from his empty cup as he said, "Meeting you again, I think, will provide me with enough memories for a while."

"Wait." Norma disappeared into her bedroom; in a few minutes, she came out with a triumphant look on her face. "See? I told you I had it. I never throw anything away." She handed George the card. As soon as his hand touched it, he felt a connection to Ann. He jerked his hand back so quickly that the card fell to the floor. He bent over and picked it up. He opened his wallet and put it inside one of the little compartments.

"Oh wait, put my number in there also. You may want to

talk to someone from your love's home town; I'm a good listener."

George kissed Norma goodbye and went to his rooming house, which was visible from the front porch of Norma's house. Walking to his lodgings, he was annoyed at himself for taking the card. As he got ready for bed, he resolved he would throw the card away. In the morning he would definitely throw the card away. He kept repeating that thought until he was fast asleep.

The next morning, a fog had settled over the town. He had to wait for the beaming sun to come into his room to fully awaken him. He got dressed; when he went into the kitchen, his hostess had a big, country breakfast, waiting for him, plus a package of goodies to take with him. George sat down, had his breakfast, took his bag of muffins, thanked her, and left. By the time he walked to his boat to start it up, the fog had lifted enough for him to continue his trip. He untied the lines as he let the current pull him out into the main current of the river. He was on his way to the three-river area of Pittsburgh, Pennsylvania.

From Pittsburgh, there is no river flowing east that was navigable. He left the boat at a marina and took a train home. The paper work on his desk was waiting for him. He would marvel at the fact that when he sat down at his desk after one of his trips, it was though he had never left. The same problems were just waiting for him to return to raise their ugly heads so that they could be solved. Each client would call to tell him the same problems in a certain tone or manner, for they felt that a particular problem only happened to them. There was never a case that he couldn't postpone for two weeks or more. The judges, as well as his clients, were more interested in his boat trip than any court case.

George had to hire a truck and boat trailer so he could tow his boat home. The trailer was easy to find; the truck took a little longer. He told a client that he would not write his will until he loaned him his truck so he could get his boat back.

A deal was struck. The next morning George drove to Pittsburgh to pick up his boat. He drove home in one, long, tiring day. The following morning, he put his boat back at his marina. He brought the trailer back to the rental company that was by his house. On the way back, he dropped the truck off in exchange for his car that his client was holding hostage. He went back to his office to start writing the will. His circular boat trip of the eastern seaboard was finished.

The story could well end here, but it doesn't. Once a certain type of person is met in a defining situation, he or she never leaves your thoughts. Whether she is near or far in a physical sense is meaningless, for she is only a thought away. One only has to close one's eyes, and he/she is in a world where everything is possible, and they are together. So was the case with George. He wanted her gone, but not so far away that he couldn't reach out in his mind to dream of her.

Chapter Fourteen

Two people may think their chances of being together have ended, but other forces from anywhere can start a chain of events that have a way of being the link in bringing two people together again. The two people—or any of the people involved—don't even know it is happening.

In this story three people met for the first time on a plane trip from London to New York. Their coming together was accidental, but from the very first moment they met, as the three of them settled in their seats for the trip across the ocean, each of them felt an attraction toward each other, and each of them knew that they wanted their lives to be intermingled. John, who sat next to the window; Evelyn, who sat in the middle; and Mongombo, who sat on the aisle, filled the three seats. The announcement to fasten seat belts for takeoff was the catalyst to start the meeting-new-people process.

"My name is Evelyn. I hope you two men don't get mad at me, but I don't fly well." As Evelyn spoke, she pulled the belt tighter around her thin waist.

Evelyn had been born in Goshen, New York. She was a very pale, feminine type of woman. She was twenty-three, with beautiful, long, blonde hair. Evelyn was the complete opposite of Mongombo, as he was very Black, had black hair, and was very muscular in build. They were both about the same height and age.

Mongombo spoke perfect, Oxford English. "My name is Mongombo. Don't feel badly, for this is only my third flight and my first across the ocean. I think if we each encourage the other, we will both make it."

Mongombo had been born in Uganda but had gone to Oxford. He was involved in athletics. In high school he had been the star of the soccer team for four years. In the last game, which was for the championship of the area, the opposing coach, who was never seen again, sent in a player whose job it was to injure Mongombo so that he couldn't play anymore. The boy did his job well, for Mongombo couldn't finish the game; for a while the doctors didn't know whether he would walk again. Soccer was definitely out. At Oxford, with the help of a specially designed brace, he could compete in skull racing.

Both Evelyn and Mongombo looked at the window seat occupant and invited him to join their conversation. John, who was in his fifties, added to the conversation by saying, "Hi, I'm John. You two don't worry about a thing. I have traveled all over the world; there is nothing to this flying stuff. Leave everything to me; just sit back and enjoy the flight."

The engines revved up, and soon they were soaring in the air.

John was the first to speak after the takeoff. "See? I told you two I knew what I was doing. We're flying." All three of them chuckled, as the stewardess came around for everyone's drink order. "Since I'm the senior member of this trio, and the most experienced traveler, you are both my guests. Order up."

Everyone ordered a drink; over the din of the engines, they all contributed to a conversation that was to last the entire trip across the ocean.

Mongombo broke the silence with, "I feel as though I am with the group that traveled to Canterbury, so I will tell the first tale. I am in the diplomatic core of Uganda. I have been assigned to our delegation at the United Nations. My job is to try to attract new business to our nation. We want companies to manufacture in our country so that we can get more of our people employed and moved into modern times."

Evelyn smiled in a coy way and added, "I am…I don't know what. My parents sent me to schools, but I just don't seem to fit in with anything." Evelyn was from New York City. She had been born and raised in the city. She went to school to unlearn her New York characteristics so she didn't come across as a hard, street-educated, New Yorker. She now sounded like she'd been raised on a farm out in the Midwest or Virginia. Her expressions and the way she held herself were not of the very crisp attitude of people in New York.

"I tried to be a model, actress, or receptionist. I work for a retail company as its forward person. I go to the stores and show them how to display our products. In London they had me act as a "meeter/ greeter" at a reception. You know, I would say, 'Hello my name is Evelyn. Can I get you anything?' I was supposed to smile when the men would all say the same crude remarks. I hated it, but I finally resolved that it's a job." The anger Evelyn was feeling became apparent. As she spoke, her facial features stiffened.

Mongombo and John looked at Evelyn; both were visibly taken back by her show of anger. John lessened the tension when he added, "I know what you mean. I hate it when the only thing someone wants is my body. It's as though she thinks I can separate myself into different parts." His comment brought a smile to Evelyn's face.

All three of the newly formed group added to the conversation as the city of New York got closer. The three of them were compatible in many ways. By means of their conversation, it was obvious that they all wanted to be rich and didn't care how they achieved it. They were all very clothes conscious, so they all bought expensive things. John seemed to be the richest, as his jewelry was admired by both of his fellow passengers.

Mongombo had a keen eye for nice things. He saw that John, as well as Evelyn, was well dressed. He kept pressing Evelyn as to what she did. "There is never any problem selling consumer goods in Uganda. As long as a manufacturer can get the products into the country, our people would buy anything.

The problem is to get the money out of the country. A special permit is needed, and it is very hard to get."

Evelyn responded, "I guess they wouldn't need someone like me."

John was listening very intently to his fellow passengers' conversation. They saw he was interested in what they were saying and that the two of them had monopolized the conversation. Evelyn looked at John, saying, "You have been listening, but you haven't contributed anything about yourself. What about you taking over for while? Mongombo and I have told you all about us. It is now your turn."

John smiled as he drained his second drink and signaled for another. Mongombo and Evelyn shook their heads "no" when the stewardess asked them if they wanted another. "I am what you would call a natural-born salesman. All I have done my whole life is sell. I know all the manufacturers because I call on them to buy their overruns. I have traveled all around the world, for selling is not only my vocation but my hobby as well. I believe that selling is war, and there are no prisoners taken. I approach a sales situation the same way people would approach a chess game. I set up complete scenes, hiring everyone in the scene to effectuate a sale."

"I guess that means you hire meeter/ greeters," Evelyn interjected.

"Yes, I do. I was going to ask you two for your phone numbers so that I can reach you for my next deal. Together, we'd make a great team. I'll rent a conference room for a day. When my customers walk in, you two meet/greet them, and I'll sell them the Brooklyn Bridge."

The conversation was interrupted by the announcement that the plane was approaching Newark International Airport: "Everyone please put your tables up and seat belts on and get ready for landing." The plane became a beehive of activity as everyone followed the instructions that had come over the intercom. The stewardess ran down the aisle, picking up what glasses there were so that by the time the landing light came on, everyone was in his seat, waiting for the inevitable bump that would announce the plane's arrival. At last it came. The roar of the engines, as the plane slowed down, attested to the fact that they were on the ground. The plane had landed in Newark. It was in the process of working its way to the terminal.

It was during the taxiing process that they were pleasantly surprised to find that they were all staying at the same hotel in Newark. They got their baggage and went to the cabstand. A cab took them to downtown Newark to the Hilton Hotel. Upon walking into the hotel, the clerk almost dropped dead when he saw this reverse "Oreo" cookie group: two Caucasians and one Black.

The clerk's facial expression showed he was relieved to see that they had each registered for a single room. He was also taken aback because he thought Mongombo, with his cropped hair, looked like a Black man from Newark. When Mongombo started to talk with his perfect Oxford English, the clerk's facial expression just gave him away.

Evelyn started to laugh. In an impish tone she said, "What's the matter?"

The clerk replied, "No, nothing. I am very sorry." His whole attitude toward Mongombo changed. He could tell that Mongombo was better educated and more sophisticated than he would ever be. Immediately, he snapped his fingers, and a bellman appeared out of nowhere. They were all taken to their rooms.

Evelyn looked at Mongombo and John as they got off the elevator and confirmed, "We will meet in the dining room at 6:30 for cocktails." They both smiled and shook their heads "yes."

When Evelyn met John and Mongombo, it was safe to say that the meeting was a marriage made in heaven. They met for dinner, and during that meeting they agreed to stay in touch with each other, for John had told them of his plan for a con. At first, Evelyn was against the idea, but Mongombo said in a stern voice, "Evelyn, get it through your head that you got three things—your body, your brain, your time. Doing things your way, it is not happening for you. You know you're too old to be a model anymore. Are you going to become a movie star, or do you want to marry some rich guy? You're going to have to make your own way in life."

Evelyn got the picture, and she said, "Ok, I'm in."

Another force, completely unrelated to the first, was coming from Bergen Pines, a nursing home in the county of Bergen. She was an old psychiatrist, who was suffering from a deterioration of the veins going to her brain. Her children wanted her declared incompetent. They'd gone to a local attorney. He recommended that they hire George to handle the hearing. The real problem of the case was that her four children were scattered around the country. The closest one lived in New York City. One lived in Colorado, another in Texas, the last in Hawaii. They did not have anything to do with each other or their mother. Their local attorney knew George. He felt that, since none of them had ever heard of George, for he was not from the area, he might be able to get them to cooperate. All of the children had to be notified as a requirement of the incompetence hearing. The attorney was right; all the children agreed to George, being the attorney of record.

When the attorney had first called George and referred the case to him, George took out a client interview sheet and started taking notes. When he heard the name of the person being declared incompetent, his mouth went dry. When he found out the incompetent was a psychiatrist from Bergen County, he could not believe it; he agreed to take the case. After he hung up, he quickly found the card of the psychiatrist that Norma had given him, the card that he was going to throw away the day after he got it but never did. He had mixed emotions when he saw the name on the card. It was the same name. George quickly thought about how he was going to find out if, in fact, it was the same person. A quick call to the licensing board confirmed that there was only one doctor with that name in Bergen County. George wasn't sure whether he should be glad or sad about the news he had just heard.

George started the paper process. He notified all of the children about the hearing. He asked the court to appoint the son from New York as the guardian. He would be designated the guardian of their mother. The only asset of her estate was a ten-room house in need of repair, which was located in Bergen County. The house was to be sold immediately. The money would be held in a trust. After the mother's death, it would be divided between the children. The woman died two days after the hearing.

The house was filled from top to bottom with everything imaginable. George was told to hire a firm to throw everything out. When George went to the house, he found the records and files of the deceased. He went through them and found her old appointment books. He turned to the date that was on the card; there was a reference to seeing a Sister X at the convent. From the book, George traced the entry to the index file, which had a record of all files; a folder had indeed been set up for a Sister X. He went to the file; it was the doctor's notes about the meeting and a videotape of the session. George kept the folder with all of its contents. He took the tape to his office, where he found his machine to play it. Just listening to the tape brought Ann back again.

When George heard the tape that was still in perfect condition, he heard Ann's voice relate what had happened to her on her seventeenth birthday. The last words on the tape was the Mother Superior saying, "The hell with the money."

After hearing the tape, it was hard for George to concentrate on what had to be done to finish the case. The company that he had hired to clean out the house never came. The real estate broker was pressuring George to get the house clean for a ready buyer, who was waiting to close the deal, but the premises had to be cleaned out. A call to the son was met with, "Do whatever you have to do; just get the damn job done. Sell the house. Get the money. Just send us each our share from the net proceeds. I want nothing else to do with my family." His client slammed the phone down.

The next day George hired a big container, which was called a roll-off. He had it put by the house. He went to the high school that his nephew attended. He hired him as well as ten of his friends to come to the house. With a crew of eleven, the house was broom swept clean in three hours. The house was sold. The money was disbursed within three days. George closed his folder on the matter.

Chapter Fifteen

When Ann had left George's Run for the last time, she was resolved to wipe the memory of the town and its people from her mind. The first thing she did was to change her name.

"Why do you want to change your name?" the judge asked.

"I want to start my life over again because, so far, it has not been too good."

"Are you doing it to evade prosecution or to avoid any debts?"

"No, Your Honor. I am not running from anything but myself."

"You know, of course, that changing your name isn't going to change anything.'

"I sure hope you're wrong."

"A judgment will be entered, changing your name from Ann to Carol."

"Thank you, Your Honor." Ann, now known as Carol, left the courtroom, feeling like a new person.

Carol worked for the New York City Department of Justice. Her talents, along with her hard work, stood out among the group with whom she worked. She was moved to Albany to work on the New York Attorney General's staff. She was moved into the governor's office to be a special assistant to the governor. He told her, "Don't worry; if I am defeated in the next election, I will make you a judge before I leave office.

The next election came around, and the governor was defeated, but the new governor pleaded with Carol to stay with him, even though he was from the opposition party. "I am told you are very good and that you're not involved in politics. Your concern is only for the state; so is mine. Stay with me; if we can't get along, I'll make you a judge.

Carol agreed. She remained with the new governor for three years; after that time, he made good on his promise and made her a Judge of the State of New York.

Carol was still single; rumors abounded that she was a lesbian. She explained that she didn't like staying in one place because she did not want to get too close to anyone. "My days of forming attachments are over."

When she was offered the job of being a roving judge, she jumped at the opportunity. Her job was one of filling in for sick or vacationing judges all over the state. She loved it so much that she resisted offers to "settle down" as a judge for a single community or court. As a roving judge, she did not have to get involved in the politics of being a judge; she just had to do her job, a job everyone thought she did very well. If a particularly oddball case came into a jurisdiction, Carol would be brought in to handle that matter. She loved the carefree life of living out of a suitcase in hotel rooms.

Meanwhile, John started on his quest to set up a con, using his two new recruits. John let word get around the manufacturers that he had an in into the Ugandan delegation. He spread the rumor that he could get a permit for one year to ship in consumer goods to the country and was able to convert the money to British Pounds. He would need a million dollars in cash for pay-offs. In one month, he had ten manufacturers' chomping at the bit. John set up a tour of the UN, which included lunch in a private dining room. Evelyn was the "meeter/greeter." Mongombo gave a presentation about the advantages available to the manufacturers in manufacturing goods in Uganda for export to foreign markets.

John warned the group not to mention anything about the arrangement to sell goods in the country while they were in the UN. The group was a little uneasy about the secrecy, but when John told them that the way he had set the whole thing up was to hire Evelyn to be Mongombo's companion, the group believed it. John did not want to touch any money until the permit to get the money out of the country was obtained. The group elected one of its own to act as the recipient of the million and to handle the actual pay off.

"Do I get my usual ten percent for setting up the deal?" John asked, as the group was getting ready to leave.

"Okay, but you have to monitor the money from Uganda to our Swiss accounts," one of the group shouted out. Another added, "And we get our million back before you make a dime. We'll cover your expense here. Come by tomorrow; I'll give you a check for the dinner, a tour, and a big tip for our lovely hostess." Everyone applauded. Evelyn's training as an actress came to use as she blushed.

The payoff was set to take place in Goshen, New York. A Ugandan delegation, consisting of the right people to sign off on the special permit, was to go on a tour of the area as a combination vacation and fact-finding trip. They were going to be staying at the Concord Hotel.

Everything was set. Evelyn was invited to be the guest of the chairman, Joel, of the manufacturing group. Joel could not understand why a beautiful girl like Evelyn would want to be seen with a Black man like Mongombo. The mere thought of her being with Mongombo just drove Joel nuts.

Joel was to bring the money to the hotel. John was not going to be there, but he made arrangements for the money. The money would be housed in a black briefcase and put into the hotel vault until it was needed. A contract was drawn up between Joel, as chairman of the group, and Mongombo, who represented his country. Mongombo would receive a ten-thousand-dollar advance for expenses. He would use his best efforts in obtaining a special license for the manufacturing group to not only manufacture but to also sell its goods in Uganda. In addition, they would be able to convert the funds into British Pounds Sterling. It was an elaborate contract. The manufacturing group wanted some degree of safety in the deal. Mongombo agreed to the terms without even reading it.

After signing it, he added, "Gentlemen, if we can work together, the terms of this contract are meaningless. My country welcomes you with open arms; we hope our relationship will last for years to come, contract or not."

Everything was set. Joel had the cash, but the other members of the group insisted that he have a guard drive him to the Concord. Joel insisted on no escort, for he didn't want to draw attention to himself. "I'll take care of the money. I don't want to attract a lot of flies; that's what a goon squad will do." Joel was very active and prided himself on his strength and agility. He was an accomplished boxer and Karate expert. He would break two-by-fours at all the company picnics. All these accomplishment didn't sway the committee. Joel got in the car and was driven to the hotel.

When Joel arrived, everything was set for the money to be put in the safe. The clerk took the brief case. He handed Joel a receipt for it. The bag was put in a separate vault, and the key was given to another man for safekeeping. The only way the key could be retrieved was by Joel's signing a release for the key to be given to the clerk; the clerk would then get the case and deliver it to Joel. Joel was impressed by the procedure.

That night, there was a famous star appearing in the Grand Ballroom; everyone was there. When Evelyn walked in with her flowing white dress, she stole the show. Even the entertainer stopped to admire the angel who was walking in. Joel immediately had her sit next to him. Throughout the night, he kept insulting Mongombo until finally Mongombo got up and left. Joel was well into his second bottle of scotch. The waiter even asked, "Sir, are you going to be all right?"

"Yes, sir. Give me my bill; I'll leave now. I think you're right, I should knock off for the night; I've had enough."

The waiter brought the bill over and Evelyn, just as Joel was handed the bill, said, “Well, thanks a lot. You chased Mongombo away! Now what do I do?”

“Why, you come with me,” he responded.

Evelyn jumped out of the chair as she grabbed Joel’s arm.” I was hoping you were going to say that.” Joel signed the paper without even looking at it. The couple left, arm in arm. When they reached the elevator, Evelyn grabbed her stomach as she said, “Oh, no, not now.” She turned away from Joel and ran toward the lady’s room.

Joel laughed to himself, “Just my luck.” The elevator arrived. Joel went upstairs to his room.

There was a knock at the door. The bellhop arrived with a bottle of champagne, “Compliments of the house.” Joel had to sign for it. He was starting to really feel the effects of what he’d drunk. He just signed his name to the slip and had the bellhop put the bottle on the side table.

He went into the other room to change for bed. The phone rang. It was Evelyn. She started apologizing for leaving like that. Joel laughed. He just said, “I understand. Call me when you get to the city. We will pick up where we left off.” Joel hung up and fell back onto the pillow and quickly went to sleep.

The next morning he got up, showered, and went downstairs for breakfast. After breakfast he was to meet with Mongombo. He called Mongombo’s room, only to be told that Mongombo had checked out. He had left a message: “Because of your rude drunken behavior, our deal is off.” Joel was wide-awake. He started thinking of what he was going to say to the rest of the group. As he was pondering his problem, Evelyn came into the dining room. She came over to him to apologize again. Joel told her to sit down. “Have breakfast with me.”

She replied, “Thank you, but I can’t stay for breakfast. I have to get back. I’m going to drive into the city. I thought I’d drive for awhile before I eat.”

“You know; that’s a great idea. I was driven here. Can I

catch a ride?" he asked.

A smile flashed across Evelyn's face as she replied, "I'd love the company. I'll meet you by the front door in a half hour, okay?"

Joel agreed. He hurried upstairs to get his bags. While in the room, he called the desk to pick up his briefcase. When Joel got to the front desk, he was told that the briefcase had been delivered to him per his request the previous night. He went nuts. He started screaming, "I never told you to deliver the case to me."

"Sir, here is your signature on the request. It is here again on the receipt for the case."

Joel started screaming that they call the police immediately. "I've been robbed."

Evelyn came in to see what the noise was all about. She saw Joel creating a big disturbance. The staff was trying to get him to calm down. They were pleading with him to go to the manager's office.

The clerk said, "It will be easier to sort this problem out in the office. The police have been summoned."

Evelyn was watching what was going on. Finally in a pleading voice, she said, "I'm sorry, but I have to leave."

"You go, honey. I'll talk to you later," Joel told her as he went with the manager. The police officers had arrived. They went into the office and Evelyn left.

That night, the new trio met. They congratulated each other, opened the case, and took five thousand each, and agreed the rest of the money would be put aside for at least six months. John proposed a toast to a new, bigger, and better deal and began to outline the next idea he had in mind.

The police investigated everything as well as everybody involved. The prosecutor, who had political aspirations, saw the potential of the case. A Ugandan delegate, a local, blond beauty, and a shrewd businessman—the crime had all the elements for banner headlines. The skillful prosecutor got the grand jury to indict John, Mongombo, and Evelyn.

The senior ambassador had been following a similar case that was being heard in New York City. He found out that George had been instrumental in defending a businessman from the area just two months prior to this indictment. When the Ugandan consulate in New York City heard of the indictment against Mongombo, it wanted George to be in charge of the defense. Evelyn and John both agreed that they would follow whatever the ambassador wanted to do.

The ambassador called George to come to the city to discuss the case. George agreed. The ambassador started the conversation with, "You understand that we want the matter handled the same way you handled that case involving…" the ambassador stopped talking. He saw that George was getting annoyed.

"Ambassador, you would not want me to discuss your case with anyone, so please don't ask me to discuss their case with you. I know what you want. Resolve in your mind that I will do what you desire."

"I know, George, but you must understand that I am concerned about the cost. I would like for you to handle the trial and use a local attorney whenever possible without jeopardizing the case."

"Sir, you have to trust me to do the right thing. Has everyone agreed to have me represent them?"

"Yes."

"Fine. I will meet with everyone and keep you informed as I go along. But I am telling you now that I will not stand for any interference. I will tell you what I'm going to do, but I do not want you to interpret that as my discussing the case with you. Is that understood?"

"Yes."

"Let me get my people started; I'll get back to you in a

week. Call the local attorney and tell him of our arrangement. I will call him afterwards." George got up, received his retainer, and left.

The next day, George asked his associate Russ to meet him in Goshen at the local attorney's office. The local attorney was named Richard. He had handled the case up to now and was not too thrilled about George being called in. He expressed his displeasure to Russ. Russ said nothing and just let Richard talk. When Russ saw it was time for George to arrive, he looked at Richard and said, "Do you have your disappointments out of your system? If not, hold them until George leaves. You can tell them to me. George is not interested in how you feel; if you want out, just say so, and you're out. I'm going to give you some advice. Keep your mouth shut. Your mind should be open. You may just learn something. The fact that you'll get paid as well is all gravy."

George walked into the office right at the end of Russ' talk. George could just feel the animosity in the room as he entered. He greeted everyone and sat down at the little conference table. He invited Russ, as well as Richard, to join him. "Richard, I know you are less than thrilled with my being here, but I am not the client; I am merely an attorney. I will run the case. I will use you if you want to stay; if not, well, let's not get into that. If you do what I say, no one need know I'm even involved in this matter unless it comes to a trial. If there is no trial, no one will even know I was here. You will, for all purposes, run the case. I will meet wherever you say, for you know the best spots, or certainly more than I do. No one is to know I am involved until the very last moment. You will see Russ around, since he will be doing some background checking for me. I will communicate only face to face with you. If anyone ever says, "George said," you call me. I've made a list of pretrial motions I want brought. You can handle the entire pretrial discovery; just give me copies of things. Here is my number. If you ever need me, I will come immediately. I hope you have the good sense to see my being here as an opportunity and not as a threat to your professionalism. I do want you to feel free to leave, but once you're in, you're in."

"What happens if I change my mind?'

Russ stood up with a smile on his face, "Let me answer this one, George. George will evaluate your request. If he feels you are doing it to harm our client, you will be dealing with me. Understand?"

"Is that a threat?" Richard shouted out.

"Man, you are stupid. You don't even know a threat when you hear one? That is exactly what it is. It is also a promise." Russ was standing less than a foot from Richard when he got done talking.

George walked over to Richard. He said in a much quieter tone, "Please don't make any threats. You're a young man with two small children. You have a beautiful wife. Your life is before you. Don't screw it up now. Now, can we get to work?"

George walked away with Russ and discussed what George wanted done. Richard was wondering how George knew he had two children. His wife was the local beauty queen at the country club, two years running. Richard reviewed the pre-trial motions George wanted brought. He really couldn't argue with them.

Russ left to get started on what George wanted, while George sat down with Richard. "Now, Richard, I want you to understand that this prosecutor brought these charges, not because he thinks he is going to win, but to get his name in the paper. He is going to want to have meetings with you. Please don't open your mouth. He has no case; so the only thing he is going to be doing is trying to get you to give him your defense, so just keep quiet. There are no deals, so don't even think about one. This case is going to be dismissed by the state, or they are going to lose. Either way, you'll be a hero."

"I am capable of making a contribution, you know" Richard

responded. "I was at the top of my class. I was the editor of my paper."

"I'm positive you are; that is why Russ told me to keep you on. He thinks very highly of you. Our clients don't. Whether you like it or not, they pay the bills, so it is their opinion that counts. If they thought you were that good, they would not have hired me to come up here."

Richard looked at the conference table for a long moment before he added, "This Russ of yours…"

"Please, don't make the mistake of thinking Russ is fooling. He is not. I know you think your friends will come to your aid, but believe me they won't. You're by yourself; you're no match for him. Once you get to know us, you won't think we're so bad. I'll talk to you." At that, George got up to leave.

The pretrial motions George wanted brought were done, and the trial date was sought. George insisted that Richard ask for one as soon as possible and insisted that he keep asking. The date was set. The trial was to start. The jury selection started on Thursday. It went quickly; the first day of trial would be the following Monday. Richard sent the jury list to Russ, per George's instructions. Thursday evening, the trial judge had a heart attack. The big question was whether or not the trial should be postponed. Richard called George with the news.

"Are you crazy? I've screamed for you to get an early trial, and now you want to postpone it because of some judge? No way. You be in the courtroom tomorrow morning first thing, screaming for the trial not to be postponed. Don't wait! Waiting only hurts us."

"How?"

George looked at the phone in disbelief. "You get an immediate trial or get the hell off the case. How does it hurt us? You're not here to question me. I get the big bucks to make decisions like this. Either go to court or file my substitution of attorney; now, get out."

Russ lived in Connecticut. His real job was running a country club. He loved working with George, which is why he did it. George called him immediately. He told him the problem. Within the hour, Russ had his plane warmed up. He was on his way to Goshen.

Richard went to court to do George's bidding. He had to see the interim assignment judge. The judge had called the administrative coordinator in Albany. He was surprised when the administrator called back within the hour. "We have a judge for Monday morning. Keep the schedule that the ill-fated judge has established for the case."

Richard walked out of court with a sense of triumph as well as defeat about the trial date issue. Outside, he ran into Russ. Russ had heard from the gossip, which always travels fast, that a new judge was assigned. Russ got the name and started making calls, for he knew George would want a bio done on the new judge. When Richard saw Russ, he went over to him, but before he could say anything, Russ spoke.

"We're going to be in town Sunday night. George wanted to know if you and your lovely wife would like to join us for dinner. We are staying at the motel down the street. They told us that the food here is the best in town. We'll be dining at seven, if you want to join us. Oh, by the way, you did a dynamite job of keeping the same trial date."

Russ got a copy of the jury panel before he left to fly home. He worked the rest of Friday night, all day Saturday, and Sunday on the new judge's bio, as well as a bio on each of the jurors. He called George to tell him that he would miss dinner Sunday night but would meet him for breakfast on Monday morning.

Sunday afternoon, George and his assistant, Barbara, left for Goshen. Barbara was a secretary, fashion consultant, and a "go-fer," all wrapped up in one package. She worked for George on certain cases. She was a paralegal in a large law firm, but they would lend her to George when he needed her.

George had rented three rooms at the motel: one for him, one for Barbara, and the third one was set up as an office. At seven, he and Barbara stopped preparing the case. They took a break for dinner. Richard showed up with his wife. The four of them sat down together.

George put everyone at ease by saying, "The business to be discussed tonight, I will do right now. Tomorrow morning, after the judge is in, I will walk in for you to present the substitution. Now tell me all about life in Goshen, New York."

"No, wait," Richard, said. "Why are you so adamant about going to trial now with a new judge that no one knows?"

"You're right," George responded. "No one knows whom we got. I would rather that than the prosecutor's having the edge with a judge he goes to parties with and sees every day. He has appeared in front of that judge many times. Richard, it is a judgment call. I can use yours or mine. Clients pay a lot of money for me to use mine. Now stop taking everything so personally. Let's eat."

The waiter came; everyone gave his or her order. As soon as the waiter left, Richard continued, "Well, I hope you're right because we have drawn a female judge. Her name is Carol. They say she is brilliant. She travels around the state as a substitute."

George looked up from his dinner as he said, "Don't tell Russ. The last female judge I appeared before, he married.

"Don't worry about that. Everyone thinks this one is a lesbian," Richard replied.

Richard, looked over at Barbara, who was busily taking notes and looking at everyone, said, "My friend called me and told me you were walking around town and even went into his men's store. Preparing for the case?"

"Yes. I wanted to see what the mode of dress is up here so that I know what George needs to wear." When Barbara was done talking, she sipped her drink that the waiter had bought.

Richard, in a surprised tone, replied, "Wear? What he will wear? What, should I put on a tuxedo? Are you his fashion consultant, too?"

Barbara didn't answer the question but started talking to Richard's wife about her children. Richard took the hint and shut up. The rest of the dinner was spent in idle conversation about life in Goshen, New York.

Chapter Sixteen

Monday morning, the town of Goshen was abuzz with gossip. The temporarily assigned judge got into town at seven-thirty and was already at the courthouse, getting ready for the trial. Everyone referred to the trial as the "Reverse Oreo Cookie Group." People were calling their friends to see what time they would meet at the courthouse and who they knew that could guarantee them a pass to the trial. Richard had been successful at limiting the number of press allowed, but he couldn't get the press eliminated altogether.

The prosecutor made sure that the right people would be in attendance. He realized that the case was not the strongest he had ever had. His analysis of his case was dependent on certain facts. He was relying on the fact that the only person who knew how much money would be in the safe was John. He had no proof that Mongombo or Evelyn knew anything about it, but he would be able to show that the three of them knew each other. They worked with one another. The dinner at the UN was the only proof, he had but he felt it was strong enough. He felt confident that he could convince the jury that there would be no other reason for a pretty girl like Evelyn to even bother with a person like Joel. Mongombo was the key player, for he was the one who was representing Uganda and had the political power to get Joel and his group into the country. His publicity manager told him, "There is no such thing as bad publicity in politics." He would say, "If you lose a case, so what. Everyone knows how lenient courts are with criminals."

All offers of a plea were refused. When the prosecutor asked why, Richard would respond with a type-written statement, "That decision is being made by someone else; he can't wait to make you look ridiculous in court."

The prosecutor started to hear rumors that Richard wouldn't be trying the case and that a hot shot was being brought in. Richard never confirmed or denied the statement but instead read the statement that had been prepared for him.

Everyone showed up on time; the packed courtroom moaned under the weight of all the spectators. The court guard was so nervous that morning that he forgot to put on his radio for communicating with the sheriff's department, in case there was trouble. In twenty-one years, he had never had to call for help, so he didn't worry about having forgotten it at home. He called his wife from the courthouse and asked her to bring it when she came to the trial. She and three lady friends couldn't wait to come; after all, her husband was the courtroom guard. They were assured great seats to what promised to be the best show ever. The prosecutor showed up with three assistants. They took their places at their table and busied themselves getting everything in order.

Richard rehearsed what he had to say when he introduced George to the court as his co-counsel. Richard didn't like the idea of being the second chair, but George had assured him that he would either be in the second chair or in the spectators' section.

The bailiff mistakenly brought the jury into the courtroom before the judge. The judge walked in to the announcement "All rise." When she saw the jury was in the jury box, she became a little annoyed. She was about to have the jury taken back out, when the courtroom doors opened. George walked in. He was wearing a light gray suit with a white on white shirt that seemed to radiate. His tie was a darker gray than his suit; his shoes were the same color as his suit. In the motel he had complained to Barbara that he looked like a pimp on his day off. Barbara quickly replied, "You want all the attention in the courtroom; well, this outfit will guarantee that."

George's shirt had his name embroidered in red thread on

the left cuff. It was easily seen when he moved his arm. His gold watch and diamond rings on each of his pinkies glistened, as they picked up the rays of the sun, coming through the top of the windows. George made his way down the center aisle as a low whistle was heard from the spectators. Barbara was following, carrying a black, leather briefcase with "George" printed on it in gold letters. Everyone stared at George, as he upstaged the entire room. When he got to the front of the courtroom, he looked up at the judge for the first time and recognized who she was; it was Ann.

They both recognized each other at the same time. Ann/Carol started to cry as she turned and left the courtroom through the door that was right behind her chair. The door led directly to her chambers.

The tears welled in George's eyes before he could turn away. He took out his handkerchief and covered his face for a moment to compose himself. He followed Ann into her chambers. The court guard didn't know what to do. He grabbed for his radio. It wasn't where he always wore it. He panicked. He suddenly remembered that when he came to work that morning, he had forgotten the radio he was supposed to always carry. The size of George with the look on his face as he followed Ann into her chambers made the guard feel it would not be wise to try to stop George by himself. He started for the chamber door. He suddenly turned around to run out of the courtroom to get help.

As George entered her chambers, the thirty-odd years that they had been apart seemed to vanish. Neither one spoke, as they embraced each other. George--in a whisper-- said, "I tried finding you, but I didn't know how; I didn't even know if you wanted me to."

She said through her tears, "I didn't. I could not live the life you wanted. Oh, George, seeing you here today…I knew you were an attorney. I've followed your career and your life very closely. I was even at your swearing-in ceremony after you became an attorney. I stood in the back of the hall, wanting to come to you, but I just couldn't. I've lived my life vicariously through you."

George responded as he held her close to him, "I'm not going to make believe that I know what is going on with you or why, but…"

The room was suddenly filled with officers from the sheriff's department. Everyone was screaming at once. Ann stepped forward and quieted the sheriff's men down by waving her arms, saying, "Gentlemen, please, there is no need for anyone to do anything. Please. What happened here this morning is unfortunate, but it did happen. Please, just everyone calm down, and the situation will work itself out. George, please wait outside, while I make this case go away. I'll see you later. Bailiff, please take the jury to the jury room; I will deal with them in a few moments."

In a quiet, orderly fashion, everyone left the chambers and did his/her assigned task. As the sheriff's men came out of the courtroom, they ran into Russ. Russ looked bewildered at the confusion. "What happened? Where's George?"

One of the spectators said, "Some man came into court and went after the judge; the sheriff had to get him. He just walked into the courtroom and chased the judge out."

The sheriff's officers cleared the courthouse at the judge's insistence. Russ walked past them into the room and shouted, "Where's George? If you guys hurt him…"

"Russ, come here. We had a problem, but it is over now. Get all my stuff and take Barbara to the motel." George turned his attention to the prosecutor and Joel. "Let me talk to you two men." Richard was still in a state of shock as he stood by the council table, not knowing what to do. George turned to face him as he said, "Richard, you join us.'

The four men went into an anteroom off to the side of the

main courtroom. George spoke before anyone said anything. He addressed Joel first, "You talk to your boys, and give me the number that it will take to make you go away. Remind them that if this case goes forward, they will have to show where they got a hundred thousand dollars in cash."

Joel, without waiting for the prosecutor to say anything, left the anteroom to find a phone. George turned his attention to the prosecutor, "You and Richard work out a deal to make this case go away. You do not want to try this case, for when you lose, your political aspirations will be gone."

"Are you threatening my office?" the prosecutor said.

Richard, by now, was with the program. He added, "No, not your office. George doesn't do things like that. No, he's just giving you good advice. Keep in mind they didn't bring him here because they had nothing else to do. Let's make a deal so we will be done with these people. This is our town. We don't need them around."

The judge went to the jury room and made up an elaborate story. She thanked them all for doing their civic duty. They were all happy when she released them. She left the courthouse to return to her motel room.

Joel came back with five hundred thousand written on a piece of paper. George went to the trio, who were standing on the side of the courtroom. Mongombo was in touch with the ambassador, keeping him apprised of everything that was happening. When George showed them the number, Mongombo consulted the ambassador, and the trio immediately agreed. George turned to Joel, "Go with the prosecutor and Richard over there and do what they say. I'll see to it that the money is delivered to you."

"No. Everyone wants to come and get his own share," he responded.

George laughed but agreed. He got a hold of John and appointed him the bagman as he said, "Richard will give you a release for everyone to sign before you give anyone any money. Get them all." George hesitated as he continued with, "What am I doing? You know what to do and how to do it. I want it completed today. Do you want me to send Russ with you? Yes, I think that is the right thing to do. Go to this motel and this room, and take Russ with you." George handed John a card from the motel with Russ' room number on it.

George joined Richard and his group as he said, "Gentlemen, you can finish this up. I have no authority here, since I never made a formal appearance in the case." George shook everyone's hand, and when he got to the door, he told the prosecutor, "When you're ready to run for office, let Richard know." Richard nodded his approval.

George found the court guard and asked, "Where's the judge staying? In all the confusion, I dropped the card she gave me." As George spoke, he went back into the chamber and looked around on the floor, as though he was looking for something. He was so convincing that the guard was looking, too. George went to the desk and saw the name of a motel written on the blotter with a number next to it. "Oh, here it is," he said. George told the name to the guard, and the guard pointed out the window to the motel. George could see the motel from the courthouse window.

George left for the motel. When he got there, he first called Russ and told him what to do. His response was reassuring as usual, "I shall do your bidding. You can count on me."

George found out from a clerk what room the judge was in and went directly to it. The motel clerk started talking, but George paid him no mind. George got to the room and started pounding on the door. He stopped, listened, and starting pounding on it again. The clerk showed up with the police; George started yelling at him to open the door. With the police as his protector, the clerk opened the door; the Judge—Carol—Ann—was on the floor. One policeman got the oxygen tank from the police car; the other called for an ambulance, while George picked her up and put her on the bed. The manager went to the far corner of the room and kept repeating, "My God, my God."

One of the officers yelled at him, "Shut up! God ain't looking."

The ambulance was at the motel in short order. The EMTs went about their duties with a zest. They took Ann to the hospital, while one of the policemen gave George a ride there. The doctors were waiting for her. As soon as the ambulance pulled up, they started doing everything at once. A bottle of pills were found by her bedside, so they were given to the doctor in charge. George was in the waiting room when one of the nurses came to him. "Why don't you go home? We'll call you when she is stabilized. There is nothing you can do here; quite frankly, you're making everyone, including me, very nervous."

George gave the nurse the number of his room at the motel and left. Richard was just walking into the hospital, as George was leaving. He went to him. "Come on. Let me buy you a cup of coffee or a drink. You look like you could use one."

George was grief stricken. Richard got George out of the hospital. He took him to the local diner. Everyone in there was well aware of what had happened at the courthouse, as well as at the motel. They strained their ears to hear a little bit of gossip before anyone else did. Over a cup of coffee, George told Richard the whole story about Ann, who was now known as Judge Carol. Richard was amazed at the story. He excused himself and called the hospital to check on Carol's condition and to make an appointment for George to see the head doctor the following morning. Richard reported back to George, "She is in stable condition. You are to meet the head doctor tomorrow morning at nine o'clock."

George went back to the motel with Richard. Barbara had packed their things and had gone back to New Jersey. Before leaving, she assured George that she would clean up the case for him. George tried to go to sleep, but nothing worked. At nine o'clock, he was in the doctor's office, being introduced to the head psychiatrist, Mario. He was a very tall, muscularly built, pompous-looking man, but when he spoke, he was very soft spoken. The voice just didn't go with the man.

"I understand you know the patient. My problem is you're not related by blood or marriage to her, so there are certain problems with my discussing her case with you. However, I must have certain information in order to help her. She has completely withdrawn from the conscious world, as we know it. She has put herself into a coma-type trance. She doesn't respond to any of the regular stimuli we use in these cases; that is why I think it is a mental reaction more than a physical one. Does she have any family?"

Before Russ left, he gave George his folder on the judge; when George looked at it, all it said was, "She must be from Mars because no one on earth knows anything about her."

"Doctor, of course I'll tell you what I know." George started telling the doctor everything, but he had to admit it wasn't much. He called his office and had the tape that he had taken from the other psychiatrist sent to the doctor. He called Norma and had the doctor interview her. When he was done, he looked at the doctor with a forlorn look as he said, "That's it, sir; I have nothing else."

The doctor nodded as he told George to go on with his life; he would call him if there were any change. "Believe me, there is nothing you can do here. I will keep you informed as to her progress. The state is going to name a guardian ad lit am; I will let him/her know you wish to be named as an interested party. I can't recommend you to be the guardian because I think you caused her current condition or else contributed to it. I think I know what has happened. As disappointing things happened to her in her life, she was able to build a little wall around them and continue with her life. Now she has just pulled down a shade over reality and has blocked everything out. When she saw you, it was all over."

George was sitting in the chair in front of the doctor with his head bowed. He was just not willing to accept what the doctor said. Finally he said, "If there is anything I can do, please call. Can I put money into an account for her in case she needs something?"

"I don't know. I will have the guardian call you. I know you care but, unfortunately, caring in this situation isn't enough. Her feelings for you are forcing her to try to forget yesterday. That repression is what the problem is. The drugs she took didn't help, but the main thing is her wanting to forget. It sad to say, but you're part of the forgetting process."

George left to return home. He tried to compute how long this saga with Ann had been going on. He met her when he was nineteen; saw her again on the way back from Mexico a year later, when he was twenty; and took a trip with the boat twenty-five years after that, when he was forty-five. He was now fifty-five, and when he saw her, the same feelings came back. Now he had to accept the fact that because she still loved him, she could not face reality. George spoke to the guardian and sent a check for twenty-five thousand dollars for incidentals for her. The money was put in a discretionary account to be used by the guardian.

The story should end here, but it doesn't. How can a story about two people ever end? How could anyone predict that a man from Uganda, a woman from Goshen, and a man from the Midwest would form a coalition to con ten businessmen out of money? To those odds, add in the odds of the action, taking place in New York, where George had handled a case that had attracted the Ugandan government's attention so that it would want to retain him to represent it. After all of that is put together, what are the odds of the judge's having a heart attack and George's being hired to handle the case? One doesn't have to be great in math to know that someone's odds of winning the lottery are better.

In reviewing what has been written, it is safe to say that the story never ends, even if it should. Death is the only true end to any story. The only reason everyone agrees on death as the end is that an individual doesn't know enough about death.

Chapter Seventeen

George followed the instructions of the doctor and left. It was a long, lonely drive home. Having to accept the idea that he was the one who was hurting Ann really bothered him. George called weekly to check on her, but he found the words "no change" were just too much for him. His once-a-month call to get an update became once a quarter and finally once every so often. George began to cringe at the sound of the voice coming over the phone. "There has been no appreciable difference in the patient's condition." These words would destroy George for weeks to come.

The doctor, on one occasion, told George that he was having her transferred to another hospital, which was totally away from everything she was used to. A friend of his had been named to the staff of a hospital in Gaspe, New Brunswick, Canada.

"Where?" George yelled into the phone. "Where the hell is that?" George paused, as he remembered where it was, and added, "It's so far."

The doctor in a calm voice responded, "We are trying to cure her, not you."

George just hung up the phone. About a month later, George received a letter, giving him the address of where the hospital was located with a notation, "Please don't come visit her right away. She needs time to adjust to her surroundings."

Time has a way of slipping by. Eleven years is nothing. In a flash, it is gone. On George's sixty-sixth birthday, forty-six years from when he first met Ann, he got in his Navigator, armed with a map of New Brunswick, Canada, and headed for the town of Gaspe.

The Gaspe Peninsula is a magnificent place to see and to view the North Atlantic in all its glory. George saw none of the beauty. His whole being was concentrating on the road in front of him. He recognized how foolish he was for even making the trip. The thought that she might be doing very well was a driving force within him. He realized that, according to the doctor, the sight of him might cause her to have a relapse. He dismissed the idea. It didn't deter him from going. He was a person possessed by some demon that would not let go of him.

He started out at five in the morning. He drove until he was so sore that he couldn't move. Going through the border was an ordeal. George became annoyed with the questions, as well as the searching of his truck, which didn't help. The border guards were not pleased with his attitude, and he was not thrilled with them. They finally allowed him to enter Canada. He stopped in a motel that would have been condemned in the States. There was a bed in the room. George could not think of anything else to say about it.

George just lay down on top of it fully dressed. He could not convince himself that he should get undressed and get under the covers. He found an extra blanket in the closet to put on top of himself to keep warm.

The following morning, it was a race to see who would be ready for the next day, him or the sun. The sun came up after he was on his way. By noon, he pulled into the town of Gaspe. Up on the tallest hill in town was a magnificent new building. It was the mental hospital. George felt ashamed of the visions he'd had of it when he was in the motel. The motel was bad; the hospital was great. The staff was of Scottish origin. Everything about the hospital and the staff said care and love and a great deal of understanding. George asked to see the doctor who was caring for Ann. The minute she saw George, she gave him the name of a local motel, as well as a fine restaurant.

"Go have a nice dinner. Get a good night's sleep. Tomorrow, if you look human, you can see her. Oh, don't forget to shave." The words were said with a smile on her lips, but they were no less true. George felt his face, as he realized he must look like a bum.

"You know I clean up pretty good. I don't know anyone in town. I would sure like the company. I'll let you order anything you want. I'll even let you take my pulse." George managed a smile. He estimated the doctor to be about his age. How many offers to go to dinner could she get in this town?

"That kind of offer could turn a girl's head. It will have to be after seven," she responded.

"Good. You know where I'll be, so just come get me. This way, I'll have time to make myself beautiful. Oh, I'm sorry; you're supposed to say that. After seven, it is." George left. He didn't realize how tired he was until he fell into the clean bed. This time, he got undressed. His last thought was, "I forgot to ask her name. I can't keep calling her 'Doctor'. "

It took a long time for the water to wake George up. He shaved, and little by little, he came alive. At ten past seven, as he was just finishing buttoning his shirt, there was a knock at the door. He opened it to the smiling, tired-looking face of the doctor.

He greeted her with, "A nice drink and a fine dinner is what I prescribe for you. I have to confess I don't have a jacket to wear to dinner. Is there an open store in town where I can buy one?"

"Are you kidding?" she responded. George locked the door and followed the doctor to her truck. They got in, and the doctor started driving towards the restaurant, but there was an eerie silence in the truck.

The restaurant was a five-minute drive from the motel. As soon as they walked in the door, the owner came over to greet the doctor and her guest. "We have an excellent fish dinner this evening."

He started to describe it, but George interrupted him, "Before we have to make a decision like that, go get us two

Manhattans, straight up. Bring out something to pick on while we drink them."

"You're not in New Jersey now. The restaurants aren't open all night up here. It is late. We have to order now, or else the cook will go home. That means we won't eat."

"Okay, you're the doctor. You're in charge. You order. As you can see, I'm not a picky eater." The doctor ordered the special and they sat down.

"I want to be honest with you. I have strong reservations about your seeing Carol, or Ann, as you know her."

"It's been eleven years. We are both not getting any younger. I would like to see her before I die. Is that so bad? You doctors haven't been able to do anything in all this time. How can my seeing her possibly have a harmful effect on her? I think you're kidding yourself. You've had eleven years to do whatever it is you want to do. Nothing has changed. I have been kept from seeing her. I think you should be more realistic." The owner bought over the drinks with a dish of cheese and left.

"You know that my nurses are all dying to meet you. Carol's medical history is well known in the hospital, for it is a unique one; however, the fact that she has such an ardent admirer as you really has my nurses wondering. When she was transferred to Canada, the money you gave her, with the interest it had earned, gave her a forty thousand-dollar account. To have such an ardent, generous admirer all this time, who can't even see her, has them all wondering. One comment was that if I didn't see my husband for one day, he would forget all about me."

"Well, after tonight, hopefully they'll get a chance to meet me tomorrow." George lifted his glass as a toast and said, "To the lovely doctor who has still to tell me her name. Or shall I keep calling you 'Doctor'?"

"My name is Stacy. Briefly, we have been trying to get her to break through this wall she has built around herself. She has trouble dealing with reality. In reviewing her history, my students went all the way back to George's Run, Ohio. There are gaps in her life that no one knows anything about. One of my students comes from Michigan so, on a trip home, she went to the town to see the school and to review the records. She even spoke to her friend Norma. You see, we can't get her to tell us about her past, so we need other people to tell us about her. After finding her mother dead, as well as witnessing her mother's beating at the hands of her father, it is understandable that she would not want to remember that. We listened to the tape you provided of the session with the other doctor, but I was under the impression they were looking for an answer to the question of who stole some money. The story of her mother's death was heard instead. The last thing on the tape is someone saying 'the hell with the money'. After her mother was murdered, there is nothing for four years. No one can tell us what happened in the convent house where she was. Her friend, Bob, whom we located, knew nothing. He said he would bring her homework to her, but after she took the test, he never saw her again, except once when she returned home for a visit. The result may well be that the murder was one block, the four years in the church another, and the theft another. That's three major events that she is refusing to recognize; that's a lot. You walking into the courtroom, as well as her overdosing, are what put her over the edge. Of course, you understand it's just a theory, but I think it's a good one."

Dinner had been served as Stacy spoke. When she paused, both of them started to eat their dinner. George had ordered a bottle of white wine from a local vineyard that complemented the dinner perfectly.

The owner started to close the place up. George went over to him to give him a tip. The owner left after George promised to lock the front door when they left.

"You are something else. No local person would even think of bribing the owner to let us stay later than closing time. My reputation is now ruined."

"Oh, I didn't mean to do that. But if you're sure it is, what's the harm? Let's stay. I slept. I'm raring to go."

"I didn't; I'm dog tired."

"I'll serve the coffee myself, and then we'll leave. How's that?" George had found out where the coffee pot was and had poured two mugs full and shut the coffee pot off as he had promised.

George continued with, "I still don't understand the tape. It makes no sense to me. The Mother Superior and the doctor gave Ann drugs and hypnotized her to find out about the robbery. The next question by the doctor would have given them the answer. Why did they stop? It makes no sense; the way they were bringing Ann along during the questioning to the next period of time would have been the time in the church convent with the nuns. The robbery didn't happen until much later."

Stacy responded, "George, you are a scary person. Now that you mention it, I agree with you, but at the time I listened to the tape, I didn't interpret their stopping as their not wanting to know what happened in the church for the next four years. The Mother Superior, by saying what she did, stopped the interview. It sounds like what you're saying is that she didn't want her friend the doctor to know what went on. I don't know if they were that friendly."

George took a sip of his coffee before he continued with, "Do you think Ann, or Carol as you know her, really meant to kill herself when she was in Goshen? Also, did your student investigator tell you that Carol was thought to be a lesbian?"

"I don't think she wanted to die, if that is what you mean. She was far too intelligent not to know that those pills she took would do that. She may have underestimated the damage they could do, but no, I don't think she wanted to die. As to the suspected affairs with other women, my student could not verify the rumor. I feel that it may have been true, but when she met you, she immediately blotted it from her mind. Another wall to put with all the other walls! The initial treatment, which consisted of hypnosis shock treatment, made her push the memory back further in her mind; that is why she is in a catatonic mental state." Stacy finished her coffee and got up, "I am really tired, and I have an early class tomorrow. Will you come to the class tomorrow? I know the nurses want to see you, and so do my students. They would love to meet you; they even may want to ask you some questions. After that, you can see Carol/Ann. But I warn you, don't expect too much. She is in her own little world. She is very reluctant to come out of it."

George couldn't hide his anticipation of seeing Ann as he said, "Just tell me when and where you want to meet me for breakfast before we go see her."

Stacy stood up and said, "Be at the hospital's front door. The road up the hill leads right to it. I'll have one of my students come fetch you. Be there at nine."

George and Stacy left the restaurant after George locked it up; Stacy drove him back to his motel. As he got out, he said, "Tomorrow at nine."

Stacy nodded her head "yes" as she drove off.

The next morning came too late for George. He was at the hospital at eight. He introduced himself as Doctor George, his rationale being that he had a doctorate degree, too. He started walking around the hospital in search of the kitchen. He saw a sign over a double door that said GARDEN WARD. He tried to enter it, but the doors were locked. Through the windows in the doors, he could see the patients were all nude; they lined up and walked through a car-wash type of set up. Another attendant was washing the room from floor to ceiling with a hose. The entire room was used as a large tub and toilet. George was shocked, for he saw most of what was happening. He could guess the rest. The patients walked through the shower. On the other side was a dryer machine. When they went through, an attendant at the far end would wrap them in a white, terrycloth robe. They left the area out of sight of George. An attendant saw George. She came to the door. George motioned for her to open the door, which she did. George stepped into the room and said, "Just watering the vegetables?"

The attendant laughed as she said, "May I help you?"

"No, I'm new here. I just want to be nosy. I see you people are busy, so I'll leave you alone. Where's the cafeteria?"

The attendant pointed the way, and George thanked her as he left. George kept walking around, for he was too upset for any coffee. He just knew that somewhere in that human car wash, Ann was being hosed down. George continued inspecting the hospital; after a few minutes, he couldn't take any more. He had to get Ann out of this place. Where? There was no place on earth that he could think of. George had to hurry to be at the front door by nine. He arrived, and the student was waiting. "I wanted to buy coffee buns for everyone, but I couldn't find the cafeteria."

"I'll show you. It is right by our class." The student said and led the way.

They entered the cafeteria. The student placed the order. When they had everything, George followed the student; within a few minutes, he and the student walked in, carrying a tray of coffee buns. The class gave him a standing ovation. Stacy just smiled as she whispered to him, "I would have bet you were going to do this."

As everyone had their coffee, one by one the students asked George about his relationship with Ann/Carol.

One student asked, "Were you having a sexual relationship with Carol?"

George responded, "Gentlemen don't discuss those types of things with other people. Our relationship was private to us. Let's just say we enjoyed each other's company very much."

The questions kept coming until George's answers started to

be redundant, for he didn't know a lot of the answers. The question about the robbery was foremost in their minds. One student was sure that the robbery and her being a nun is what started the chain of events. Another added, "She was becoming a nun and going to bed with a hired lover; that's what I call class."

Not one student laughed as they saw George's face turn to stone. One girl added, "Excuse him. He can be a real jerk at times. I just have one question for you before you leave. How did you get that tape of the session she had with the other doctor?"

"I stole it. I would do anything to help her." George's abrupt answer shocked the class, which left the room in an eerie silence.

Stacy thanked George for coming; the two of them walked out of the class. "Go to the solarium at the end of the hall; I'll have them bring Carol to you. I'll meet up with the two of you in a few minutes."

George did as he was told; soon the female attendant whom he had met in the Garden Room that morning walked into the room, holding a piece of rope. Carol was holding the other end and following behind her. Carol had on a wrap-around dress. Even in her condition, she still looked like an angel.

The attendant said, "If you want to go for a walk outside, you can, for it is a beautiful day. Hold the rope; she will follow you."

It was all George could do to keep from crying. He thanked the attendant and took the end of the rope from her. George led the way out of the solarium into the warm sun. It was the end of September. The day was warm and sunny, but more importantly, it was his birthday. He remembered back to the first birthday he had spent with Ann in the motel down the street from the little club they had gone to. George started talking, but he could see that Ann was not responding at all.

He led her away from the hospital toward the far end of the property. The hospital was built on a hill. From it, the Gaspe Bay could be seen. The sun was reflecting off of the water and almost blinded him. He walked, holding the rope, with Ann following as though she were an animal of some sort. George was trying to build up enough nerve to turn and face her, when he felt a hand slide onto his arm. Ann was beside him. She had put her arm in his. The two of them were walking arm in arm. George stopped to face her. He stared into a dull, lifeless face.

She put her arms down by her side and stood with her eyes closed; the sun from the water was bright on her face. George moved around until he was shielding her from the reflection of the sun. She opened her eyes. With a lifeless gaze, she looked at George. George stood in front of Ann. He looked into her lifeless eyes; he could only remember the way they had once lit up his soul. She was dead, yet she was standing before him. There was no hope left in George of her ever-being Ann again. Envisioning her in the Garden Room was too dehumanizing for him. He looked at her for what seemed an eternity, as he accepted the fact that he had to do something. He had to do it now. Suddenly, she started to talk in a shaky voice.

"George, please kill me." George couldn't believe what he was hearing. She continued, "Don't let God do it. If you love me, you do it. God took you from me. Don't let him have me, too." George didn't understand what Ann meant by the words; she was mumbling in a voice that was barely audible.

"After my mother died, I was in the church. They did whatever they wanted to do to me for four years. I became pregnant. When they tried to perform an abortion, I almost died. I was sent to a hospital in Cincinnati. When I was with you, I knew we could never be together, even though I wanted to be. I tried to kill myself, but I didn't have enough strength to do it. Please, you do it, for I don't want to be like this anymore. I knew you would come for me, but I do not want to go with you.

Your life has been my life. I would not want to jeopardize it. There is nothing left on this Earth for me, so please, if you love me the way I know you do, please do what I ask."

"But you are not in a coma or whatever they told me you were in. Your strength will come back. I'll get you out of here." The pleading sound that was in George's voice did not have any effect on Ann. She stood facing George, showing no outward signs of life or emotion. The tears were running down George's face, but he could not turn away from Ann. It was as though Ann had him in a trance.

"I do not want to see what you have done with your life. I have lived with the thought that I will never be a part of your life. Please, George, do what I ask. Don't leave me in this place or on this Earth any longer. Please."

George put his massive hands around the long thin throat of Ann. He knew that with a slight amount of effort Ann's slim, bony body would go limp. As George was facing with his hands on her, a smile came over her face. Her last words were, "When you come to my grave, please always come alone, for it may be the only place you and I will be alone together. Thank you."

"No, I'm not going to do this."

George walked out towards the end of the hill and looked out on to the St. Lawrence Seaway as it entered the interior of Canada. Ann was following behind; each step she took was done with a lot of effort. The wind picked up, and George had to brace himself not to be blown back. Suddenly, Ann grabbed his arm and said in a voice barely audible over the wind, "Why did you have to come here? I had resolved that my life was over, and I do not need a reason to be mad at God."

The words hit George as hard as any physical blow he had ever encountered in his life. He turned and faced her, and in a voice louder than he intended, he replied, "Why is it always about you? Do you ever take my feelings into account? You don't want to be mad at God. What about me?"

"You have led a full and rewarding life. You married, had children, and have been financially successful. How many people can say that?"

"You're measuring my life next to your standards. What about what I wanted? I would have …" George was caught up in too much emotion to continue talking.

It took all of Ann's strength to reply, "I made the choices I did because I did not want to include you in my problems. My life was dictated to me, and I did not want any of the things I did to affect you in any way. I resolved to stay here to take my punishment for what I had done. Why couldn't you just leave it that way? I think God sent you here to punish me more."

"Is it inconceivable to you to accept the fact that just maybe He answered my prayers?"

"No."

"Well, I think he did. Come on, we are getting out of this horrible place. Look at you! I don't understand how you can stand being like that."

The wind was blowing harder and Ann had to hang on to George, or she would have been blown over. The wind was taking the breath out of her lungs, and she started to cough. George half dragged and half carried her back into the building. All of the attendants were busy making sure all the patients were inside and the outside equipment was securely tied down. As the staff was scurrying about, George with Ann still in his grasp, made his way to the exit door. She tried to pull away from him, but his grasp was far too strong for her to break away.

In a choking voice, she said, "If you don't let me go…" her coughing was too intense for her to finish the sentence. George paid her no heed and dragged her outside into the wind, which had increased tremendously, and fought his way to his car. Ann's coughing increased as the velocity of the wind made it too difficult for her to breathe. The light jacket she had put on when she first went outside with George was being blown right off of her. She was totally dependent on George to get her into his car. The wind was blowing with such force that it was very difficult for George to close the door to the car. With a great deal of effort, he finally managed to do it. He went around the car and had the same difficulty getting into his side. Finally, they were secure inside the car, which was being shaken by the wind. They watched in awe at the trees' being blown about like so many matchsticks. George started the car and inched his way out of the parking lot and toward his motel room, which was a few miles away.

The road was littered with all kinds of debris, and avoiding it took all of George's skill and attention. Ann opened the door, and George had to stop and grab her before she fell out of the car. He grabbed her with such force that she had a black and blue mark where his hand had been.

"I don't want to go. Why can't you just leave me alone?"

"Because I don't want to; now shut up and don't try anything stupid like that again." As George spoke, he could see the mark he had left where he had grabbed her. He finished the drive to his motel, and with a great deal of effort due to the wind, he got her inside. She was trembling so much that he took her shoes off and put her in bed under all of the blankets he could find. There was a coffee maker in the room, so he quickly made her a cup and had her drink the hot liquid. After a few minutes, she stopped coughing and trembling and seemed as though she had at last relaxed. A smile crept across her face, and she said, "It's been a long time since we have been together like this." She made a chuckling sound as she turned over and went to sleep.

George just smiled as he went to the far side of the room. He picked up the phone to call Stacy, his doctor friend. His speech was short as he said, "I got her out, but I think you better come and look at her."

The doctor knew exactly what he meant and said she would

be over within the hour. "That is, of course, if you tell me where you are."

George looked at the phone, stunned by her remark, but he soon realized that she didn't know where he was staying. He quickly gave her the address and settled down to await her arrival. His mind was working overtime, as he tried to figure out what his next move would be. He had to get Ann out of the country and into some place where she could get her strength back. After that, he would do whatever he had to do to keep her safe from harm. He smiled at that thought. For the first time in a long time, he felt good about himself.

The shaking of the door and windows of the motel interrupted his concentration. There was a loud crash right outside his door, which woke Ann up. "God's telling you that what you are doing is wrong."

George looked out the window and saw that the canopy over the office door had been ripped off the building and blown across the yard, hitting two cars. The wind was now accompanied by a heavy downpour, which made it hard to see anything. "Well, don't you worry about it; because of my close affiliation with Him, he will soon forgive me."

The storm stopped just as quickly as it had started. There was a dead calm. George looked at the pathetic figure in the bed and added, "See, I told you so. I am going to go to the office and rent the room next door. You stay in bed until the doctor comes."

As George was crossing the parking lot, there was a big argument between the car owners and the motel manager about the extensive damage that had been done to their cars. Just at that moment, the doctor pulled into the lot. As the doctor got out of the car, she said, "Come on, I can't stay long; the hospital is calling me."

Without waiting for a response, George opened the door to the room, and the doctor walked in. She turned and faced

George and said, "This will go much faster if you aren't in the way." George went over to his car to inspect it for any damage. He was lucky his car was untouched by the storm.

Within a few minutes, the doctor came out and motioned to George to walk to her car. As he approached the car Stacy said, "Your friend is very weak and undernourished. I think it is because she wants to die. I gave her a shot that will put her to sleep and some vitamins to build her up." As she spoke, Stacy reached into her car and took out some pills and handed them to George. "When she wakes up, give her two of these every four hours. Follow me, and we can go to the general store, and I'll get her some clothes to wear."

George asked, "What happened at the hospital after I left?" Stacy replied, "I was in the solarium with two of my students. They went looking for you and Carol. When the attendant said that she was with you and that the two of you were probably outside, I started yelling for everyone to find the two of you. I thought you might kill her."

One of the attendants was shocked and said, "He's not a doctor? He was in the Garden Room this morning."

I asked him, "Did he see her in there?"

He replied, "I don't know."

"Did he see what you do in there?"

"Yes."

"Find them. He is going to kill her."

George interrupted with, "You thought I would kill her? Why?"

Stacy stated, "Because I knew you loved her and you couldn't stand to see her living like this."

Someone set off an alarm, and everyone was looking for the two of you. Within seconds, there was a crowd running around, looking for you and Carol. When I arrived at the office, I realized what I had started, and I sent everyone away."

Stacy struggled with herself to find a delicate balance

between her oath to help people and what she thought had happened. She reached out of the car and pulled George to her as she said, "I know you love her; I know you want to put her out of her misery. I can't even blame you for doing what you did. I know she wanted you to help her. Because you did that, she isn't suffering anymore. Please take care of her; I will do whatever has to be done to make it right with the hospital."

George was still in a daze, as he stood looking at Stacy.

"George, don't hurt the one thing that she loved. She loved you so much that she gave you up because she didn't feel she could give you the life you wanted. Leave now, and leave everything to me. Remember you are living out two lives—hers and yours."

"What about the police?" George asked; he couldn't take his eyes off of Stacy.

"She will become another 'DIME marking' in our books; no one will know what happened here. This is Canada, not the United States."

George got in his car and followed Stacy down the street to the general store. In a short time, the doctor went around the store, picking up items for George to take back with him. She handed them to him as she said, "I'll come back as soon as I can."

George paid the bill and returned to the motel. He rented the adjoining room and went inside. Across the street from the motel was a restaurant that George made a mental note of for later. He opened the door between the two rooms and settled down on his bed; he suddenly felt very tired from the day's activities. He left the door between the two rooms ajar. He put the clothes that he had bought on a chair in Ann's room and was soon fast asleep on the bed in his room.

A gentle hand smoothing his hair down awaked him. He awoke with a start. He opened his eyes and saw Ann smiling at him, "I'm glad you are my protector. I'm sorry, but I woke up hungry, and I don't have any money." She kept talking, but George was so glad to hear her voice that he didn't pay any attention to what she was saying. He did hear her final sentence when she said, "As usual, you aren't listening to me. Some things just don't change."

She got up and turned around to show off her new outfit, which was a ridiculous flannel dress that just hung on her frail, bony body. The exertion of spinning made her lose her balance, and she fell on the bed. "I don't think I can go out for dinner. Would you mind if we ate in?"

"Not at all, my dear; you stay right here, and I will go out and purchase us a feast." With these words, George was out the door and walking toward the restaurant. As he walked in, they were getting ready to close. George was faced with the reality that he wasn't home, and up here in the Gaspe Bay Peninsula, restaurants don't stay open late. "Sir, this is an emergency; please, make me up a couple of dishes of whatever you have ready, and I'm out of here." As he spoke, he took some money out of his pocket and was handed a box of covered dishes and was sent on his way.

He walked into the motel room and was met by Stacy, who greeted him with, "I'm just in time for dinner, I see."

The table was pulled away from the wall, and the task of opening all of the different covered dishes was accomplished with everyone's help. The doctor's somber voice interrupted the festivities as she warned Ann: "You better take it easy; your system has to get used to the spices that are used."

The doctor motioned to George to walk her to her car. As soon as they were outside, she said, "I put a 'dime marking' on Ann's record so no one will be looking for her. I wouldn't stay around here too long, so…"

"We'll move tomorrow. I will take her into the States. I shouldn't have any trouble at the border; anyway, I hope I don't."

As he spoke, the doctor wrote an address on a piece of paper and handed it to George. “Tomorrow, I am going to my home in Vermont. Meet me at this address, and I will take her across the border. The border patrol is used to me bringing patients home with me. I doubt that I will be questioned; I’ll see you tomorrow...”

As Stacy got in her car, George asked, “What is a ‘Dime marking’?”

“Oh, the hospital uses it. It means that someone was ‘Dead in the Morning’.” With those words, the doctor left, and George smiled as he went back into the motel to see to his ward. Dinner was over, and Ann went back to bed after warning George, “Don’t throw anything out.”

Left alone, George went to bed, happy in the thought that Ann was feeling better and that the doctor was going to help him get her out of the country. The next step would be to talk the doctor into letting Ann stay in her Vermont house until she was strong enough to make plans for the future. With those comforting thoughts, George drifted off, for--at last--he was at peace with himself.

His introduction to the next day was more violent. “Get up; you have problems. The hospital did a complete check of all the patients, and they know Ann is missing. When the photo check started, my friend pulled the ‘Dime marking’ I had entered. He thought he was doing me a favor. If he had just left everything alone, there would not have been any problem, but when he removed the marking, Ann was listed as missing. Get up and get her out of the area; you know--out of sight, out of mind.”

On that note, Stacy left George’s room and went through the common doorway into Ann’s room. Ann had heard the commotion and was sitting in a chair, trying to comb her hair. The doctor commented, “You can always tell when a female patient is feeling better; the first thing she does is comb her hair.” The two ladies laughed as the doctor took Ann’s blood pressure and checked her other vital signs. "I am always in awe of seeing a patient, who wants to live, walk away from Death's door. A good meal and a good night's sleep have done wonders for you. But, please, just take it easy for awhile until your body catches up to your mental well-being."

The doctor had brought coffee with her, and Ann and she chatted about a shopping trip, while George was still having trouble facing the day. They could hear him stumbling around in the room. The sound of the shower marked another milestone in his preparation for the day, and after a few more strange sounds, he knocked on the common door and walked into the room.

As he sipped the coffee the doctor had given him, she started to repeat her earlier statements until George held up his hand and shouted, "Enough. You said you were going to your house in Vermont. Can you take Ann with you, or do you want me to get her into the States? I think I can bring her in by water, if you think you'll have a problem. I'll get a boat and bring her in down the locks and into Lake Champlain. You can meet us in Burlington. Decide what you want to do, and let me know. Right now, let's go out for breakfast and get out of this motel."

With those words said, the doctor helped Ann pack her things in the paper bags, and George went to his room and packed his things and threw them into the car. He came to Ann's room and took her bags and put them into Stacy's car. He sat in his car until the Stacy and Ann appeared. They got into the doctor's car and drove off with George following behind.

There was a little restaurant on the way to the border, where the doctor stopped. It was in a little town and in the center of the shopping area. Food came first, but afterwards, the local store was visited for a brief shopping spree. George commented to himself, "I am glad she is feeling better."

The two ladies came out of the store, and George had to look twice, for there was a marked difference in Ann. They came to his car and the doctor said, "I'm going to drive to my house in Vermont. Here is the address. I don't think your following us is a good idea, so meet us there." The two ladies got into the car and drove off. For some reason George felt very uneasy. The relationship between Stacy and Ann just didn't seem right to him. It seemed that they had formed a stronger bond than he thought possible for the short period of time that they'd been together. He shrugged his shoulders and just chalked up his uneasy feeling to his constant pessimism.

He drove around for a while before starting for the border. The day was bright, compared to the previous day when the storm had hit. As he drove, he started to plan out what would have to be done in order to get Ann back into the main stream of life. Her identity would be no problem, since she had all of the necessary documents from when she was a judge. Her affiliation with the church would have to be defined, but George didn't think that would be too hard, for he had done a lot of work for the church and still had some good contacts in it. It might cost a little more by way of contributions, but he didn't feel the task would best him.

He had estimated the drive from the hospital to the doctor's house would be about six hours. At his current rate of speed, he would make it in that time with no problem.

The scene in the doctor's car between her and Ann was much different. They were having a discussion that was quite different from the one that George thought they were having. Ann started with, "Please help me get away from George. He means well, and I know he has my best interests at heart, but I don't want to be part of his life, and I am just not strong enough to break away and stay away from him. Can you help me, please?" Her words were said in a tearful voice. At times, she was crying so hard that she had to stop because she was starting to choke.

She composed herself as they crossed the border into the United States; once away from the border, she continued with her plea. "I realize I am asking a lot, but I have no one to turn to. If I can get back to George's Run, I still know people there who will help me get back into the good graces of the church. My friends Bob and Norma will help as soon as I get back. Once I am back with the church, I will have the support I need to finish out my life by making some contribution to pay for my existence here on Earth. Take me to a train station because I think they'll ask too many questions in an airport, and I will be able to make my way back to my hometown. I will need some money, but I swear to you that as soon as I am home, I will send it to you. Please don't take me to your house because once I am there, I know I will not have the strength to do what I know should be done. Please."

Stacy was stunned by the words, and she was not too sure what she should be doing. Aside from Ann's physical weakness, which seemed to be disappearing by the minute, her mental attitude became stronger at the same miraculous rate. Ann was clear as to what she wanted to do and had worked out a plan in her mind on how to achieve the results she wanted. She even had the presence of mind to remember that traveling by train was much easier than to travel by plane. What to tell George would be another problem, but the good doctor knew she was in a much stronger position to deal with George than Ann was. Within a very short time, she resolved that she would help. The doctor pulled into the next store she came to and got directions to the nearest train or bus station. She helped Ann plan her trip and gave her enough money to do it.

The trip segued from a bus to a train and back to a bus, which took her to her hometown of George's Run, Ohio. While on route, she was able to contact her old friend, who still lived there and who met her at the depot and took Ann home with her. The trip proved much more strenuous than Ann had anticipated, so she stayed in bed for her first three days at home.

Norma contacted the convent where she'd first entered the

church, and much to Ann's surprise, she was accepted back into the order with great enthusiasm. The "old guard" had died off, and the new regime was more tolerable towards what had happened, much more than Ann ever expected. The only proviso was that she would have to leave the order and volunteer for a new group that was starting up in a small town in New England. She stayed at the mother house for a period of three months, where she regained her strength and renewed her vows. Her physical, mental and religious strength flowed back into her faster than anyone could have ever hoped or predicted.

The new church needed a teacher and an administrator to help develop the parish. Ann was suited for both of these positions. She changed her name again and was at peace with herself at last, and all thoughts of George were tucked away and only visited on special occasions.

When George arrived at the doctor's house, no one was there. He drove into the nearby village and had dinner in a quaint, little restaurant. After the long drive and the second bottle of wine, which he had shared with the owner, he went out to his car and promptly fell asleep. There was a chill in the air, and after a few minutes, the owner came out with a blanket that worked very well in keeping the annoying cold air at bay. The next day, the late morning sun awoke George with a start. He went inside the restaurant, and the owner's wife gave him a cup of coffee. "I came out to wake you, but I didn't have the heart. You looked so peaceful that I could not bring myself to shatter such a tranquil scene."

They both laughed as George returned the blanket and thanked her for her kindness. He drove to the house, and with a little effort woke the doctor up. "You get dressed and I will make us breakfast." Stacy walked away but could not bring herself to wait any longer; she came back into the kitchen with a stern, determined look on her face. It was the kind of appearance she saved for when she had to tell someone he/she was going to die.

"George, there is no nice way to say this, so I am going to tell you straight out. Ann is not here. She told me the whole story about how you two met and begged me to help her get away from you. She went home, I think, and she wants to return to the church. That is her life, and she wants to return to it without your interference. Please accept the fact that you can't always have your own way and your life without her is and has been full. She is still seeking the happiness you have found. I realize that what has happened is not what you wanted …"

George put the coffeepot down and walked out of the house. Stacy started to follow him but stopped when she got to the doorway. She watched as George got in his car and sat there for a long time. His head was bowed, and Stack got a chill from thinking that he was crying. Finally, he started the engine and pulled out of her yard. He drove down the mountain and past the restaurant and out of the village. He turned the car towards George's Run, but after a few miles, he made a turn and headed toward his house. His thoughts so confused him that his driving was very erratic. A state trooper pulled him over and gave him a warning but let him go. That interruption brought his focus back to his driving. It was a long, lonely drive back to his home and an even more lonely existence, realizing that Ann would be where she wanted to be and that place was not with him. He tried to rationalize that what he was doing was the right thing, but no matter how hard he concentrated on the fact that they were apart and that is the way she wanted it, he still felt emptiness in his life that he was not used to and didn't like.

Through a friend of his who was a priest and who knew everyone, George was able to keep track of Ann's whereabouts. It took a constant effort for him to stay away. The years passed, but the hurt never did. His wife died, and soon afterwards his priest friend passed also. George felt for the first time the pangs of loneliness that he had only heard of or read about. The hurt became so great, that one day he decided to go see her. At first, he resolved that he would not show himself and that he would not talk to her. On the day he left to go to the church where she was, he knew that she would have to be strong enough for the both of them, for any willpower he had left was gone. Their relationship had gone full circle, for now they were in the same position they'd been in when they first met. She a nun and he … he could not come up with a word that he felt described himself. Their life was one of brief encounters, and now that their lives were coming to an end, they would both have to accept the fact that they didn't know how much time they both had and that whatever time was left was going to be spent as their lives had dictated. They were going to be separated from each other.

When George arrived at the church, he could not bring himself to go inside. He sat on a bench outside the tiny church and watched the other parishioners come and go. He looked up and came face to face with Ann. In her habit, only her face showed, but it beamed from an inner source of light. At first, she nodded and he nodded, for he was not sure what he should say or do. Finally, she walked over to him and in a quiet voice said, "His plan was that we not be with each other, so please share my happiness and fill your life with the contentment I feel now."

She smiled and walked away. George walked back to his car and headed home. He knew he would be back but resolved that his return would be as a parishioner of the church, not as a scorned lover. He looked skyward and thought about all the events that had occurred between him and Ann. Finally, he had to concentrate upon his driving, for the other drivers out that day were not sympathetic to his plight, and they showed their displeasure by constantly blowing their horns. He still did not understand why the events unfolded the way they did. He silently said, I guess these things happened to me when God wasn't lookin'. At the end of that thought, he said, "AMEN."

Chapter Eighteen

George was sitting at home one evening about three months after seeing Ann. The memory of her was his constant companion. No matter what he did, she was always with him. He didn't feel any guilt for what he'd done; he felt only contempt toward a God that would do this to him. He kept asking himself, Why did he punish her so? Why did He make me think that nothing else mattered other than my loving her? At that moment, nothing in George's life meant anything to him.

The chiming of the doorbell did little to awaken George out of his stupor. The constant ringing of it made him look up from his desk to see two men standing on his porch and looking at him. The way that the room was set up, George had placed his desk so that he could see the entire street in front of his house. When the sun wasn't shining on the window, making it like a mirror, the people riding by could look in.

At the front of his house (that he also used as an office) there were thirteen steps' leading to the street. There were nine steps from the street to the first landing, and there were four more steps from the landing to the front door. When standing on the second landing, one could look right into the room. It was on this landing that the two men were standing. When George and the men made eye contact, they waved. George got up and went to open the door.

"May I help you?" he said as he opened the door to speak to the two men.

"Are you George?"

"Yes, I am."

"We are from the police department. We would like to speak to you." As they spoke, they showed George their gold badges.

George stepped back from the door to allow the two men to come in. George's movements were very rigid as he opened the door wider. He stepped back away from it. One of the officers asked, "Are you alright?"

"Yes. Please come in." George pointed to the two red leather chairs that were in front of his desk and said, "Please sit down." He shut the door as he asked," May I get you anything?"

Both men just shook their head "no."

George sat down and looked at the two men. They looked at each other as if they were debating who was going to speak. They had told George their names, but looking at them, George couldn't remember who was who.

Finally the older one asked, "Did you know a Carol. Her name was Ann before she changed it."

"Yes."

"How well did you know her?'

George had his head down and stared at his desk as if he was expecting a message to be flashed across it, telling him the answers to the questions he was being asked.

"How well did you know her?" Although the detective raised his voice, it scared his partner more than it did George.

"I'm sorry; I can't help you, gentlemen, but if you have any other questions, please feel free to call me at any time." When George finished talking, he pushed himself back from the desk as he got up. He started toward the door.

"Did you hear what I said?"

"You said you were going," George responded.

"I asked you how well you knew her, not that I was going. Look, we can do this here or down at headquarters."

"Do you have an arrest warrant?"

"We can get one." Now the detective who had been silent joined in. "We came here to see if we could clear up a few questions we have. We have been asked to look into this matter by the Canadian government. If you're arrested, you'll be sent back to Gaspe. Now are you going to cooperate and tell us about your relationship with Carol/Ann?"

"No. Our relationship was our business and is none of yours. If the Canadian police want to talk to me, tell them to call me or I will go up there. But you two guys are just here to be busy bodies. Now get out."

"We came here..."

"You came here to get me to incriminate myself. Now leave, or I will call the police and have you arrested for trespassing."

The two detectives looked at each other and shook their heads, for they did not know what to do. They walked to the door. "We'll be back to put you under arrest and take you out in cuffs."

"Good. You do that." George shut the door in their faces.

He went back to sit at his desk. As the officers went outside, they looked back into the room to see George sit down at his desk and resume the position he'd been in when they first saw him.

The two detectives applied for an arrest warrant. The judge knew George. He refused to sign the warrant until he spoke to the detective in charge. The interview started with the judge asking, "Did you go see George?"

"Yes, but he refused to answer any questions. He would not cooperate with the investigation at all. He told us it was none of our business what his relationship with Carol, or Ann as he knew her. He said if the Canadian police wanted to talk to him, they should just call him."

"Well?"

"Well, what? I don't think that George should be allowed to talk to an officer that way. We were asked to speak to him on behalf of the Canadian government. I don't think that as police offers, we should have someone talk like that to us."

"What did he do wrong? He has no obligation to talk to you. If you just want to use him as a hunting expedition, why would he answer your questions? I will not sign this arrest warrant until you have something more than that? You haven't even stated why you want to talk to him about Ann. From now on, let everyone refer to her as Ann so that there is no mix up. Did the Canadians tell you why they wanted him questioned? Where did she die? I mean, is she dead? It's not clear from your papers whether or not she is."

"She is dead, and he was the last one to see her, he and some Doctor Stacy."

The judge made a notation on the papers before he continued, "Where?"

"At the mental hospital in Gaspe, New Brunswick, Canada; she was a patient there. I think."

The judge became very annoyed. "Before I allow you to arrest an American citizen, you are going to have to give me more than that. Was she under the doctor's care? Is the doctor raising an issue about how she died? In short, gentlemen, other than the fact that you didn't like the idea that George reminded you that he didn't have to speak to you, why do you want to arrest him?"

The two detectives bowed their heads and left. On the way back to their office, they started trying to analyze why George would take the attitude he did. They were supposed to meet with their chief. One of the officers said, "George knows we're not going to go away. He can slow us down, but eventually he is going to have to talk to us. What makes him think he is above the law?"

A voice came from behind them. The two detectives recognized it as belonging to the police psychiatrist. "He is punishing himself much more than we can ever punish him. What can we do? Put him on trial? Who is going to convict him of anything based upon the evidence we have? No Canadian jury--they are tougher than our juries, yet they have a bigger bleeding heart than our juries. I read the folder the Canadian

Police sent down. She was less than a vegetable. The fact she was still living was a miracle. Who is going to go to the expense of a trial if, at best, all we could prove is a mercy killing if we win? The odds of that happening are nil. Believe me right now; if we convict George of anything, he would probably thank us. If we do convict him, he isn't going to get the death penalty, and at his age, I doubt he would get any time at all. Any time he would get would be on a prison farm. No. George is staying out of jail because he believes he can punish himself much more than we can."

The psychiatrist walked away before either detective could respond. They went to their office to start on another case. They sent a note to their chief, asking for further instructions. The chief picked up their note, made sure the two detectives were watching, and tore it up.

The following month, three Canadian detectives visited the chief of police. The meeting was arranged through the Governor's office. The men came in. After the usual introductions, they got right to the point: they wanted to interview George. "He is not under suspicion; it is the doctor in charge we are concerned about. We want to question him with regard to a Doctor Stacy." When the three men spoke, it looked like each had a part he wanted to say.

The chief looked in amazement as he said, "As you know, George does not have to speak with you. I know about him, but I can't say that I've ever had any dealings with him. When my detectives were at his house, he threw them out. I could not get an arrest warrant. The judge down here didn't think we had enough evidence of a crime to support an arrest warrant. Do you have anything in addition to what you sent us down last time? What are you looking for? All I can do is call him and ask him if he will come in."

"Would you do that? We are concerned because the percentage of patients who die while under Doctor Stacy's care is higher than any other doctor in Canada. She works in a mental institution. A pattern of deaths has emerged. Once a patient is beyond help, he/she winds up on their DIME list. That means the person is found dead, and they don't know what to do with the body. We have performed autopsies on some of the bodies, but it is hard to tell what the cause of death was."

The chief thought a moment, "What can we lose; I'll call him and ask." The chief asked his secretary to place the call.

"Hello," George answered. His day started off with his sitting at his desk in the front room, watching the commuters going to work as he read the newspaper. Today, he had his cleaning woman in. Her name was Margie. She was a bubbly type person that made a whole room bright when she walked into it. On the days she cleaned, she would come over early to make breakfast for George and herself. The house had the aroma of freshly brewed coffee. She walked in with a cup for George, just as he answered the phone. She placed the coffee next to him.

"George, this is the chief of police. I have members of the Canadian police department in my office, who would like to question you. Now you know you do not have to come in but well, you know, neighborly relations and all..."

George remembered the last time he'd had a run in with the Canadian police. They had arrested him in Detroit when he crossed the border back into the States after a trip to Canada. "I'd love to help out, but I'm not coming there. They are five minutes from my house. Bring them over here, and we can talk here. In fact, come right now. I have to go out this afternoon, so if it is convenient for them, have them come now."

The chief looked at the men, "Do you want to go now?"

They all nodded their heads yes. "OK, I'll send one of my men with them. There are three of them. They will be right there."

After George hung up, he yelled out, "Margie, we are going

to have four guests for breakfast. You better make more coffee."

From the kitchen he heard, "Ok, boss, fresh coffee and fresh muffins, coming right up. Should I change into my maid's outfit?" Margie was the type of person who loved her little jokes. She quickly put the coffee on the stove to brew a bigger pot. She put the muffins in the oven before she dashed upstairs to change her cleaning outfit for something more presentable. George's office was also his home. Downstairs was his office, and upstairs was his living area. It consisted of four rooms and two full baths. Two rooms were his. He'd made them into a master suite for himself. The other two were spare rooms. Margie would always bring a change of clothes with her to change into when she was done cleaning.

The doorbell rang just as Margie came down the steps. She opened the door as she bid the four men to come in. George recognized the detective who'd been there last time. He did the introductions. George led everyone into the back part of the house.

The kitchen area consisted of a counter behind which there was a stove and refrigerator/freezer combination. In front of the counter was an enormous oval-shaped oak table with eight chairs. Margie had set the table for coffee and buns. The smell of the fresh coffee and hot buns just made the room smell delicious. Margie showed everyone to a seat and went to check on her baking. George had just had a double oven installed. One of the Canadian detectives, who was a gourmet chef as a hobby, just marveled over the double ovens. He stopped admiring them when his boss called the meeting to order. Everyone sat down around the table. Over the table was an enormous brass chandelier. It was the final touch to the room.

As soon as everyone was comfortable, Margie poured the coffee and put the muffins on the table with butter and jelly. When she was done, she excused herself and went upstairs.

George looked at his group. "Gentlemen, I am all yours. Just tell me what you are questioning me about and why."

"You were the last one to see Carol in Gaspe. You knew her as Ann. During these discussions, we are going to refer to her as Carol. Is that alright with you?" Without waiting for an answer, the detective continued. George listened, but other than an occasional grunt or nodding his head, he said nothing. When the detective finished talking, he showed George a picture of Carol. George had a hard time choking back his tears. He got up from the table.

"Excuse me for a moment." He went into the bathroom, which was located off the kitchen area. He was back in a minute. He picked up the picture and looked at it again. He could feel the tears' welling in his eyes. "Gentlemen, I don't know if I was the last person or not, but why all the questions?"

"The doctor who was her attending physician has an unusually high death rate among her patients."

"Well, that makes sense; she only gets the ones that no one else wants or can do anything with. Are you accusing her of mercy killings?"

"We are not here to discuss the pros and cons of mercy killings. In Canada, they are against the law. It is also against the law in your country. When you left her, was she alive?"

"You define "live," and I'll answer. In my definition she was dead when I last saw her."

"You knew her for years, didn't you?"

"Sir, I think I may have seen her two or three times at the most in the last twenty-five years. If it is that important, I could probably figure out the number of times I've seen her if you want me to. I mean I can't do it today, but I will, and I'll forward it to you."

Another detective, the one who was fascinated by the ovens, blurted out, "You set up a fund for her of over twenty thousand dollars. What was that for?"

"To appease my conscience; I felt responsible for her being

in the hospital."

"Do you have such resources that you can just hand out twenty thousand dollars to appease your conscience?'

"The table and place setting you're eating from cost over a thousand; that should tell you something." The "gourmet chef" picked up the small plate for his muffin that Margie had baked and turned it over to see the name on it. He shook his head in agreement.

"Did you know she was a nun? She was accused of embezzling a large sum of money from the church?"

"I heard about that about twenty years ago, but I don't know if it is true or not. Gentleman, I am not trying to be evasive with my answers; it is that I just don't know. My knowledge is based upon someone like you, telling me the stories about her being a nun and about her being a thief. I don't think anyone ever charged her with a crime; instead, it was just a lot of talk. Now you're telling me that you think her doctor put her out of her misery and you want to call it murder. You want me to help prosecute her. I think you are nuts. Have you ever met Carol? Did you ever know her?"

The oldest detective was annoyed at George's response. "As I told you when we came in, we are not here to discuss the issue of mercy killings with you. It is against the law."

"So is questioning a defendant without his attorney's being present. If you ever talk to Doctor Stacy, I am her attorney, and you are not to do it without my being present. I am hereby putting you on notice that I represent her."

The oldest detective stood up in a rage. "That means nothing to us. You are not a member of the Canadian Bar. You are not."

George just waved his hand as he added, "I think this interview is over. I hope I have been of some help. If I can be of any further service to you, just let me know."

One by one, the group left after expressing their gratitude

for George's hospitality. They marched out the door in single file past Margie. They all complimented her on her muffins. Margie looked at George before she turned to go upstairs once again to change back into her cleaning outfit. On her way up the steps, she said, "You should stay in the law business. That is the most life I've seen in you in a long time.

George placed a call to Stacy. She answered the phone with, "I know why you called. They are up here talking to a lot of people, too. I am leaving here and going to work in a hospital in New York State. I'll send you a note as soon I get there."

"George added before she hung up, "Keep in mind that I am an attorney in New York, as well as New Jersey."

"Believe me, I will remember that."

George heard no more about the matter. He quietly got back into the waiting line in God's waiting room.

Epilogue

The drive back home from Vermont was a long, hard drive that George wished would be over. His Ann was now in a religious order. He had rescued her from the Garden Room of the hospital, and for that he was glad. Stacy was still in Canada and Vermont. She promised to look after Ann whenever she could. Somehow that thought gave George no peace of mind. He was ashamed at himself for not going after Ann; at the same time, he was mad at himself for not being smart enough to know what else to do. The drive home was endless.

Bob and Norma still lived in George's Run, Ohio. They stayed in touch with Ann. Sister Edith died two years after Father O'Neil passed away.

Detective Josephine was dismissed from the police department for certain infractions that were never made public. She works as a security guard on one of the gambling boats on the Mississippi River.

Detective Larry became Captain. He retired to a ranch he bought in Montana.

Doc John was killed in a traffic accident two years after the Ann incident. He left no survivors. It was later found out that he was dating his sixteen-year-old assistant in the office. The girl's mother was trying to prove that her grandchild was the doctor's, but the blood type was wrong. She sued his estate anyway, but the case was thrown out.

Andy married a Puerto Rican girl. They moved to her parent's house in Puerto Rico. He was never heard from again.

Mary Lou married and had three children. Her life was a hard one, for her husband was of the opinion that she should support him. After fifteen years, she divorced him. She was going to use George to represent her in the divorce, but she was too ashamed.

Janet just disappeared. She graduated from college, moved to the West Coast, and never had anything to do with her family or friends on the East Coast. The fact that she moved so abruptly broke her mother and father's hearts. They could never accept the fact that their only daughter did this to them.

Sal married Monique. They run the hotel in Miami Beach that now only caters to retirees.

Curly retired to Mexico in a small town on the Pacific Ocean. He tells everyone that he has had enough excitement for two lifetimes. He continued to speak of George until the day he died.

Adele was shot by one of her customer's right in the hotel. No one knows why or who did it.

Jean and Maude moved to New York on the east side. Jean married a New Yorker and had two children. Her mother lived with them. She became the built-in babysitter for about five years. One morning, she announced she was leaving. She moved out and went back to New Orleans to live with a friend of hers down there. Her daughter's family went to visit her for the first couple of years, but they soon stopped when the kids got older and didn't want to go any more.

José died a quiet death in the lobby of the Del Prado hotel. He just fell over while on one of his many inspection tours of the hotel.

Maria moved to her uncle's house and married his competitor's son. In time, they owned the largest and most prestigious bull ranch in Mexico. Their bulls were even featured in the arenas in Spain.

Mongombo was recalled to Uganda and was never heard from again.

Evelyn traveled with John for a while. They were both convicted of a stock fraud deal and received twenty years each in a federal prison. John died in jail; Evelyn married one of her guards. She was paroled six months after the wedding and a month before she had triplets.

Joel, like all businessmen, just faded away. His friends, as well as his competitors, shunned him. He could never understand why they were so mad at him. He had lost just as much as they did.

Richard still practices law in Goshen. Every so often he will mention some of the things he learned from George. He never felt George was a good lawyer, but he sure knew the business end of the law business. He hired a fashion consultant to help him pick out his wardrobe, for he still remembered the way George looked when he walked into the courtroom that day.

Barbara retired and stayed home to raise her two grandchildren. She would tell her friends, "George left me with memories enough for all of you." After a few glasses of wine, she would always entertain her guests with "George stories," as they became known. They liked the one about Ann the best.

Stacy moved to New York State and worked in a mental hospital. The police questioned her, but nothing came of it. She and Mario are still friends. They alternate about who will go visit whom. Mario asks Stacy, "Why didn't you ever get married?"

Stacy would reply, "I never met George until after he was hooked on Ann." Mario's come back would be, "I would have loved to know Carol when she was Ann."

Stacy, not to be out-done, would reply, "The problem is that I don't think George ever knew Ann either. He only met the Ann who had started to become Carol."

They would end the discussion with both of them saying, "Poor George."

Russ still lives in Connecticut, is retired, and hates every minute of it. Every day he waits for a call from George so that he "can spring back into action."

George retired to write his life's history. At least, that is what he told everybody; but what he was really doing was waiting for his turn in God's waiting room. He wanted to ask God, "Why weren't you lookin'?"

The End

About the Author

George Delmarmo is a retired accountant and attorney living in Brick, New Jersey. He has traveled extensively while representing an international list of clientele. His experiences varied to all types of assignments that required his special mixture of talents. He started writing to fill the void in his life created by his retirement. He has written a series of books, which are a reflection of his travels and experiences. He is a member of the New Jersey as well as the New York bars and is a licensed accountant in the state of New Jersey.

Memoirs of a Retired Modern-Day Mercenary, George

George is a retired mercenary, who at the end of his career started writing his memoirs.

To contact George please send an e-mail to:

hogfarmer@aol.com

Books by George Delmarmo

A Heart Never Heals: The story of a girl George sees in a vision. She appeared to George while in Italy, working on a case. She was walking out of the Mediterranean Sea. The vision is so vivid that he visits the Vatican to confer with a Cardinal, seeking an explanation of what he saw. The Cardinal advises George to start from the very beginning of the events of what brought him to that spot at that time. George relates the details of his journey. When George returns home, he finishes the case before he starts on his maddening quest to find his vision.

All About Mary: The story about the extent that the police will go to entrap someone. The tactics police use and which are used against them create the backdrop of the story. Emotions such as love and affection are used like any other tool. The legality of an act is only a wisp of air and so many words when the party in charge tries to use it for his own benefit. The main character is an attorney in the prosecutor's office who changes her name and her persona in order to get her man. The results she achieves wind up being her own downfall.

Cooperstown Diamonds: The story of a man who lived his life to the fullest by manipulating everyone around him. He was the kind of man who lived his life according to his rules, and somehow everyone just let him do what he wanted. By using his personal charm and cunning, he built for himself his own world and loved every minute of it. He would be accused of many things, but with the help of his friend, he was never found guilty of any wrongdoing. He could play his life as one would play a fiddle, just for his pleasure.

The Darkest Day: This novel deals with a family's problems regarding divorce and abortion. It also deals with a woman who decides that she is going to become the matriarch of the family. Her domination destroys the family, for no one in the family wants her to assume such a role. What the members of her family want are secondary to her unmerciful quest to become the dominant factor. She learns too late the folly of her choices. The financial viability and the stability of her family are destroyed before her very eyes, but this does not deter her from her quest.

Deception by Marriage: The story of a man and woman who use marriages as a method of getting what they want out of life. They have no regard for the human tragedy they leave behind. They have no sympathy or concern for the people around them. Divorce and abandonment are used as tools and a convenient method of getting in and out of situations that no longer interest them. The children, as well as spouses, they leave behind are of no concern to them as they go through life, searching for what they feel will satisfy them for the moment.

End of the Light: The story deals with one man's encounter with the supernatural. The love of one man is traced throughout his life and the life of the woman he loved. Their affection for each other lasted throughout both their lives. Although she died years before him, he was still close to her until his death years later. After her death, her spirit stayed in the lighthouse where they first met until he joined her. Try as he might, he could not forget or get away from her. The story is sad for he never wanted to.

Hate Crimes: The story revolves around a group of people who use the acts of the police to create a resort-type setting. People are invited to participate in some of the infamous shootouts. The story examines the actions of police and criminals alike. After studying them, the acts are used to train a group of people to enforce what should be done rather than what the law allows. The training of different groups of people blends in with the resort-type atmosphere that the story is set in. The training is sometimes used to thwart the police's efforts to stop crimes.

It Begins… It Ends: The story of a murder case set in an actual setting. It shows the investigation and defense of a suspect while life still goes on. Although a lawyer takes on the case, his own personal life, as well of his associates, still continues. Each element of the story is set in the middle of all the activities that take place as an ordinary part of living. The story also points out the errors that can be made in gathering evidence. These errors, whether done by omission or commission, can get a person convicted. The story stresses the defense attorney's job.

Last of the Last: The story of a man who pleaded guilty to a crime he didn't commit. At the time, it was cheaper to do so than to go through a trial. After the plea is entered, the government changes the terms of the plea. The change deals with the prison he will be sent to. The man decided to agree to the terms anyway. He contracts a fatal disease. The closer he gets to death's door, the more he can't deal with his plea as a mark on his soul. George is hired to have the guilty plea set aside.

Mississippi After Dark: The story of a series of unexplained disappearances and deaths. The police feared that a serial killer might be responsible. He had to be stopped. The question was how. No outsider law enforcers were welcomed in the state, least of all the FBI. The state was concerned with their public image if the story leaked out to the media. They did not want the federal government's serial killer division officially involved. The State's concern was created by the popularity of the movie, Mississippi Burning. George was hired to quietly find the killer and to end the killings.

Outraged in Mexico: The story of a town and its people caught up in violence and manipulation of a system that was ruled by one man. When they could take no more, they rebelled against the tyranny and recaptured their lives. The retribution they took against those who had enslaved them and the effort the people put forth to rebuild their lives is what makes up the basis for the story. The people involved are constantly forced to decide what values they want to nurture and what to disregard. They are forced to change their values to rid themselves of their oppressors.

Rape: The story of a young man who is accused of rape. The case causes the boy and girl to examine their own minds as to whether or not a rape occurred in the legal sense and in the moral sense. The state becomes so relentless in their quest to convict the boy that they forget that their job is also to protect the innocent. The ethnic and religious backgrounds of the two people are difficult to keep out of the case, as they are both caught up in the whirlwind that is created whenever the crime of rape is charged.

2.8 Seconds: The story of an alleged plot to assassinate the Pope during his visit to Venezuela. The people of the country were divided as to the value of having the Holy Father visit the country. George was hired to find the people involved, as well as to make sure that the assassination did not take place. Neither the church officials nor the authorities want to be connected to the investigation in any way. His assignment also was to include developing an assassination plan that circumvents all the precautions taken by both the church, as well as the government security forces.

When God Ain't Lookin': The story covers the lives of two people who meet, part, and reunite again. The characters are from two different worlds. Ann is a nun who is not sure she wants to be a nun because of the hypocrisy she has found in her order. Although twenty-five when she first meets George, she looks much younger. George is a twenty-year-old young man when they meet and has no idea that he is dating an older woman who is a nun. Their meetings over the years cause much joy and sadness for both of them.

Yellow River: The story of the "Enforcers" leaving Hong Kong when it was returned to Chinese rule. They were the Chinese who helped the English control Hong Kong during England's rule. The "Enforcers" were hated by their own countrymen and feared by everyone else in the world. They feared nothing. They had no ties to any faith, family or country. They were ruthless and yet well educated by watching the British. The "Enforcers" were allowed to leave Hong Kong and enter Canada and America, as long as they were penniless. They had to find different ways of bringing their wealth with them.